Solace Island

(Book One of the Solace Series)

Sara Flynn

Sweetberry Press

Sweetberry Press
www.sweetberrypress.com

Publisher's Note: This is a work of fiction. Names, characters, places, and incidents are a product of the author's imagination. Locales and public names are sometimes used for atmospheric purposes. Any resemblance to actual people, living or dead, or to businesses, companies, events, institutions, or locales is completely coincidental.

Solace Island/ Sara Flynn. -- 1st ed.
ISBN 978-0-9958118-0-5

To Nancy, who went above and beyond.

I am so very, *very* grateful.

One

Maggie Harris had her cell phone jammed against her right ear, a finger stuffed in her left, but still, Brett's voice was an indistinct murmur. "Sorry, honey, could you please speak a little louder? It's kind of noisy in here." That was an understatement. The club was packed with writhing, sweaty bodies, undulating to the pounding pulse of the music, not to mention the shrieking laughter of her eight bridesmaids and assorted female family and friends.

Maggie felt a tug on her arm. It was Carol Endercott from the office, who had been knocking back shooters since they had arrived an hour ago. Maggie didn't know her well, but the woman's husband had walked out on her and their kid after ten years of wedded bliss. Probably not the best person to invite to one's bachelorette party; however, Carol had overheard Maggie and Sarah making plans and Maggie didn't have the heart not to include her.

"Magsters," Carol slurred, leaning close, stumbling slightly. "Come on, girl, off za phone. It's pardy time!" She wore a big, sloppy smile, her mascara was smeared, and wisps of blond, frizzy hair clung to her perspiring face. "Let's have fuuun!" she bellowed like an elephant in heat.

Maggie held up a finger. "One moment, Carol," she mouthed. "It's Brett."

"Ooooh …" Carol said, throwing up her hands and tiptoeing backward, eyes wide, like a cartoon character removing herself from a bomb site. "The luuuvebirds … I bettah give you some privacy, seeing as how yer talkin' to za *fab*ulous Mr. Nolan!"

"Yes, well …" Maggie smiled at Carol. "Thanks. I think I'll just …" She tipped her head toward the bathrooms and started moving past Carol.

"Good idea!" Carol said, giving Maggie a crazy-hard nudge in the ribs and an attempt at a wink. "I'll tell the gang you're in za potski having phone sex, so they won't barge in at an inopportune moment," she bleated and lurched off.

"Jeeze," Maggie said, watching her leave. "I am very grateful not to have a drinking problem."

"Huh?"

"Nothing, Brett. Hang on a second," Maggie said. She started weaving her way through the crowd.

Once in the restroom, she heaved a sigh of relief. It was cooler in there; almost peaceful. She could still hear the thump and roar of the music, but it was muffled, muted. "Thank goodness," she breathed. "You still there?"

"Yeah," Brett said, his voice mostly clear, just a little static.

"What time is it?"

"Uh … ten fifteen. Look, babe, I wanted to—"

"Ten fifteen! Oh my gosh, we've only been here an hour? I'm pooped already. How long do you think I need to stay? Don't want to be rude, or anything. Everyone's come from so far away. But I gotta say, this going to clubs, drinking copious amounts of alcohol, the meat market of these places? It's not really me." Maggie laughed. "Well, you know that better than anyone, don't you? Honey, I am *so* glad we met."

"Yeah, well …"

"I can hardly wait until this is over. Maybe I can drop by after, if it's not too late, and snuggle in bed with you. Oh my goodness, my feet are sore," Maggie said, slipping off her heels, the polished concrete floor cool and soothing under her feet.

"That might be a problem."

"I know, right? I don't know what I'm going to do tomorrow! I don't know why I let my sister talk me into those strappy, sparkly heels to finish off my wedding ensemble. I should have stuck with my original idea and bought those glittery Doc Martens. Nobody cares what you're wearing underneath and then I'd be comfort—"

"Margaret," Brett cut in. "I need you to stop talking for a minute. Can you do that?"

"What?" Maggie's breath caught in her chest. He'd used her formal name, and his voice sounded strange. "Are you all right? Is everything okay? You didn't get in an accident, did you?"

"No, I'm fine, I just want to—"

"Oh, thank goodness!" A wave of relief rushed through her. "How horrible would that be—you having to hobble up the aisle in your handsome tux on a pair of crutches."

"Can you shut up for a second? I've been trying to tell you something for the last five minutes, but you just keep jabbering on and on."

Wait. Did Brett just tell her to shut up?

"I've been doing a lot of soul-searching the last couple months," Brett said. "And I just ... I can't do it."

Maggie's stomach lurched as her world, her future, suddenly swerved off course. She felt both removed from her body and hyper-aware of her surroundings, like she was an alien observing her own life. The water dripping from the faucet, the beating of her heart, loud, loud, loud. Her mouth like chalk, throat constricted.

"Can't ... You can't do what?" she asked, but she already knew.

Two

*A*re you sure you're going to be okay?" Rosemund Harris asked. There were violet shadows under Maggie's mother's eyes, as if she too hadn't been able to sleep for the last three nights as well.

"I'm totally fine, Mom," Maggie said, managing a smile. She glanced at the departure display board. Good. Their flight to Tampa, Florida, was on time. Another couple minutes and her parents would have no choice but to go through security.

Her sister, Eve, had taken the red-eye back to New York last night and the plane's departure had been delayed twice. While they waited, Eve managed to extract a promise that Maggie would go on vacation with her. Who knew what kind of concessions her parents would've wiggled out of her had their flight been delayed.

By some miracle, Maggie had been able to maintain her composure through contacting the guests, canceling what services she could and donating the rest. She still had to contact the registry and arrange to return the enormous pile of gifts so credit cards could be refunded. However, she needed to sort through the presents so she could personalize the thank-you notes that had to be written. There was too much to do. No way in hell she was going to allow herself to fall apart now and start bawling in the middle of the Phoenix Sky Harbor International Airport.

"I want to kill that son of a bitch," her dad said. Her dad had always been even-tempered and slow to anger, but he was angry now. She could tell by his voice.

Maggie dragged her gaze from the departure board to her dad, standing beside her mom. Ed Harris's large hands, hardened by years of construction work, were clenched, and worry had etched deeper grooves in the lines on his face.

"Dad," Maggie said, reaching out and patting his arm, "really, it's all right." Her parents looked around five years older than they had a week ago, and for that alone, she wanted to kill the bastard herself. "I'm just sorry you flew all this way for nothing—"

"Nonsense," her dad said, his voice gruff.

"We're grateful we were here," Rosemund said, pulling Maggie in for a hug. Her mom was small, a tiny bird of a woman, but seriously strong for a woman of any age, let alone one in her sixties. All those years pitching in on-site, running wiring, lugging pipes, installing pot-lights, had kept not just her mom but the whole family fit.

Maggie felt her dad's arms encircle the two of them. A part of her longed to give herself over to the comfort of her parents' support, but she couldn't. She didn't want to shatter. "Not every occasion," her mom continued as if Maggie wasn't standing stiffly in her arms, "is going to be a happy one. But it's the spending of time, the sharing of experiences, that is the glue that bonds a family together."

The boarding announcement for the flight to Tampa came over the loudspeaker just in time. Maggie blinked her eyes hard and pulled away. "You gotta go," she said, her voice cracking slightly. "You don't want to miss your flight."

There was a final hasty hug and then her parents left, turning to wave a few times before disappearing from sight.

Three

*D*on't you think you are being a little unreasonable?"
Brett said, leaning forward and steepling his tanned,
manicured fingers on the desk in front of him. *Their* desk.
He was smiling that smile that used to make her melt.
Funny how two weeks of hell can change one's perceptions, she
mused. She'd always thought he blow-dried his "sun-
streaked" blond hair a little too poofy, but she had never
noticed before just how practiced his smile was.

Her sister Eve had. "He's too slick," she'd said, when
she first met him. "Too smooth. I don't trust him."

Maggie had waved her worries aside. "Are you kidding?
He's perfect."

"Yes, and that's what worries me, because *no* one—
Maggie, look at me. No one is perfect."

And now, standing in the Camelback East Village office
that she and Brett had shared, she saw what Eve had seen
all those years ago. Five years and four months of her life
Maggie had wasted on this narcissistic, insensitive creep. *A
frigging five-year engagement. Ha! That should have been a clue.*

"Just because I decided I didn't want to marry you
doesn't mean I don't want to continue working with you.
We're a great team. I'm the ideas man and you implement
all the details. Take that derelict church, for instance.
Turning it into a high-end condo development was a

brilliant idea, if I do say so myself. Pre-sales are moving extremely well. Yes, I know you're doing a lot of work, but we're going to make a shitload of money on this one. Comfort Homes is just starting to hit the big leagues. Seriously, sweetie, you're making a mountain out of a molehill."

"First," Maggie said, holding up her hand, palm thrust out like a traffic cop, "I am *not* your 'sweetie.' Second, even you, with your pin-sized brain, must know that calling off a wedding the night before it's supposed to occur would not, under any circumstances, be classified as a *molehill*!"

Brett opened his mouth to speak, but Maggie steamrollered right over him. "If you were having all these doubts, why did you insist on making it such a big event? I wanted something small and intimate, but no! You felt it was necessary to invite *three hundred and eighty-six* friends, family members, and business colleagues to *our* wedding! Some of them could ill afford to fly themselves out here and put themselves up in a hotel, but they did it because they wanted to show us their love and support. My mom and dad re-booked their world cruise vacation because they wanted to be here for our special day. Did that even cross your mind, how you inconvenienced so many people? Then, you get cold feet, and you don't even have the balls to stand up like a man and let people know. What a jerk!"

"A guy's entitled to—"

"*You* are entitled to *nothing*. Not after leaving me to make excuses and explanations, and to settle the accounts. Oh, by the way, did you and Kristal enjoy our honeymoon holiday?"

Brett blanched.

"Yes, I know all about that. Carol enlightened me. Amazing how loose the lips of everyone at the office got once the shit hit the fan. I gather your little fling has been going on for some time. The silver lining, I suppose, is that I finally understand why you pushed so hard for her to get the VP Sales position." Maggie had been trying to keep her voice calm and modulated, to present herself as a woman in control, but it wasn't working. She could feel the deep waves of anger rising. "Well, I hate to break it to you, buddy-boy, but this?" she said, swirling her hands in the air. And it was as if the movement lit a match to the dynamite stockpiled in the pit of her stomach, because she heard herself bellow, "WAS *NOT* a frigging *MOLEHILL!*"

Brett shifted uncomfortably. "Toots, come on. You're being unduly harsh——"

Maggie snatched the John Fitzstien metal sculpture from the desk and brandished it, eyes narrowed. "Don't you 'Toots' me, you son of a bitch, or I'll bash your brains out and enjoy every second of it."

Brett shut up.

"Now," Maggie continued, slamming the sculpture down on the desk with a satisfying *thunk*, enjoying the nervous expression on his face way more than she should, "this is the way it's going to go down. Either you buy my half of the company, at fair market value——"

"That's ridiculous. You're the one who wants to walk away. So leave. No reason I should be penalized and give you half of my company——"

"Our company."

"—just because your feelings got hurt," Brett continued, shrugging. "I understand. I'd be emotional, too, if I was going to be missing out on all of this," Brett said, gesturing to himself.

"Why, you self-satisfied, pompous peacock," Maggie said, shaking her head. She couldn't believe the nerve of this guy. "Yes, I *am* feeling a little emotional, but not because I'm going to *miss* you. Was it painful? Yes, but I'm glad my blinders were ripped off. I am angry I had such terrible judgment and didn't see through you. I am pissed off that I let you talk me into plowing my entire inheritance from Great-Aunt Clare into the start-up costs for this company. *Our* company. It's amazing to me that I never noticed the timing between her death and our engagement." Maggie had thrown that last comment in, hoping that she was wrong. That there had been something genuine in their relationship. That it hadn't been all about money. That Brett had truly wanted to marry her, and that the timing of the reading of her great-aunt's will and his sudden burning desire to get engaged and start their own company was a coincidence. But she could see from the expression on his face that it wasn't.

Maggie had thought that she was fine. That now, seeing him clearly, any kind of emotional tie would no longer have its talons sunk into her. But the knowledge that she had been played all those years was like a fist to the gut. "Did you ever love me?" she heard, barely audible.

Damn. She hadn't meant to say it out loud. That was a mistake. She knew it instantly. She could see Brett's mind ticking it over, figuring out how to use her vulnerability to his advantage. She'd seen him do it many times when they were negotiating contracts for the company.

"Won't work, Brett," she said, before he could open his mouth. "Don't even bother."

He shrugged, giving her that boyish smile that used to make her go weak at the knees. "Maggie … Come here. You look like you need a hug."

"Over my dead body," she said, taking a step back and crossing her arms. "Back to business. The seed money was mine. You didn't put a red cent into the start-up."

"I didn't have——" Brett started to say.

"I don't want to hear your sob story, and neither do the courts. I've put my money, my sweat, blood, and tears into this company. Count your blessings I'm only asking for what we wrote down in the original contract. And yes, I still have it."

Brett's fingers were tapping a staccato rhythm on his desk. He always did that when he was irritated.

Maggie didn't care.

He leaned back in his chair, swiveled right and then left, eyes on her. "We have no idea what that would be."

"No worries." Maggie reached into her purse and pulled out a file. "I had ten whole days to cost it out while you and Kristal were frolicking in the sun." She slapped the file on the desk and slid it over to him.

"Forget it," Brett said, crossing his arms, shaking his head. "Not going to happen."

Maggie shrugged. "Either you buy me out, or I'll talk to Pondstone Inc. They were sniffing around last year, and I'm sure they would love to own my controlling shares. Though I can't promise they won't decide you're useless and toss you out on your highly toned ass. That would be their call." She arranged her features into a polite, civilized veneer and then straightened. "Are we clear?"

No answer.

"Good." Maggie dusted off her hands. "I'll give you a couple days to mull it over. If you decide to move forward with the purchase of my shares, two weeks should be sufficient time to arrange a loan from the bank."

"Two weeks," Brett choked out.

"Yup," Maggie said over her shoulder, as she headed toward the door. "Better get cracking." Her hand closed over the brass doorknob. It was odd to think that after all these years, she would never walk through these offices again. "Oh, wait." She turned and went back to the desk. "I'm taking this," she said, scooping up the sculpture and shoving it into her purse. "A souvenir."

Then she left with her head high. *Too bad Mom and Dad couldn't have seen me in action*, she thought. They *would've been so proud.*

Four

*L*eaning her back against the rail, Maggie tilted her head back and shut her eyes, enjoying the late-afternoon sun. She could feel the thrum of the ferry's engine vibrating through the deck below her feet. The breeze off the Pacific Ocean was brisk, stinging her cheeks and making her snuggle deeper into her sweater. She was grateful for her hat. It was cold almost to the point of discomfort, but still she didn't go in. Yes, the passenger lounge, with its thick, smeared windows, was heated. But people were in there, families and couples laughing and living life, huddled next to the old radiators.

She took a deep breath, filling her body to the very brim, then exhaled and opened her eyes. It was better out here. The view from the top deck was glorious. The deep, green-gray water rushing past the bow of the boat, leaving a frill of white in its wake; the birds spiraling higher and higher, then swooping down again; the purple-blue, shadowy shapes of islands beyond islands; and the sun partway through its downward arch toward the horizon.

"I'm glad I left," she said out loud, tossing the words onto the wind, her throat suddenly constricted. "That spoiled trust-fund rich bitch Kristal can have him. Good riddance to bad rubbish, I say, because I really don't care." And then, inexplicably, her eyes filled and overflowed. It must have been the cold wind, or the sun sparkling too brightly off the water—whatever it was, it was too much to bear. And she had to sit down and give way to it, sobs coming hard and fast, ripping through her body.

Five

*L*uke Benson slid the last batch of bread dough into the retarder-proofer to rise overnight. Some bakers swore that one should proof dough for one and a half to two hours, but Luke preferred the flavor and consistency that occurred with a long, slow rise.

He straightened, rolled his shoulders to release the slight tension that had accumulated there. Glanced out the window at the bay that beckoned beyond. The sun had already disappeared behind the mountainous peak of the neighboring island. Streaks of orange and gold with traces of purple slashed across the sky. He was grateful for the lengthening days that March had brought. It would be forty-five minutes to an hour before darkness descended on his Pacific Northwest paradise, and he felt restless. In need of some kind of physical release.

He'd sworn off women after his last train wreck of a relationship had detonated in his face a year and a half ago. A hard run would have to suffice.

He grabbed his sweater, slipped it over his head, and exited through the back door. His wolfhound, Samson, was close on his heels.

Rather than go down to the beach, Luke turned right out of the door and took the path that ran along the bluff.

It would make for a smoother run. Especially given the dimming light.

He did a couple of stretches, then started at a slow jog, gradually building speed. The old injury in his leg complained violently, but as usual, he ignored it. He knew from experience that it was better to move than to not. For the first five minutes, there was always resistance. It would give way to the pleasure of the run, and he would enjoy the feeling of his lungs expanding. He picked up the pace, the sound of his sneakers making contact with the packed dirt of the trail accelerating, air rushing past. He could feel his heart pounding, blood surging through his body, his arms and legs slicing through space. Samson galloped ahead, both on and off the trail, coming back to check in, and then disappearing again, following some scent or another.

Sometimes they would arrive back at the cottage together. Other times, they'd go their separate ways, and Samson would arrive at the door much later, muddy, happy, and uninterested in dinner.

Darkness was starting to settle around Luke, but his body was into a rhythm now, and he was reluctant to turn back. So he kept running. And as he did, his mind drifted past thoughts of the physical exertion to the ferry ride home that afternoon and the woman weeping on the outside upper deck. He didn't know her. She must have been one of the multitudes of tourists that descended on the island.

It was odd that he'd had the urge to go to her, offer comfort.

He hadn't. That would have been weird. Clearly, she had gone up there to be by herself.

He'd stayed in his truck. Trying to fix the world was not part of his job description anymore. It was a waste of time. Most things were unfixable. He had sat there on his worn leather seats, Samson beside him, the dog's large body sprawled across the width of the front seat, his shoulders and shaggy gray head warm and heavy on Luke's lap.

Luke stumbled over an exposed tree root and lurched forward, causing crippling pain to shoot through his left quadriceps. He managed to catch his balance.

He shook his head. Tripping was unlike him. Usually he was hyper-aware of his surroundings. That was the problem with regrets and the past. If one dwelled on them, they could devour the present. A waste of time. Let it go. Be in the present.

Again, Luke was back in his body, aware of his breath and his limbs moving. Thankfully, the strain and burn from the old wound, where the bullet had entered his left thigh and exited again, was easing. This allowed him to focus again on the thump of his sneakers pounding on the path.

But within a few minutes, his mind had veered back to her. *I should have gone and offered help*, he thought. *Solace. No one should have to weep with that intensity alone.*

By the time he reached The Point, it was difficult to see. Night had fallen. Fog was rolling in, turning the trees and the Olympic mountain range beyond the bay into blurry charcoal ghosts, silhouettes against the sky. Luke glanced up. Soon, even the moon and stars would be obliterated.

Although he was still heated from running, he could tell that the temperature had dropped considerably. His breath was turning into puffs of condensation as it left his mouth.

"Think we'd best take the road back," he said to Samson. "No cliff to accidentally plummet off."

It had seemed like a good idea to stop in the little town and pick up a few supplies. Then, once Maggie arrived at the rental cottage, Rosemary & Time, she could tuck in and wouldn't have to venture out until after Eve arrived in the morning.

Eve *loved* Solace Island and had stayed at Rosemary & Time many times. "It's magical, Maggs. Just what you need to soothe your aching heart and soul."

Which Maggie had thought was over-poeticizing the situation. "I'm not sad, Eve," she had said. "There is no aching going on. I'm angry. There is an enormous difference."

"Ah ..." Eve had said.

Like her big sister knew better. Which made Maggie angrier.

However, after her embarrassing meltdown on the ferry, she had to admit that perhaps her sister was right.

It was interesting, actually, because the minute Maggie had driven her car off the ferry and onto the road that led away from the small town of Westford and Westford Harbor, she felt something lighten in her chest. The lightness grew as she followed the winding road past craggy mountains, lush valleys, and thick wooded areas.

When she had arrived in the small, picturesque town of Comfort and purchased groceries, she found she was reluctant to leave. The idea of being in an empty, unknown cottage, alone with her thoughts, was more than a little daunting.

One thing had led to another. She enjoyed a delicious organic latte at Solace Given, which was full of warmth and baked goods and chatter. She nursed her drink for as long as she could, savoring the warmth of the mug in her hand, the creamy, spicy goodness as it trickled down her throat, warming her inside and out. When she had drunk the last drop, she went out onto the street and wandered through cute little shops full of whimsy and handcrafted goods.

In hindsight, Maggie realized there'd been flaws in her hanging-out-in-town plan. Who knew it would get so dark while she ambled up and down the aisles, plopping groceries into her cart? Now she was careening down a bumpy dirt road, praying she wouldn't get a flat tire or end up in a ditch.

She was out in the middle of nowhere.

She hadn't thought to purchase a flashlight or matches and emergency candles. She wished she had. It was kind of spooky. She hadn't realized just how dense, dark, and looming the forest was. Eve was nuts, vacationing out here. They could die or be carried off by a bear, and it would be years before anyone found their bleached bones.

If only she had located the cottage in daylight, then she wouldn't have had to deal with not knowing where she was going. Her night vision had never been the best, but out here in the boondocks, it seemed to be practically non-existent.

Apparently, the good folks of Solace Island didn't believe in the modern magic of streetlights. Sure, the main town of Comfort had a couple scattered around, but out here? Zilch.

Maggie had never realized quite how dark the night could get. It certainly never got this pitch black in Phoenix, and the stupid thick fog that had rolled in only exacerbated her vision challenges.

Thank heaven for GPS.

She glanced down at the dashboard of her rental car, and her heart sank.

"You've got to be kidding," she muttered.

Yes, the GPS screen was still lit up, but between the last time she had glanced at it and now, it had stopped functioning. It showed a lazy blue arrow sailing in the middle of nothingness. There was the outline of where the land ended. Apparently, the ocean was somewhere to her left, but there were no roads showing on the GPS. No markings. Nothing.

"Seriously?"

Really, it was ridiculous for her to feel so surprised. The way things had been unfolding for her in the last few weeks, of course her GPS would malfunction right when she needed it most.

"GPS ... fiancés ... what next?"

She blew out a puff of air. Tried to make her hands not grip the steering wheel so hard.

"No big deal," she said. "I just need to find a place to turn off. I can plug the address into my cell phone. Problem solved."

She drove further.

There was no turn-off.

"No worries," she said, sounding extra loud and overly cheerful. But she had to do something to counterbalance the slight panic that was beginning to bubble up. "Ho hum

... a little fog. It's dark, and you don't know where you're going. So what? What do you care that there are thick woods all around you, and maybe bears and mountain lions? Hungry mountain lions ..." This sort of talk was *not* helping.

"Stop ... right ... now," she told herself firmly. "You're a grown woman of twenty-seven, not a frightened five-year-old. So you don't know where you're going, and there's a slight glitch with the GPS. So what? You could have been in a crash. Your car could have caught on fire. There are a million things worse than this minuscule problem."

The fog shifted, and for a second Maggie could make out a driveway up ahead on the left before it was swallowed up in the mist again, but she had seen it. It was there: a place to pull over. Slowly, she drove forward, trying to peer through the darkness and fog, her body hunched over the steering wheel. Ah! There it was! She eased her rental car into the drive and turned the engine off and her emergency lights on. She got her cell phone out of her purse and hit the power switch.

The signal strength bars were non-existent; however, the phone was searching.

"Come on," she said, giving the phone an encouraging jiggle.

The jiggle seemed to help. The *searching...* disappeared. Unfortunately, the tiny, depressing words *No service* arrived in its stead.

She sat there for a few moments while the reality of her circumstances set in. She ran several scenarios through her head. She shouldn't continue on. The fog made driving dangerous and house numbers hard to read, and she wasn't sure she was still headed in the right direction. Walking would be a mistake, as visibility was an issue. She might get hit by a car. And then there was the small matter of wildlife roaming about, looking for dinner. Maggie quickly realized that her best option was to stay put. She would wait for the fog to lift, and then she could be on her way.

She didn't know how long she'd be stranded. However, she had seen a wilderness survival show on TV once. The host had stressed that if one found oneself stranded in the wilds, one must find a way to maintain one's body heat. Otherwise, hypothermia could set in. The handsome host, with gleaming white teeth, had shown how to make a bed of leaves and branches. Ha! Maggie could do better than that. Granted, it was a bit chilly, but there was no need for her to roll around in dead leaves and muck. She had a trunk full of resources!

She got out, opened her trunk, and rummaged around in her suitcase until her hands landed on a few items that seemed to have a little bulk and warmth. She grabbed them and walked speedily—okay, she *ran*—back and hopped into her car, slamming the door behind her. She locked the doors. Yes, there didn't appear to be a living being for miles around, but one couldn't be too prudent.

Then, she carefully wound the articles of clothing around and around her, paying special attention to her head. She had once heard that a lot of heat escaped through the top of one's head.

Yes, it was a little scary being stranded in the wilderness, but Maggie felt good, too. Like an adventurer. A problem solver. A woman in control.

Six

*G*reat," Luke growled, glaring at the abandoned car blocking his drive, its red emergency lights flashing. "There's a perfectly good turnout twenty yards down the road, but this idiot decides to abandon his car here."

Samson approached the car, smelled something by the trunk, batted the trunk with his enormous paw, then followed the scent around to the driver's side of the car, sniffed some more, and let out a loud, sharp *woof.*

There was a shriek from the car. A head with some sort of strange headdress appeared at the window, face drained of all color, eyes wide, mouth a round O. He caught only a flash, and then there was another shriek and the head disappeared. The car rocked slightly from some sort of vigorous movement inside. From the high pitch of the shriek, Luke was able to ascertain that the owner of the oddly garbed head was definitely female.

Maggie lay as flat as she could on the floor of the car. It was an impossible task, because the gearshift was poking into her ribs. When she had been rummaging for clothes in the trunk, she should have thrown the groceries far away from the car. The smell of the food must have attracted the bear.

"Please go away ... please go away," she prayed.

Now the bear was banging on the door! Oh dear ... oh dear. It wasn't going to go away. *Wait!* Maggie had an idea. The bear must be hungry: better it feast on her groceries than on her. She pushed off the center console—her ribs thanked her—and keeping low, she fumbled under the dashboard until she felt the trunk release button. *Ahh ...* She could hear the trunk fly open.

"Whaaa?!"

The bear had said *whaaa*?! That didn't make sense. Bears don't talk.

She must have seen incorrectly. It was a person, not a bear! A person who could help!

Maggie slowly raised herself up and peeked out the window. A tall, fierce warrior of a man was standing outside her car. He looked grouchy as hell. Strong, too, like he could snap a person's neck with his bare hands. But the weird thing was, Maggie knew deep down to her core that she was safe with this man. The second she saw his face, the words *Oh, it's you* flashed through her mind. She didn't know what that meant, or why those particular words had arrived. It didn't matter. She was safe. She was no longer alone. She wasn't going to be eaten by a bear, because if anyone could beat off a wild bear, it was this man.

The car door burst open, a woman tumbled out, and recognition flashed through him. It was the weeping woman from the ferry, although she had changed, had added to her clothes, making for a most peculiar ensemble. What he had thought was a headdress appeared, on closer inspection, to be a flannel pajama top with a sock-monkey print. One sleeve was loose and flopping around her face.

She was also wearing a fuzzy pink bathrobe and a pair of red woolen long johns that were wrapped several times around her neck and shoulders.

"Oh, thank goodness!" She seemed excited, talking fast and loud, but underneath was a lazy trace of silk and whiskey in her voice that his body apparently found arousing. "You have no idea how relieved I am to see you."

What are you doing? he told his stirring nether regions firmly. *The poor woman is clearly unhinged. Weeping violently, and now this? She needs your compassion, not an erection.*

"I thought you were a bear!" she continued, oblivious to the battle he was waging below. "A bear. Can you imagine?" She was waving her arms around like a bird trying to take flight. "That's why I opened the trunk. I have groceries, you see, and——"

Samson chose this opportunity to amble around the car and rise onto his hindquarters to nudge her face with his wet nose.

She emitted a squawk that would raise the dead. "AAAAHHH! Bear! B-b-b-bear!"

The next thing Luke knew, she had catapulted into the air, as though shot out of a cannon, and landed in his arms. Clinging to him for dear life, her body nestled against his chest as if she belonged there. Even through her layers of apparel, he found himself hyper-aware of the soft, womanly curves hidden beneath.

She smelled good, a mix of tea, fresh-cut grass, and honeysuckle. His cock went from partially to fully erect. This was not good. Not good at all.

"Ma'am," he growled, his tone sharper than was called for. "Ma'am. I'm going to ask you to climb down."

"There's a bear," she whimpered, her face turned toward his chest, her eyes squeezed shut.

"That's not a bear. It's a dog." Her added weight was causing his thigh to ache rather badly.

"It's not a dog!" Her voice was getting shriller. "It's too big for a dog!"

"Ma'am, there are no bears on Solace."

"What?" She looked up at him, and even in the dark, he could see moisture clinging to her lashes.

He gentled his voice. "It's my dog. Samson."

Samson looked up at Luke and cocked his head.

"Lie down, boy."

The large wolfhound lowered himself to the ground with a soft groan.

"Ma'am. If you could open your eyes."

She peeked over his arm.

"See, it's a dog. He's lying down. He won't hurt you."

"He's so enormous," she said, her arms still wrapped tight around his neck.

It felt nice to hold her. Felt right, somehow. He hadn't realized, until that very moment, how much he had missed human touch.

However, his thigh was throbbing quite violently, and if he didn't put her down soon, they would both crash to the ground.

"Yes, now, if you could just get down. Please?" It wasn't so dark that he missed the stain of color that raced across her face.

"I'm sorry. I'm *so* sorry," she said, scrambling out of his arms. "Thank you for your ... um ... forbearance. I didn't mean to ..." She took a deep breath and let it out. "Hi," she said, sticking out her hand. "I'm Mag—"

It was then that apparently she noticed the pink arm of her bathrobe. Her horrified gaze traveled up her arm to the red long johns wrapped around her shoulders. Her hand shot up to her head. "Oh no," she moaned, ripping the pajama top from her head. "Ha ha ..." she laughed nervously. "How embarrassing!"

But Luke couldn't speak, couldn't reassure her. The sight of glorious, thick waves of auburn hair tumbling over her shoulders had poleaxed him, rendering useless any previous ability he'd had to form words.

Seven

Maggie woke to the sound of the screen door slamming, followed by footsteps. Where was she? She squinted blearily around the room, at the white-washed walls and polished pine floors with cozy area rugs. The bed was very comfy with its fluffy, white duvet. Was she on her honeymoon? *Don't remember the wedding,* she thought, a yawn overtaking her. *Brett must be in the bathroom.*

"Maggie?" she heard her sister call. *Her sister?* And then reality landed with a thump. She wasn't on her honeymoon. There would be no honeymoon. She was at the Rosemary & Time B&B on Solace Island.

"Maggie?"

"In here," Maggie croaked, rising up on her elbow.

Eve burst into the room, her ebony hair swirling around her, a big smile on her face. "Rise and shine," she said, pulling back the crisp, white curtains. Sunshine flooded the room.

"What time is it?" Maggie asked, rubbing her eyes.

"It's time," Eve replied, scooping a pair of jeans and a blouse out of Maggie's suitcase and tossing them to her, "to go to the Saturday market. Why do you have this metal," Eve held the Fitzstien metal sculpture up and squinted at it, "thingy in your suitcase?"

Maggie glanced over, enjoying the little surge of satisfaction she felt. "Because it's mine," Maggie said. "Can you put it on the dresser? I want it to be the first thing I see when I wake up."

Eve walked over and plunked the sculpture down.

"Speaking of ..." Maggie yawned, stretched, and then flopped back down and pulled the hand-stitched Belgian duvet up over her shoulders. "We don't need to go to the market. I already got some groceries." She yawned again and shut her eyes. "Bacon, eggs, bread for toast ..." She snuggled down, nice and cozy; her pillow was still warm. "Fresh coffee beans, too. Weird name: Jacobin. Tastes good, though ..." She could feel her sleep wave descending. "Nice to see you ... just gonna ... sleep a little ..."

"Oh, no, you don't!" Eve grabbed Maggie's covers and yanked them off. "Sleeping too much is a sign that you're sliding into depression—"

"I'm not sliding into depression," Maggie mumbled, fumbling for the duvet, trying to pull it back up.

Eve had a firm grip on it.

"Come on, Eve, I didn't sleep la—"

"It's not going to happen," Eve replied, adamantly. "Not on my watch. That little two-faced, cheating weasel isn't worth one more precious second of your life."

She hoisted Maggie to a sitting position then crouched so their faces were level, fierce determination on her face that softened to something else. She gently smoothed Maggie's hair out of her face.

"I love you, honey," she said, wrapping her arms around her sister and kissing the top of her head. "And I'm going to do my damnedest to see you happy again."

It sounded like a vow, and when Eve put her mind to something, nothing and nobody was going to change her course. She was a lot like their dad, in that respect.

So Maggie got up.

The Saturday market was apparently a big deal. A multitude of stalls with everything a person could want—fresh-baked goods, local farmers with beautiful, fresh organic produce, stalls with unique clothing, handcrafted jewelry, cheese makers, adorable handbags made of repurposed tweed suit jackets, and more.

The place was hopping.

"Where did all these people come from?" Maggie asked, as they made their way through the crowd.

"All over," Eve said. "The Saturday market is famous. People take the ferry from Seattle and from the surrounding smaller islands. Locals. Tourists. Pretty much everybody comes to Saturday market. Umm … yum! Taste this."

"I'm not hungr—" Maggie started to say, but as she opened her mouth, Eve popped a bite of carrot cake in.

It was the best bite of carrot cake she had ever tasted. It was moist, delicious, with plump raisins and not too sweet. Cream-cheese icing was slathered on top. She could taste fresh butter, vanilla, and icing sugar as well. And salt? Yes, that was there, just barely.

"Wow," Maggie breathed, for the whole combination somehow managed to blend together in the mouth and strike a perfect balance. "Um ... maybe I am hungry," she said, which made both of them laugh.

"Here you go." Eve broke her slice of cake in two. "Isn't it the best thing ever?" she said, handing the larger piece to Maggie.

It didn't take long for both pieces to disappear.

"So," Eve said, licking the last of the frosting off her fingers. "Back to last night. You had fog, no phone service, and no GPS. That's crazy! How did you manage to find the cottage? It's kind of off the beaten track."

Maggie felt her face heat up. "It was pretty challenging, but ..."

"Oooh ..." Eve had turned to admire a display of cream-colored mugs. The interiors were robin's egg blue. On the creamy exterior were a couple of small birds, hand-painted black silhouettes sitting on a twig. "I love these!" Eve cooed.

This was not the first stall where Eve had found something she loved. The reusable cloth bag Eve had shoved into Maggie's hand as they exited the car was officially full.

"I'm sorry, Maggie," Eve said, handing her purchase to the vendor to be wrapped. "You were saying?"

Maggie shrugged. "Oh, some grouch happened by and begrudgingly pointed me in the right direction. I was only a couple of driveways off. I'd have found it fine without the fog." She didn't mention that the grouch had been handsome as sin, or that she'd been wearing her fuzzy pink bathrobe and a pajama top on her head. Nor did she say anything about how she had leaped uninvited into his reluctant arms—his arms and chest had seared themselves into her memory. Hard, warm, strong. He had smelled of clean sweat, night air, and ocean breeze with a tinge of spice. A part of her had wanted to stay there, her face buried in his chest, taking in his scent, listening to the steady thump of his heart.

Sleep last night had been impossible. She kept being bombarded with alternate waves of mortification and arousal.

"Poor you," Eve said, with a sympathetic laugh. "Too bad he wasn't a hottie." She plopped her wallet into her purse and somehow managed to create space for her paper-wrapped mug in Maggie's carryall.

"I don't want a hottie," Maggie muttered, feeling slightly guilty, because last night's guy definitely had been one.

"Don't be ridiculous. Every girl wants a hottie."

"Not me," Maggie stated firmly. "I just got out of a terrible relationship with one, and look where that got me. No, I'm never going to allow myself to be vulnerable like that again. So if that's part of your let's-get-Maggie-happy scheme, you can forget about it."

Eve snorted. "Excuse me, little sister," she said, patting Maggie on the shoulder in the condescending way that only an elder sister could master. "I'm sorry, but Brett? He was *not* a hottie. Believe me. If you had ever experienced one," Eve said with a grin, "you'd be lining up for seconds."

Suddenly, Eve clutched Maggie's arm. "Now that," she said, leaning her head toward her sister, gesturing with her chin, her voice suddenly hushed like she was in church, "is what I call a *hottie*!"

Maggie scanned the crowd milling around them. "Where?"

"There," Eve said. "Right there. Straight ahead."

Maggie laughed. "I hate to disappoint you but I see no—"

"Are you blind? Straight ahead." Eve grabbed Maggie's chin and turned it. "There. Right there! See. Behind all those stacks of gorgeous-looking artisan bread is an even gorgeouser-looking man." And that's when Maggie saw *him*. "Is *gorgeouser* even a word? I don't think so. No matter. You see him now, don't you? Don't try to wiggle out of it," Eve said, with a smirk, shaking an admonishing finger at her sister. "I've known you since you were a babe in diapers. You see him, and you feel that jolt as well." Eve sat back on her heels and looked him over like he was a prize horse on the auction block. "He's cute," she said, tapping a finger on her lips. "I wonder if he's married?" A group of people had paused, blocking Eve's view, but that didn't stop her. She stepped to the side and craned her neck to see around them. "Don't see a ring."

"Eve, no! I'm not—"

"I feel like some bread!" Eve said, laughing triumphantly. "Come on! He's the perfect antidote for your depression. A get-over-Brett fling!" She grabbed Maggie's hand with a surprisingly strong grip and dragged her toward *his* booth.

Eight

S he was here.

The woman from last night. The one he had held in his arms and then sent on her way.

The minute the fog had swallowed up the red glow of her taillights, he'd had to call on his inner reserves to stay where he was. Every cell in his body was urging him to chase her down, drag her out of the car, and discover what her full, luscious lips tasted like.

He hadn't slept. Couldn't. Plans, plots on how to accidentally bump into her had kept him awake. He needed to see if last night had been a freak incident caused by circumstances, the adrenaline of the run, her throwing herself into his arms, the privacy of the fog surrounding them so that the world stopped and started with her every breath.

Maybe it was just an accidental attraction made mysterious by the night air and the bruised sorrow that seemed to surround her. Someone had hurt her deeply that was clear. It must have aroused his protective instincts, which had been over-developed with his old line of work. If he could see her again, in broad daylight, things would be fine. He'd be able to stop thinking about her and settle back into the peaceful life he had carved out for himself over the last year and a half.

She was staying at Ethelwyn and Lavina's B&B down the road. Ethelwyn often borrowed tools. She had his bolt cutter at present. To her house, he'd take the scenic path that swung right past the guest cottage. Maybe he'd bring Samson, too. Samson knew her scent now, so he'd probably want to say hello.

Once Luke had his plan in place, the desire for sleep made itself known, but his three a.m. alarm was going to go off in eighteen minutes. He would need to get up, remove the dough from the proofer, finish the prep, and begin the rotation of baking in his multi-deck oven. Not enough time for a satisfying sleep.

Now, oddly, he didn't feel tired. Watching her walk around the market, her hips swaying to music that only she could hear, he could tell his attraction to her was not a fleeting thing. No, he wasn't exhausted at all. He felt adrenalized, invigorated. Fatigue would probably set in later tonight.

At first, Luke had thought that the dark-haired woman with her was a friend. But as he watched them make their way through the market, he could see a similarity, although physically they were quite different. The tilt of the head, the way they moved their hands when they spoke, how they leaned toward each other, made him think perhaps they were sisters.

"Excuse me?"

Luke tore his gaze from the women. Time to get back to the task at hand. Customers were starting to line up around his stall. He was glad the local community had embraced his product. It was satisfying to watch the loaves fly off his table. It was coming up on eleven o'clock, and already two-thirds of his baskets were empty and stacked upside down in the corner. By noon, everything would be sold, and he could pack up his table, baskets and tent, and go home.

"Yes?" he said.

It was Zelia Thompson, who owned Art Expressions Gallery. To an untrained eye, her flowing, colorful garments, chunky jewelry, and wild mane of curly hair proclaimed a free spirit, but below that surface was a shrewd businesswoman, strong to the core. He admired that in a woman. They had almost hooked up once. She had had tickets to an outdoor concert, came by his stall, wanted to know if he'd like to go. Americana country-soul. Why the hell not? The music had been surprisingly good. The violinist from Italy was especially talented. A storm had rolled in, and she had an umbrella in her tote. Their shoulders bumped. He turned his head, and she was there, her mouth rising to meet his.

It had been a surprise, and she was a beautiful woman, so he had returned her kiss, but it hadn't felt right. So he had shifted his body back to face the stage again.

She hadn't held a grudge. Still came around, regular as rain, to buy his bread.

"I'll have four of your Asiago cheese buns," she said, then turned to her companion who, wearing a large hat, sunglasses, and holiday clothes, looked to be visiting from elsewhere. "They're to die for. Everything he produces is." She smiled, leaned toward her friend. "Well," she purred, supposedly speaking to her companion but watching him through lowered lashes, "I've only had an amuse-bouche.

Haven't yet sampled everything he has the ability to produce, but never say never ..."

Luke bagged the cheese buns. "That'll be twelve dollars."

"Oh," Zelia said, playfully shaking her finger at him, "I'm not done with you. We'll have some croissants, six plain and six chocolate—"

"Six of each?" her friend said, looking startled.

"Absolutely. They're the best croissants on the island— nice and buttery, with just the right amount of crisp. Once you eat one, nothing else will do. He only sells at Saturday market—won't let me come to his house," she said, with a sigh. "So I have to buy enough to last me the week. I freeze them so I won't eat all of them in one sitting." She turned back to Luke. "I also want a French baguette and one of those delicious round loaves of sourdough rye."

"Sure." Luke counted out the croissants and plopped them into a bag. He was sliding the baguette into a paper sack when he became aware of a shift in the air around him.

He looked up, and there she was. And, yes, the other woman was most definitely a sister. Different hair color, but they both had the same large, almond-shaped eyes with a slight tilt at the corners and an unusual shade of green. *An emerald green*, he thought, getting lost in her eyes, enjoying the luxury of daylight. *Yes, emerald with tawny flecks of brown and gold scattering outward from the iris like shooting stars.*

"And the sourdough rye?" he heard Zelia say.

"Absolutely." He handed her the baguette, bagged the rye bread, and passed that over to her as well. "Thanks.

Appreciate your business," he said, turning back toward the two sisters.

"Uh ... Luke?"

He looked at Zelia. "Yes? Did I forget something?"

She laughed. "Yeah. What do I owe you?"

"Hmm ..." Maggie heard her sister murmur in her ear. "Either his bread is manna from God, or the hordes of women clustered around his booth means you're going to have some competition."

"You are delusional," Maggie muttered through clenched teeth, trying to discreetly wiggle out of her sister's vise-like grasp. "Eve, stop pushing me forward."

The woman had called him *Luke*. The name fit.

The exotic beauty was now handing him money, the tips of her fingers drawing an invisible painting along his palm. Her nail polish was an unusual color, purple so dark it almost looked black. Maybe a custom blend. She seemed the artistic type. Probably created it herself.

She looked like the kind of woman who didn't need to read *Cosmo* to find out what a man liked.

Although sometimes *Cosmo* was wrong.

Embarrassingly wrong, Maggie thought, her mind flying back to the time she'd carefully wrapped herself in saran wrap —as per Cosmo's suggestion— donned heels and greeted Brett with a chilled bottle of chardonnay, two wine glasses and a smile. *"Irresistible"* she was not. When Brett had finally stopped howling with laughter, he plucked the bottle of wine from her hand. "You're nuts," he said, shaking his head. He had pried a glass from her numb fingers, then gone into the living room and turned on the game.

Remembering that evening made Maggie feel like she had swallowed a mouthful of congealed lard.

"There you go," Luke said, giving the woman her change.

She said something Maggie couldn't quite hear and laughed, a low, husky laugh that made Maggie want to kick her in the shins. A ridiculous impulse. Why should she care if this woman was all but dry-humping his table? She watched as the woman walked away with her friend, confidence in every step. Maggie sighed. What would it feel like to be her, to be able to put an outfit together like that and wear it with panache? To say, *I want that man*, and go after him. To know that—

"Hello there," a man's voice said from behind Maggie's shoulder.

She felt her sister elbow her in the ribs. Maggie turned back to her sister, to him.

He was looking at her, the corners of his mouth quirking up. There was amusement in his eyes and something else, too. A languid sensuality throbbed off him, even more potent than she remembered from last night. She tried to ignore it, but the heat coursing through her body was saying, *Whoopee! Let's party!*

"You make it to the B&B okay?" he asked.

Maggie didn't need to glance over. She could feel her sister swivel and stare at her.

"Yeah, sure," Maggie said. "Thanks for your help. Sorry about—"

"You know each other?" Eve cut in. "You've met?"

"Yeah, last night," Maggie said with a shrug. "It was super brief. Didn't, uh, get around to introductions or anything. I, uh, I asked for directions. He gave them. No biggie—"

"How very fascinating," Eve drawled. "You failed to mention—"

"No, I told you," Maggie said, shooting her sister a cease-and-desist glare.

"Not *really*," Eve said, a big smile on her face, eyes twinkling. "But not to worry. As for that pesky matter of introductions? Easy to solve. I'm Eve Harris, and this," she said, gesturing toward Maggie like she was doing the reveal of a shiny new car on a TV game show, "is my sister, Maggie."

Nine

I know you mean well, but you really have to stop." Maggie was pacing as best she could. The cottage living room wasn't big to start with, and Eve had plopped down in the middle of the floor, surrounded by bags filled with her loot from the market. "Eve? Eve, look at me."

Eve glanced up. "Uh-huh," she said, calm and unperturbed.

"I can't ..." Maggie said. "I don't want to date."

"And you don't have to," Eve said, using her I'm-a-reasonable-woman voice. Which she *so* wasn't. "Tonight is certainly not a date. We invited a nice neighbor over for dinner to thank him for saving you in your hour of need. Simple, neighborly courtesy. Stop stalking about, wringing your hands, Maggie. You're making me dizzy."

"You don't understand," Maggie moaned, slumping to the sofa. "Even if I *were* open to dating—which I'm *not*—it would *never* happen with him!"

"Why not?" Eve was unwrapping earrings now. Dainty, delicate bits of silver and multicolored glass. "You don't think he's handsome?" she asked, holding the dangly earrings up to her ears and turning her head this way and that.

"Of course he's handsome!" Maggie said, frustration building. "The guy should have a warning label stamped on his forehead, for Chrissakes. That's not the point—"

"Aha!" Eve said, gleefully spinning around to face her sister. "So you *do* think he's handsome! Your taste is improving, little sistah. Your taste is improving—"

"The *point* is," Maggie said, talking over her sister, trying, needing to stop this runaway train in its tracks, "that even *if* I were interested, *he's* most definitely not."

Maggie must have been more forceful than she realized because Eve actually stopped talking. The only noise in the room was the tick of the old-fashioned clock on the fireplace mantel.

Eve studied her face. "You don't know that," she finally said, but Maggie could see a smidgen of doubt creep into her eyes.

"I do," Maggie said, suddenly weary.

"But why? You're a beautiful woman."

Maggie snorted.

"You are," Eve insisted. "And intelligent and kind. Any man would be lucky to date you."

"You're my sister," Maggie said. She wanted to go to bed. Or have a glass of wine. Or eat some chocolate. Or do all three. The beginnings of a headache were threatening to form. Maggie dropped her head into her hands, started to massage her temples, her forehead.

"Are you crying?"

"No, of course I'm not crying—"

"That asshole!"

Maggie heard her sister shoot to her feet, packages tumbling. "Eve, no. It's nothing like—"

"What did that Luke-guy do? Did he say something mean? I'm gonna kill him!"

"Eve …" Maggie got up. Even that seemed to require so much effort. She took her sister by the shoulders. "He. Didn't. Do. Anything." She couldn't be clearer than that. "He's just not interested, is all." Maggie gave a disparaging laugh. "And even if he were, he wouldn't act on it."

"Why not?"

"I'm pretty sure he thinks I'm crazy."

"Now you're being ridiculous! You're the most stable person I know."

"He doesn't know that."

"Please," Eve said, rolling her eyes. "All he has to do is look at you. Everything about you screams sensible."

"Really?" Maggie snapped. There was no reason to get snippy with her sister, but Maggie couldn't help the sarcastic tone creeping into her voice. It wasn't Eve's fault Maggie made such an ass of herself. "You want to know what I was wearing when I met him? Hmm?" she demanded.

"You know, now that we're on the subject," Eve said, "I was thinking it would be fun if you let me do a makeover on you. You're so beautiful, and perhaps if you had the right—"

"Eve," Maggie said. "In this instance, a makeover is *not* going to help. You want to know why?" Maggie held up a finger. "Stay there. I'll be right back."

She returned a moment later, wearing her fuzzy pink bathrobe, red long johns mummifying her shoulders and neck, and the pajama top tied around her head with a sleeve flopping in her face. "There. See. Are you satisfied?

This is what I was wearing. *This* was my brilliant first impression! *This* is why he would have no possible choice but to conclude I'm a little deranged."

Eve didn't say anything. Just stared at Maggie, her eyes wide, hands flying to her mouth.

"Are you joking?" she finally said.

"No," Maggie replied.

Eve shook her head like she was trying to make sense of what she was seeing. "But, why, Maggs?" She looked so confused. "Why would you be walking around like that? What on earth got into you?"

"I was trying …" Maggie had to shut her eyes. Why was she feeling so emotional? It wasn't like she even wanted to date this guy. She puffed out a breath and looked her sister. "To be a wilderness adventurer."

"In a …" Eve said, "… in a pink bathrobe?"

And suddenly the humor of it—her ludicrous outfit; Eve's woebegone face—made Maggie start laughing.

A split-second later, her sister was laughing, too. One wave of laughter building on another, until finally they were laughing so hard their legs gave out and they fell to the floor. And whenever the laughter started to abate, one of them would yell out, "I was trying to be a wilderness adventurer!" And that would trigger yet another bout, until their eyes teared up and their bellies and cheeks ached too much to carry on.

"You were right though, Eve," Maggie said later, as she was removing her "wilderness adventurer" garb. "I do love this place."

"Me, too," Eve said, sitting cross-legged on the bed. "Wish we could live here always."

"Yeah." Maggie nodded, hanging her robe on the bathroom door hook. "Wouldn't that be cool?"

Ten

*L*uke had taken a cold shower and chugged three espressos, hoping it would help. But he was still staggering on his feet. Why had he agreed to go? He never accepted invitations of any kind on Saturday nights. By five or six in the evening, he usually crashed and burned, and that was when he'd actually got sleep the night before.

"This is not going to end well," he told Samson, who was lounging alongside the fireplace. "It's too late to cancel. They'll already be cooking. I don't know what do. Don't want to fall asleep at the table. That would be rude."

Samson was no help. Just cocked a shaggy eyebrow at Luke, yawned, and let the warmth and glow of the fire seeping through the stone hearth lull him back to sleep.

Luke glanced at the clock. 6:43 p.m. Another forty-seven minutes before he was supposed to arrive. Their cottage was a five-minute walk away. Maybe he should take another cold shower, get another espresso. Luke yawned, tipped his head back so it rested on the back of the sofa. He stared up at the ceiling. *No sweat,* he told himself. *Buck up! You can do this.*

Maggie was feeling pretty good. She had called Brett and done a little more arm-twisting and, miracle of miracles, he had agreed to buy her out. He tried to push back on the numbers she had given him, but she didn't budge. All that was left was for her lawyer to read through the final document and for Brett to arrange a loan.

It was a nice feeling to have that behind her. The happiness clung to her throughout the dinner preparations, a joyous voice inside saying, *new beginnings, new beginnings, fresh start* as she puttered around the kitchen.

She had made a marinade of olive oil, garlic, fresh ginger, maple syrup, soy sauce, kosher salt, pepper, a squeeze of fresh lemon, and a dash of cayenne. A beautiful wild salmon fillet was resting in it. She would wait until Luke arrived to put the fish on the grill. On the stove, black rice simmered in chicken stock, half an onion added for flavor, which she would remove before serving. Then she would add a dash or two of salt, some pepper, and a dollop of butter.

Eve had put together a salad. The table she had set looked pretty. They had found a white linen tablecloth in a drawer. The fresh flowers Eve had bought at the market were nicely arranged in a glass milk bottle. It seemed an odd choice for a vase, but once Eve had placed the flowers just so and tied a pale lavender ribbon around the top, Maggie had to admit the arrangement was very charming. Eve took after their mom in that way; could make the plainest thing beautiful. *Maybe I'll let her do a makeover*, Maggie thought.

Chardonnay was chilling in the fridge, and a bottle of Cabernet stood on the counter. Everything was ready.

Maggie went into the living room. *I might need to add another log to the fire.* Of course, no logs were required. She had, after all, added a log a few minutes ago. The fire was roaring enthusiastically in the fireplace, and the room was already quite warm. Maggie opened the window and let in the night breeze.

The driveway was empty. She glanced at the path across the field in the direction of Luke's house. Nothing. She looked a little longer, hoping he was just around the bend, his approach obscured by the dark, blending with the trees.

He didn't appear.

She glanced at the clock on the mantel. 8:15 p.m. "Be damned if I'm going down this road again," she muttered under her breath. She returned to the kitchen and took the salmon out of the fridge.

"He here?" Eve asked, pushing back from the table, replacing the chair, and giving the flowers one last tweak.

"Nope," Maggie said, as she went out the back door. She opened the lid of the heated grill and threw the salmon on. "He's not coming."

"You don't know that," Eve said from the doorway.

Maggie turned to look at her. Eve looked so beautiful, framed in light spilling out of the kitchen; so hopeful. Maggie hated to disappoint her, but facts were facts. "Eve, it is eight-seventeen. The man is forty-seven minutes late."

"Maybe something came up?"

"Then he should have called."

"I think you're being unduly harsh. I didn't give him my phone number. Did you? No? I didn't think so."

Maggie set her jaw. "Then he should have had the common courtesy to drop by to tell us. He knows where the cottage is. So that leaves us with two possibilities." Maggie held up a finger. "A. He's an inconsiderate jerk who has no respect for anyone's time but his own and thinks it perfectly fine to show up extremely late to a dinner party. Not okay. Or," she held up a second finger, "B. He's the type of guy who makes plans and then bails with no apologies. Again, not okay. I just got out of a relationship with a self-involved asshole. I have no desire to start dating another one."

Eve looked at her, a smile spreading across her face. "You're right," she said. "He is a dickhead. I'm glad he didn't show up, because that means more of your amazing cooking for me. I'm starving! And if he has the gall to show up now, we'll kick him to the curb."

Luke woke to a wet nose and a headbutt. "Go away, Samson," he mumbled, trying to keep hold of his sleep wave.

Samson gave him another nudge, accompanied by a short, rumbling *woof.*

He must have crashed on the sofa before taking Samson out for his final nightly hurrah. "Sorry, boy," he said, pushing himself forward, getting to his feet, groggy and a little disoriented. The two of them headed for the back door.

Outside, he stretched slightly, still a little woozy, enjoying night sounds and the peaceful twinkle of the stars while Samson went through his ritual of christening various bushes and trees.

He rolled his shoulders. They were a little sore. Always were after Saturday's bread-baking marathon. Took a toll on the lower back as well. He twisted, rotating his body from side to side, loosening up his spine—and that was when he remembered.

The dinner.

"Damn!"

Samson looked over, tilting his head to one side.

"Jesus. What time is it?" he shouted, running for the door and wrenching it open.

Samson gazed mournfully after him, as if to say, "You're screwed, you sorry bastard."

Luke dashed into the kitchen, grabbed the bouquet of flowers and the bottle of Malbec and sprinted out the door.

"I'm so sorry … I'm terribly sorry …" Luke muttered, as he ran. It took a bit of juggling with the wine and flowers to tuck in his shirt properly and comb his fingers through his hair to smooth it into some semblance of civility. "It's indefensible to arrive so late." Luke took a shortcut through the back field. "What time is it? Late. It's probably late. Damn."

When Luke arrived at the Rosemary & Time cottage, all was silent. The windows were dark. The blank glass panels stared at him like shuttered eyes. Not even the tiniest hope of light spilled out.

Eleven

*T*he housekeeper walked across the Spanish-tile floor of the hall on quiet feet. She had learned early on that rubber-soled shoes were a must.

There was company, and an order for hot hors d'oeuvres had wakened the staff from a dead sleep. The cook was incapacitated with a migraine, so Maritza had covered for him. "You rest," she had said. "It's simple. I'll warm up a few things. No big deal." It was 2:35 a.m., but never mind, they all looked out for one another. It was necessary when working for a crazy.

However, now she was having severe misgivings.

A guttural scream erupted from behind the closed study door, followed by the sound of something shattering. Maritza hoped it wasn't another piece of that beautiful Waterford Crystal. It hurt her heart, sweeping up the shards. Why not break something inexpensive?

She stood there with the silver tray of hot hors d'oeuvres. Should she go in or should she run back to the kitchen and come back later? It was always a dangerous proposition to place oneself in the line of fire. Nevertheless, she had a job to do. She had just lifted her hand to rap on the door, when something crashed against it. Something large and breakable.

"Who the hell does she think she is? Threatening to sell to Pondstone Inc.? I'll kill the bitch first," the voice snarled, the fury and venom in it palpable. But it was the maniacal laughter that followed that caused the tiny hairs on Maritza's arms and at the back of her neck to quiver and the nausea to rise in her throat.

She did an about-face, moving as swiftly and silently as she could back to the safety of the kitchen. She was sorry about Tim's headache, but he was going to have to get up and take the food in. There was no way in hell she was going to enter that room.

Twelve

*E*ve reached for another piece of Maggie's hot coffee cake with the fragrant cinnamon, brown sugar, pecan, and butter topping. "This is truly amazing," she said, slicing the cake open and slipping a slab of butter in the middle to melt. "I don't know how you take a little of this and a pinch of that and make such heaven on earth."

"Glad you like it," Maggie said, feeling a warm glow spread through her chest. She liked creating delicious dishes. There was something so comforting about having a nice hunk of warm coffee cake to go with one's cheddar and chive scrambled eggs.

She took a sip of her coffee, the aroma rising with the steam, accentuating the flavor, and watched Eve take another mouthful of coffee cake.

Her sister's eyes drifted shut.

"Mmmm …" Eve moaned. "So good." Suddenly her eyelids flew open. "I've got it!" she yelled, standing up and slamming her fork down on the table. "Oh my God. I am a genius!" She threw up her arms and did a victory dance around the kitchen.

"What's going on? You're going crazy." Maggie laughed as Eve grabbed her arms and pulled her into a wild polka around the room.

"I just had an epiphany!" Eve said. "You and I are going to get a stall for the Saturday market!"

"A what?"

"A stall. You know, like the bonehead breadman has. A stall. And you're going to sell your to-die-for baked goods!"

"Wait a minute, Eve, we're only here for two more weeks—"

"That's the beauty of it," Eve crowed. "We have two whole weeks to give it a test run. See if it's a possibility. Yes, you'd be doing the baking, but I could help." Eve was waving her arms around again. She always did that when she was worked up. "You'd just need to point me in the right direction and tell me what to do. I could buy the supplies, do the dishes, decorate the stall, deal with customers—no problem. I love it here. You love it here. I can paint here. Every time I come, I'm inspired."

"I know, but to move—"

"Maggs," Eve said, suddenly serious, "I can't ..." She shook her head, eyes dark. "I can't go back ... I'm ..." Her mouth twisted slightly, an expression Maggie hadn't seen on her before. " ... Not happy there."

"I thought you liked living in Brooklyn," Maggie said, feeling as if the world had shifted on its axis somehow. "The luxury of having world-class art just a subway ride away, and the shows and the restaurants and—"

"Pffft," Eve said, looking weary. "I'm thirty years old, and what do I have to show for it? A loft in Brooklyn that I share with three people—"

"Three? I thought it was just you and Carmen."

"It was," Eve said drily. "But her boyfriend, Joey, moved in. Which was fine. A little crowded, but fine. But then she decided she was polyamorous, and Dylan moved in." Eve walked over to the table and plucked the piece of coffee cake off her plate. "Sure, that brought the rent and utilities down, but ..." She took a bite of her cake, her other hand cupped below it to catch crumbs.

"*Carmen* is polyamorous?" Maggie was trying to wrap her mind around the idea. In high school, Carmen had been a skinny string bean of a girl who wore large-framed glasses and blushed incessantly. She was two grades ahead of Maggie, but both of them had frequented the library during lunch hour.

"Wow," Maggie said. "I always thought her cheeks flamed like that because she was super shy. You know, prim and proper. But maybe she was thinking wildly experimental things even back then."

"Yeah, it surprised the hell out of me, too, but hey," Eve shrugged, "it is what it is. No judgment. It's inconvenient, is all. Her old boyfriend Joey's going along with the 'lifestyle,' but I can tell his feelings are hurt. All that emotion is ricocheting around the place and making it impossible for me to settle into the work. I try, but it's forced; I'm unable to achieve any kind of depth with my painting. I have no privacy. There's too much noise-of-the-intimate-sort when they're getting along and too much drama when they aren't. And four people sharing one bathroom, two of them grown-ass hairy men. Yuck."

"Wow." Maggie shook her head in disbelief. "I had no idea. At Christmas, when Mom and Dad were quizzing you, you didn't mention any of this. The Brooklyn-loft life sounded like nirvana."

"Yeah, well, I didn't want them to worry."

"But work's good, right? You're enjoying teaching—"

"I hate it," Eve said.

"You hate it?" Maggie squeaked. She could feel her eyebrows flying upward. "I thought you found it fulfilling, helping other people discover their inner artist."

"Nope," Eve said, starting to laugh. "You should take a look in the mirror, Maggie. You look so funny, like a cartoon character going 'GAZOINKS'!" Eve swallowed the last bite of her cake and licked smidgens off her fingers. "I thought I'd like teaching, but the reality is actually rather grim. I went to Yale, for crying out loud. It has the best art programs in the country. I worked hard. Did everything I was supposed to, and then some. I studied with the best. Graduated top of my class, Maggie. You would think that would account for something. So, what am I doing? What is my big, fancy career? A mercy job one of my profs got me. Four days a week, I'm on the train six and a half hours: three hours and fifteen minutes to get to New Haven and the same to get back. And for what? To teach after-school art to a handful of bored, overprivileged kids, most of whom have no desire to be there."

Eve sat back down at the table with a sigh, her shoulders rounding. She pushed her plate away, making room for her elbows, and rubbed her face.

"On my days off, am I painting? No. Who has the time? Gotta pay the bills, after all, so I'm a cocktail waitress at Trapeze. The tips are good, but putting on that smile and those heels to work at that club night after night?" Eve looked up at Maggie, who was still standing in the center of the kitchen. "It's soul-destroying, Maggs."

Maggie wasn't sure what to say.

"But enough about me," Eve said, seeming to shake off her melancholy. "What about you? What would you be going back to? Huh? Do you really want to go back to living in Phoenix? The only reason you moved to Arizona was because Brett wanted to. You're selling your share of the company, so there's nothing to keep you there."

"I know, but ..." Maggie protested weakly, feeling slightly dizzy even contemplating it. Brett had moved to Arizona shortly after Great-Aunt Clare died, and Maggie had followed. "I've built a life there."

"Yeah. A life that sucks. You don't need to go back to that. Let's throw it out and start new."

"But you can't just—"

"Why not?" Eve said, her face flushed with passion. "We are the creators of our own destiny." She flattened her hands on the table and she pushed to her feet. "It's up to us to save ourselves and build the life we want. And I want this!" she said, thumping her clenched fist to her heart. Maggie could see in her sister's gaze expectant hope and a bit of a dare. "What about you?"

A million things flew through Maggie's head: all the reasons why it wouldn't work, why it was a bad idea, that her baking wasn't good enough, that she didn't want to let her sister down, why it was an unrealistic pipe dream ...

"Okay," she heard herself say. "I'm in."

"Oh no." Eve slumped back in her chair and stared at her laptop computer. "This is not good."

"What?" Maggie asked, looking up from the list she was compiling, of baked goods she could make for their new venture.

"Apparently only residents of Solace are allowed to have stalls."

"Well, we're residing here, for the next two weeks at least. Can we use this address?"

"No. That won't cut it. This is a temporary accommodation. In order to qualify for a stall, we have to show two items proving this is our primary residence. Local driver's license, phone or water bill, et cetera."

"That sucks," Maggie said, as the buoyant feeling that had been carrying them through the last few hours started to dissipate.

"Darn." Eve exhaled loudly and dropped her head into her hands, her elbows clunking onto the table. "I was really excited about this."

"Me, too," Maggie said, and in the saying of it, she could feel the truth of her statement. "Look, maybe there's a way around it? If we explain we're contemplating a move—"

"Nah," Eve said, sliding her laptop across the table to her sister. "Take a look. It's pretty cut and dried. Even if we were residents, we'd be put on a wait-list, and wouldn't be guaranteed a spot. If we did luck out and get one, we'd have to outlay a serious chunk of change to buy a tent and table, because apparently, they aren't included." She stood up. "I'm depressed. Gonna go back to bed."

"Eve …" Maggie said. She had hoped that once she opened her mouth, more comforting words would follow, but nothing came. The facts were the facts.

"Don't worry," Eve said, heading toward the bedroom. "A half-hour nap and I'll be good as new." She turned and looked at her sister, and smiled wanly. "It was a crazy idea to start with. We'll have a nice vacation with long tramps through the woods, seashore ambles and delicious food. We're lucky, really."

There was a knock at the door.

"Hell's bells," Eve said. "Can you deal with it? It's probably one of the owners. Lovely ladies but long-winded, and I'm in no mood for a chat."

"Sure," Maggie said, rising to her feet.

"Thanks," Eve said, and disappeared into the bedroom.

Maggie opened the door, and Luke's breath caught in his throat. She was a vision of loveliness, with her rumpled auburn hair tumbling down her back, strands glinting copper and gold in the sunshine. She was wearing jeans and a crisp white blouse and was barefoot.

She stared at him for a moment, the welcoming smile on her face fading. "You," Maggie said, her voice flat, her eyes narrowing.

"I'm sorry," he said quickly, thrusting last night's flowers and wine into her hands before the words he could see bubbling their way to the surface could escape her mouth. "I accidental/ly fell asleep, but that's no excuse."

"No," she said. "It isn't."

She started to shut the door.

He needed to talk fast. "It was incredibly bad manners to stand you up." The door was almost closed now. "And I hope you'll give me a chance to make it up to you." His voice was building in volume to try to reach through the now-shut door.

He waited.

Nothing.

Damn.

"Anything at all," he called. "Just let me know." Even though it was clearly a lost cause. Samson nudged him. "Yeah," he said, giving his dog's scruffy head a pat. "I screwed up." He sighed and headed up the path. "Come on, boy," he said, slapping his thigh, but Samson ignored him and continued snuffing at the door. "Samson, come."

Samson loped over reluctantly.

"Hey," Luke heard her call. He turned around.

She was standing in the doorway, arms crossed in front of her chest. No smile, but at least she was there.

"There is something you can do." She said it like a challenge, a gauntlet thrown down.

"Sure," he said, even though the expression on her face made him a trifle uneasy. "Whatever you want."

Thirteen

*I*f Luke had been thinking with his head, instead of another, more insistent part of his anatomy, he would have said no. Would have walked away.

But he hadn't.

And he was paying for it.

He glanced at his watch. The Saturday market would be in full swing by now, but was he there? No. He was sitting in Ethelwyn and Lavina's guest cottage, with a truckload of fresh-baked bread waiting in the drive, watching Maggie and Eve race around the kitchen like chickens with their heads cut off.

"Can I help?" he asked for the umpteenth time.

"No!" they both shouted in unison.

Let it go, he told himself. *If penance was easy, they wouldn't call it penance. You'll get to the market when you get there.* He made a conscious effort to get out of his head and drop back into his body. To feel the chair under him. To smell the delicious … *Dear God.* Maggie had dashed to the oven and was bent over, lifting truly succulent pies off the rack. His mouth was watering, but he wasn't sure if it was the aroma from the pies or the way her dress clung to her body, caressing her buttocks and thighs.

"Hey, Luke?" Eve's voice cut through his mental meanderings. He looked over. She was rigging some wire on the back of an eye-catching, whimsical sign. "Actually, if you would hold this while I tie and clip it, and then bring it out to the truck?"

"Sure," he said.

The sign turned out to be quite cumbersome and heavy. It wouldn't have presented any difficulty a year and a half ago.

Would he always view his life this way? Divided into two distinct compartments: before the "accident" and after?

When lifting the sign, he made sure to take the bulk of its weight on his good side, planting his left leg carefully. How those two women had managed to get it into the kitchen in the first place was beyond him.

He didn't bother mentioning that there wasn't an appropriate place in his stall to attach the sign. The weight of it would send his tent crashing to the ground. No need to add to their already sky-high stress level. Perhaps he could figure a way to jerry-rig something.

Once the sign was safely stowed in his truck, he took another look at his watch and sighed.

Luke had a preferred way of doing things. A throwback, he supposed, to running a corporation with more than eight thousand employees looking to him for guidance. In those days, he'd had to be time conscious, highly organized, and incredibly detail oriented.

Not so much anymore.

He stretched, enjoying the morning sunshine on his face.

On a normal Saturday, he would arrive at the market at 7:45 a.m., an hour and fifteen minutes before it opened.

That way he could back his truck into a parking spot that was only forty-five feet from the entrance. Even a ten-minute difference in arrival time could morph that distance into a hundred to two hundred feet further to travel—important when one had a lot of stuff to haul.

He'd set up his table, then take his mug and amble over to Claude's booth to snag a double espresso. Returning to his stall, he'd sit back in his chair, enjoy the smoky taste, and watch the market come to life around him. When the early birds showed up a half-hour before the official start, he'd have everything in its place. He had perfected his layout. Didn't have to waste time looking for things. Could just reach and grab. Bang—here's your bread, your croissants, and that'll be $22.50, please.

His cell phone buzzed. He pulled it out of his worn jacket and glanced at the number on the screen. *Figures.* "Yep," he said into the phone.

His brother's familiar voice filtered through. "How you doing, Luke?"

"Fine."

"Where are you now?" Jake asked. "No, let me guess. Sitting in some two-bit stall, selling bread for a pittance. Jesus. If I hadn't seen it for myself, I'd be laughing my ass off. Haven't you had enough of this introspective-contemplation-of-the-inner-working-of-your-navel?"

"Nope."

"Look," his brother said, "I'm not making light of what happened. Adyna was a piece of work, and what she did was truly messed up. I'm sorry she's dead but—"

"Drop it," Luke cut in. Still couldn't believe he had been so stupid. The invincible Luke Benson, founder and

CEO of Benson International Security Inc., had fallen for the oldest con in the book; his fiancée's "*brother*" had actually been her lover, and the whole thing had been a setup from the start.

He should have left. Should have turned around and shut the door when he found her, sprawled back on his desk, her scarlet silk evening gown shoved up around her pale hips. But he hadn't. His legs had refused to move, his brain unable to compute what he was seeing. A man, kneeling before Adyna, his hands spreading her thighs wide, his tongue working her over, fingers inserted inside his wife-to-be.

"What the fuck?!" Luke had yelled.

Adyna had jerked up onto her elbows, her mouth and eyes wide "O"s. The man had spun around and that was when Luke had seen his face: Jasper, Adyna's *brother*, diving for his jacket, the gun, the flash—

Jake was still talking. "But that's over and done with. No need to abandon the multibillion-dollar security company you founded and built."

"Didn't abandon it, baby brother," Luke said, shaking the memories off. "I passed the reins over to you. The company's in good hands. Thriving, actually."

Silence. Jake always had had a difficult time accepting a compliment.

"Are you happy?" Jake asked.

"Happy?" Luke snorted.

"All right, maybe that's pushing it. But are you okay? Are you content?"

Luke thought about baking bread. Good bread. The line of people waiting Saturday mornings to purchase it. He thought of his dog, his old pickup truck, the home he'd found, the sunlight dancing on the water, the sound of its gentle lapping as it met the shore. And then Maggie came out of the house, as if on cue. Her arms were laden and a triumphant smile lit up her face.

"Yeah," Luke said. "I am."

"We're ready!" Maggie called. Her sister, similarly loaded down, was following behind.

"Who's that?" his brother asked.

"Sorry, you're not coming in. There's static. Can't hear. Gotta go," Luke said, and pressed the red *end* button on his phone.

"**There** you go," Maggie said, sending the last of her pies off to a good home. She swiped her forearm across her face. She felt sweaty and gritty, and her feet were sore from standing on the asphalt. But none of that mattered.

"Congratulations," Luke said, the deep rumble of his voice sending tingles to all of her nerve endings. "You sold out. Maggie and Eve's Home-Cooked Comforts is an unequivocal, smashing success."

"A good deal of that success belongs at your doorstep," she said, glancing up at him. He really was easy on the eyes.

"I didn't bake it."

"No," Maggie said, smiling at him. "But you shared your tent and table with us—"

"Didn't really have a choice."

"And you helped us carry our stuff and set up and didn't get too grouchy when we got in your way—"

"Again," he said, eyes twinkling, holding his hands up like she was a highway robber, "didn't have an option."

"Well, you certainly didn't have to send your customers over to our line."

"Or," Eve chimed in, "need to make a big show of stealing coffee cake squares and eating them loudly, proclaiming how tasty they were."

"Just telling the truth, lady. Just telling the truth," Luke said, with a laugh. "Not my fault if people were eavesdropping."

"Eavesdropping?" Maggie snorted. "They could have heard you five stalls down."

Luke leaned over Maggie, causing her pulse to accelerate. "No need doing something if one doesn't do it well," he murmured.

Maggie knew he was talking about helping to introduce her baking to the hungry hordes of Saturday market attendees. However, the silky velvet of his voice caused her mind to fly to more intimate things that he probably also did very well. She turned quickly and started packing up their boxes, hoping he wouldn't notice the hot blush that she could feel flooding her face.

"How about a celebratory dinner?" he asked. "Not tonight," he hastily added. "Saturday night plans, as you now know, are a washout. But how about tomorrow?"

Maggie turned. "You are nuts," she said, poking a finger in his chest—his hard, warm chest, "if you think we're going to cook for you again." She wanted to linger there, to spread out her hand, explore, and stay awhile. However, she was not some wishy-washy woman driven wild by the sensation of the steady thump of his heart beneath her finger. She was a woman in charge. She removed her finger, and stuck it behind her back for good measure.

"I was thinking," he said, his voice having gone husky, "that I would cook for you."

"It's really not necessary," Maggie said. "You're letting us use your stall. That's more than—"

"Dinner?" Eve butted in. "What a great idea. What's your address, and what time do you want us? Actually, here." She shoved a paper and pen at him. Where she had got it from so fast was a mystery to Maggie. But that was Eve. Whatever she wanted somehow appeared at her fingertips. "Write it down, or we'll never remember. Phone number, too. Thanks!"

As Luke scribbled his info down, Eve smiled like a cat with a mouse under her paw. "That's so lovely of you to invite us. It'll be fun, huh, Maggs?"

"Yes," Maggie said through gritted teeth, trying to catch her sister's gaze so she could signal to Eve that she was overstepping.

Eve, however, stubbornly refused to look in her direction. "Wonderful!" Eve chirped. She took the paper with the info on it, gave it a quick glance, and tucked it into the pocket of her jeans. "Seven o'clock it is. This is so exciting! And here's our phone number," Eve said, handing him a scrap of paper. "Actually, it's Maggie's cell. I could give you mine, but it would be kind of pointless, since I rarely check it. You want us to bring anything? Dessert?"

"We aren't bringing anything," Maggie said.

"Oh, that's right," Eve said, still smiling. "This dinner is to celebrate and to make amends for standing us up."

"Letting us crash his stall was making amen—"

"Nonsense," Eve said, briskly. "He feels that cooking dinner for us is necessary for the easing of his conscience. It would be surly and rude to deny him the pleasure. Isn't that right, Luke?" Eve said, turning to him with a triumphant smile.

"Yes," Luke said and Maggie suspected he was trying his damnedest not to laugh.

"Fine," Maggie said. "I'll come."

"And enjoy it?" Eve said.

"You missed your calling," Maggie muttered. "You should have gone into law." Eve just grinned at her. "Fine, yes. I'll enjoy it."

"This is lovely," Eve said, clapping her hands. "I am so glad, Maggie, that you've decided not to hold a grudge. Dinner at seven it is. Oh wait!" She slapped a hand to her forehead. "I forgot. I have a previous engagement tomorrow night."

"We could do Monday night, if that would work better for you?" Luke offered.

"Oh, no, no, no," Eve said, batting his offer away. "It's all set. Don't let me spoil the fun. You two have dinner, and I'll join you some other time."

Before Maggie could get a word in edgewise, Eve had snatched up a stack of boxes and disappeared in the direction of their car.

Fourteen

*T*here," Eve said, adding a finishing dab of lipstick to Maggie's lower lip. She leaned back and squinted at her sister, then broke into a smile. "Oh, Maggie, you look so beautiful! Here …" She gave Maggie's shoulders a little squeeze, then turned her around to face the mirror. "What do you think? Do you like it?"

"Oh my …" Maggie stared into the mirror. "Oh my …" She lifted her hand to her hair, ran her fingertips along her cheek. "I look … I look …"

"Beautiful," Eve said with quiet satisfaction in her voice. "I've been wanting to do this for so long."

"Wow." Maggie sighed happily. "I can't even believe it's me."

"Well, it is," Eve said, with an affectionate smile. "So you better get used to it. Now go knock 'em dead."

"It's just a—"

"Yes, I know," Eve said, in a soothing tone. She plucked a smoky-gray cashmere stole from her suitcase and draped it around Maggie's shoulders. "Dinner with a friend." She gave Maggie a gentle nudge toward the door. "Off you go, Maggs. Have fun."

Maggie walked to her car in a daze. The silky ink-blue dress that Eve had convinced her to wear was swirling around her legs. The cashmere stole caressed her shoulders and neck. It was difficult to wrap her mind around the fact that the vision she had seen in the mirror was actually her. Eve had been begging to make her over for years. Why had she resisted?

She looked different. She felt different. Maybe if she had agreed to the makeover sooner, Brett wouldn't have cheated and dumped her. *No!* she told herself firmly. *Stop right there! It was not your fault. He was a jerk. Love is love. And if he loved you, it wouldn't have mattered what you looked like.* Maggie opened the car door. *As Eve would say, "Do not waste one more precious second of your life on that dickhe—"*

"Wait!" Eve bellowed, bursting out the front door of the cottage and charging over to the car. Something in her fist was fluttering behind her like a miniature foil-wrapped flag. "Here! I forgot to tuck these in your purse."

"Wha ...?" Maggie started to say, but then Eve was close enough, and she saw what they were. "No!" she roared. "I'm just going for dinner!"

But Eve tossed them through the open window and started jogging back toward the house, her hands up, palms out in a don't-shoot-the-messenger pose.

"Just in case," Eve called. "You never know. Better safe than sorry!" She was back by the cottage now. "Love you. Bye. Have fun!" She blew Maggie an extravagant kiss and disappeared into the house, shutting the door behind her.

Maggie sighed. Seriously, her sister was nuts. There was no way Maggie was going to be having hot, mind-blowing sex with Luke—or anyone else, for that matter. At least not in the foreseeable future. She shook her head. *My sister is a well-meaning, meddling pest,* Maggie thought, as she opened her purse and stuffed the condoms inside.

Luke heard the sound of tires on his gravel drive. But it wasn't until Maggie's car rounded the bend and he could see her inside, behind the wheel, that he let out the breath he hadn't known he was holding.

She had come.

A feeling of rightness and satisfaction surged through him.

She had come.

"Hello," he called as she opened her car door.

"Hey there," she replied.

She stepped out of the car, and he felt as if he'd been hit over the head with a two-by-four.

She was stunning. A vision. A goddess come to life. The last vestiges of light from the sunset made her auburn hair glow more brightly than burnished copper, creating a halo effect around her face.

And what a face.

He had known she was beautiful, but it was as if the special essence that was uniquely Maggie had been compounding and multiplying since yesterday afternoon.

He opened his mouth to say *welcome, you look beautiful.* But what came out was, "Gah …"

He shut his mouth.

"Pardon?" she said, tipping her head. She started walking toward him.

She had a damned sexy walk.

Luke decided in that moment that his Abstinence-from-Women policy was officially at an end.

That was …

…If she'd have him.

Before she'd walked into his house, she hadn't known what to expect, but given that he was a man who sold loaves of bread at a stall, she sure hadn't expected this. His home was amazing. The living room alone had rendered her practically speechless, with a soaring ceiling and large, arched windows that captured the ocean stretching out before them. The Olympic Peninsula was beyond that, mountains almost purple against the last vestiges of the setting sun, streaking the sky with color.

"How do you get anything accomplished?" she asked. "I think I would just stand here all day and drink in the view."

He laughed. "I must admit, I do spend an inordinate amount of time doing just that."

"Gorgeous," she said. "Simply gorgeous."

She turned to take in the rest of the room. Exposed wood beams following the curve of the ceiling; deep, comfortable sofas, their gray upholstery echoing some of the color in the stone fireplace along the wall. Samson, lounging beside the fire, lifted his shaggy head and regarded her solemnly. *Good heavens*, she thought. The stunning rug the dog was sprawled on—with its lush, deep reds, rust-oranges, and golds—looked to be an antique Persian Kashan. Actually, she would have put money on it. Kashan rugs were way out of her price range, but she'd been lusting after one for years, so she knew a Kashan when she saw one. "Uh," she said. "You might want to get your rug checked out. It could be quite valuable."

"Umm ..." he replied.

"Where did you find it?"

"Around," he said with a shrug.

Around! Why couldn't she have that kind of luck? She wanted to take off all her clothes and roll around on that beautiful rug, try to absorb it into her skin.

She didn't, of course. "Lovely," she said, quite politely, and moved on.

"**D**elicious," Maggie said, polishing off her last bite of steak. She was amazed she'd managed to eat anything while sitting opposite him, given how shy she'd felt when they first sat down. But now, she didn't feel nervous at all. Something else was thrumming through her body, and it certainly wasn't nerves.

"Glad you enjoyed it," Luke said, topping up Maggie's wine glass. "Steak, baked potato, and grilled asparagus. Nothing fancy." He stood up to clear the table.

She flirted with the idea of helping with the cleanup, but she had slipped off Eve's borrowed heels while they sat at the dinner table. Besides, this was his apology dinner, so why ruin a good thing?

"It tasted good," she said, taking a sip of her wine. "Sometimes simple is best."

He carried the dirty dishes over to the deep farmhouse sink with its polished-chrome culinary faucet. Her dream sink.

Actually, she thought, leaning back in her chair, if she had spent hours poring over kitchen magazines, ripping out pages of her favorite designs, none of them would have come close to this one. His kitchen was perfection. Long stretches of uncluttered surfaces, mostly white marble shot through with strands of gray. But there was also a lower countertop of beautiful wood. Which must be where he kneaded and shaped his bread. There was a stainless-steel countertop as well, which would be fabulous when dealing with chicken or fish and so on.

And then, of course, Maggie thought with a smirk, the ultimate cooking accessory: a gorgeous, long-limbed, hungry panther of a man. She took another sip of her wine and enjoyed the view: the way he moved; his crisp, white, button-down shirt with sleeves rolled up; faded jeans that clung in all the right places. The man had a good ass. Looked mighty fine coming or going.

"That's generous of you to say. Actually, I make amazing bread, but the rest of my culinary skills are pretty basic. I'm a one-trick pony," he said, rinsing off the plates and placing them in the dishwasher.

Oh, I doubt that, she thought, feeling way too turned on for someone who was supposed to be recovering from a broken heart.

He ambled over to the fridge, slightly favoring his left leg.

Has he pulled a muscle, or is it something more permanent?

"Would you like a slice of cheesecake?" he asked, opening the refrigerator and taking out a bakery box. "It's pretty good. Comes with raspberry compote."

"Sure," she said. "Far be it from me to turn down cheesecake."

She watched him plate the dessert. The way the man maneuvered in his kitchen was sexy as hell. She took another sip of her Cab, savoring the hints of oak and black cherry and the spicy finish that lingered in the mouth.

She wondered what he would taste like.

She took another sip of wine. Given the direction of her thoughts, she should probably have put her wine glass down, but she didn't. The wine was too delicious. Complex. Smooth. Expensive. He must have used a good portion of his bread profits to pay for it. She wiggled her bare toes under the table and took another sip, because not drinking this wine would be a crime against all that was holy.

"Whipped cream?" he asked.

"Hell, yeah," she said with a grin. She felt really good and warm inside. This was fun. Eve was right. She should get out more. Date a little.

Maggie was quite pleased that she had managed to make it from her car and into his house without tripping. This was a bit of a feat, because Eve's feet were a size and a half larger than Maggie's. However, Eve's suede stilettos matched perfectly with the dress she had lent her. So they'd stuffed a wad of toilet paper into the toes of the pumps and stuck double-sided tape on the back of her heels. Worked like a charm.

When Eve had begun assembling her outfit, Maggie was concerned that she might appear overdressed. But when she got out of the car and walked toward Luke she knew, by the look on his face and the predatory hunger that flared in his eyes, that Eve had been one hundred percent correct.

It felt nice to be pretty.

"Yeah, it was pretty tough," she was saying, and it wasn't that Luke wasn't listening, or didn't care. He was listening, and he did care, and if he ever ran into her ex, the asshole would be sorry. But Jesus, Luke was finding it hard to focus. "In hindsight," she continued, "I realize he did me a favor. Better that his true nature come out before the wedding rather than after."

"Yes, definitely," Luke said, watching as her lips closed around another morsel of cheesecake smeared with whipped cream. Then the fork slowly slid out of her mouth, her eyelids falling to half-mast.

He shifted, needing to make room in his jeans for his cock, which had moved beyond moderate swelling.

"Mmm …" she moaned, the tip of her pink tongue darting out to capture a drop of raspberry compote that lingered on her lush lower lip.

Okay, now he was in trouble. There was certainly nothing moderate about what was going on in his pants now.

"So good," she murmured. She sighed happily, opened her eyes, and leaned back in her chair, her arms stretching up as she arched like a contented kitty. Which, unfortunately, served to thrust her pert breasts out and upward, only exacerbating the already desperate matters in the cock department. "Anyway," she said, with a half-yawn, apparently oblivious to the effect she was having on his raging hormones, "that's why I'm not looking to dive into another relationship. Not now. Maybe never."

She paused, clearly replaying that last sentence in her head. Her face flushed, she moved her hands to her lap as her spine yanked all the languor out of her.

"Not that you are," she said, hastily. "Looking for a relationship, that is." Her words tripped over one another as her face got rosier and rosier. "I didn't mean to insinuate you were. Or, *if* you were, that it would be me you were looking at. I *know* we're just friends. Not even friends—acquaintances, really, seeing as how I just met you last week. Ha ha ha!" She was making laughing noises, but he could see embarrassed misery in her beautiful eyes.

He reached across the table and snagged the hand that had flailed in the air with the *ha-ha-ha* noise. The rightness of her hand in his made every cell in his body slam to a halt. He knew he should let go, but he couldn't seem to make his hand release hers.

However, she wasn't pulling away. It was like everything in her had paused as well, although her eyes seemed to grow even bigger in her face. He could drown in those eyes.

"Maggie," he said, carefully, gently. "No pressure." She reminded him of a wounded woodland creature that he didn't want to spook. "But," he continued, "just to clarify, I would be lying if I said I wasn't interested in pursuing a more intimate relationship with you."

She swallowed.

"I understand, given your circumstances, that you don't feel ready."

"Yeah." She nodded, and he saw a flash of uncertainty and sorrow flicker across her face.

"No worries," he said. "I'm not going anywhere. If you want a friend, so be it. If you decide you'd like to try for more, I'm your man."

"Thanks," she said.

He let go of her hand and watched it disappear under the table, back into her lap. And he envied her hand. Wished that was him sliding under the table, nestling his head where her hand was now resting. Actually, a bit higher than where it was resting.

The kitchen was silent.

A muffled clatter behind the freezer door as the ice-cube maker dumped a new batch of ice, the sound of water running as it refilled.

Smooth, Benson, he thought, disgusted with himself. *Way to mess it up before you even get started.*

Maggie's mind was spinning. He *wanted* her? He was *interested* in an *intimate relationship* with *her?*

Holy mother of God.

Now what?

She felt almost dizzy with need. Which didn't make sense *at all.* Need for what? Disappointment between the sheets was what. And yet, mixed in with the caution and fear, was a jubilation, too. *I'm a woman,* she thought. *I'm attractive.* Over the last five and a half years, Brett had repeatedly pointed out her defects, her unfuckability. And yet. Even knowing she sucked in the sack, she had an inexplicable desire to climb over the table and attach her mouth to Luke's. She almost laughed at the thought. Wouldn't he be surprised?

Wouldn't *she?* Maggie had never done anything like that in her entire life.

"What?" he asked, looking at her with those dark, intense eyes.

"Oh," she said. She must have smiled. "I just …" She suddenly felt shy. "I wanted to thank you. I know that's not why you said the things you did. And I'm sorry I'm at such a messed-up place in my life. But …"

She looked at him, wishing they were closer and, at the same time, glad that they weren't. Because if they had been … oh my. She would sift her fingers through that unruly, wavy lock of chocolate-brown hair that had fallen onto his forehead. And maybe trace a finger along the peak of his ear for good measure. He had handsome ears.

"Anyway, thank you," she said.

For what? he thought. *I don't know what she's thanking me for. How do I respond?* He was trying to figure that out when she placed her hand on his, where it was resting palm down on the table.

Both of his hands were.

On the table.

Palms down.

Luke was trying to keep them in line. Didn't want them doing something stupid like grabbing her again.

"I can't tell you," she continued, "how much it healed my heart, hearing you say you desired me."

Suddenly, he wanted to punch something. Her ex's face, if he ever met the bastard. "You're a beautiful, smart, sexy woman. Why in the world would you think otherwise?"

"It's just …" Her voice cracked. She wouldn't, couldn't lift her gaze to him. But he didn't need to read her eyes, because he saw first one and then another tear make a slow descent down her cheek.

Forget keeping your hands on the table. The woman needs a hug. He rounded the table. "Come here," he said, extending his hands.

He wanted to scoop her up, wrap his arms around her tight. But in this particular instance, permission was required.

"Just friends," he said.

She tipped her head up, studied his face with tear-filled eyes. She must have seen that he was speaking the truth, because she smiled faintly and took his hands. Once she was standing, he wrapped his arms around her and tucked her head up against his chest. And it was as if the physical contact caused some deeply held sorrow to break free, because she started crying in earnest.

So he stood there, his head bowed over hers, holding her close.

Almost as if they had become one person, and she was grieving for what had happened to both of them, because he wasn't able to.

Fifteen

*M*aggie wasn't crying anymore, but she didn't want to leave the comfort of the shelter of Luke's arms, tucked up against his chest. He smelled good. The steady thump of his heart was reassuring. She exhaled.

"How are you doing?" he asked, his voice rumbling in his chest.

"Good," she said, releasing her grip on Luke's shirt. It wasn't so crisp or clean any longer. She tried to smooth the wrinkles with her hand, but they were pretty entrenched. His body seemed to stiffen. Maybe he had glanced down and seen the tearstains and wrinkles, too. She hadn't pegged him to be anal about that kind of thing. However, sometimes it was hard to know what would piss somebody off until you were too deep in a relationship.

"Sorry," she said. "I made a mess of your shirt."

"Not to worry," he answered. "It's just a shirt." He sounded like he meant it, too.

Oh, she thought, gladness filling her heart. *This is another way he isn't like Brett.*

"Hold on a sec," he said. He reached one arm behind her, and the next thing she knew, he had tucked a couple of Kleenex tissues into her hand. "Just in case."

There was no *in case* about it. Her eyes needed mopping, and her nose too.

She felt a little embarrassed wiping her nose in front of him, but at the same time, she was thankful for the tissues.

When she was done, he held out his hand. "Here," he said.

Hell, no! She was not putting these goopy things in his hand. "I'll do it," Maggie said. "Where's the trash?"

"Under the sink."

She threw the used tissues away, even though it had meant leaving the warmth of his arms.

"Do you want tea or coffee?" he asked. He looked so adorable, with his tear-stained shirt and rumpled hair.

"No, thanks," she said. "I'd better get going."

She crossed to the table and stuck a foot under it, sweeping around until she made contact with one and then the second shoe. She scooted them out from under the table with her foot, stood the shoes upright, and slipped them on.

They felt bigger than she remembered.

Luke was looking down with a puzzled smile. "Uh ... I think you dropped something," he said, pointing under the table.

Maggie glanced down. *Oh, Jesus.* The two little scrunched-up wads of toilet paper that she had stuffed into the toes of Eve's shoes were staring back at her. They looked a little worse for wear.

"Oh my," she said, snatching them up. "Ha ha ..." She lunged for her purse on the counter, wanting to shove the toilet paper inside. But without the toilet paper stuffed into the toes, the shoes were way too loose. She wobbled on her heels, took one step, and tripped.

She did manage to snag the handle of her purse on her downward journey and stuff the toilet paper inside.

Unfortunately, when she shoved the toilet paper inside, the streamer of gold-foil-wrapped condoms flew out.

"Oh no!" She watched in horror as the condoms soared up into the air.

An inelegant grunt escaped as her body landed hard, knocking the breath out of her lungs. Didn't matter. She was on the move. She flipped onto her belly and tried to grab the condoms, but the damn things skittered out of reach across the polished wood floor until they came to their final resting place ...

... At the toe of Luke's sexy-as-hell, well-worn boot.

Shit.

He looked down at the shimmering gold packets lying at his feet. No way to miss them. It was a *long* strand of condoms.

"Hmm," he said. "I'm good. But ... uh ... " He paused and cleared his throat. The corners of his mouth were struggling not to break into an all-out grin. "Ten times in one night might be just ... uh ... a bit beyond even *my* capabilities," he looked over at Maggie sprawled out on his floor, "but I'm happy to give it a go."

"Kill me now," Maggie groaned, rolling onto her back and squeezing her eyes shut tight.

Sixteen

*H*ow'd it go?" Eve asked. She looked cozy, sitting cross-legged on the sofa, a mug of tea on the side table, a small fire glowing in the fireplace.

Maggie plopped down beside her. "What are you working on?" she asked, glancing over at Eve's laptop.

"Hey, I'm on vacation. No work for me. I was just playing around, checking what local rents are here on Solace. They're really reasonable. We could rent a two-bedroom house for less than my portion of the rent back home."

"Eve," Maggie said, "moving here is a long shot. You know that, right?"

"I know," Eve said with a grin, batting away Maggie's concern like it was a pesky but harmless gnat. "I'm just having fun building castles in the air." She scooted closer and angled her screen so Maggie could see it better. "After indulging my real estate curiosity, I posted a couple of pictures of us on Instagram." She scrolled down. "See, here's us at our stall at the market. Cute, huh? And here's you racing around cooking."

"Technically, it's not our stall. It's Luke's. He's sharing it."

"Pfft … semantics," Eve said, waving her off. "And look, these photos haven't been up for more than an hour, and we already have thirty-two likes and six comments."

"Wow," Maggie said. "That is a lot."

"Yeah," Eve said. "People love Solace Island, and they are *nuts* for the Saturday market. I don't know most of these people, but the hashtag solaceisland and hashtag saturdaymarket called them out of the woodwork. Look, here's some guy who lives in Amsterdam. Amazing, huh? The world is such a small place. Hmm … He's kinda cute, too." Eve shut her laptop and placed it on the coffee table in front of them. "Well, enough about my successes," she said, turning to face her sister. "How'd the evening go? What was he wearing? What was his place like?"

Maggie shrugged.

"Did your new look knock him off his feet?"

"Well," Maggie said dryly, "someone was off their feet, but I don't think it was him."

"Oh," Eve said, clapping her hands. "So you do like him! I'm so glad. You know, when we were at the market, I could *see* the two of you together. So clearly. It was like you were a couple already. And the chemistry? Oh my God. Sparks were *flying!*"

"Whoa, whoa, whoa," Maggie said, holding up a hand. "When I said 'off their feet,' I meant me. Literally."

"What?" Eve looked confused.

"I fell," Maggie said succinctly.

"You fell?"

"Yup. Flat on my face. A big ol' belly flop with a skid, like I was heading for home plate. Although instead of home plate, I was lunging for these," Maggie said, plucking the condoms from her purse and letting them dangle from her fingers. "I did find out, however, that he's a quick counter."

"Oh," Eve said weakly. "So he's good with numbers. That's nice. You both like numbers. That's something you have in common."

"He's even faster than me. It took one brief glance for him to compute that there were ten condoms. Not nine. Not twelve. Ten." Maggie sighed, then stuffed the condoms back in her purse.

"I'm sorry, Maggs," Eve said.

"Nah, don't be," Maggie said, reaching over and patting her sister's hand. "Actually, I found it rather sweet that you were looking out for me. Brett's the only guy I've ever slept with, and we were monogamous—"

"No, sweetie," Eve said, her eyes sad. "You weren't."

It took Maggie a moment to absorb that truth.

"Wow. Yeah. You're right. I just *thought* we were." She slumped back into the sofa. "I mean, I found out about Kristal, but only after Brett and I had broken up. I was so oblivious. He had an affair in my own office, right under my nose. Who knows who else he fucked? He could have gone through our entire female staff, for all I know." Maggie leaped up from the sofa. "Jesus! If he didn't wear a condom, I could be carrying all kinds of STDs!" She shuddered, waving her hands like she was trying to flick slime off. "Ick! What-do-I-do? What-do-I-do? I feel so dirty."

Eve got up, gave her sister a hug. "We'll go to a clinic tomorrow, and they can check you out."

"Okay," Maggie said, taking a big breath and letting it out. "You're right. No sense borrowing trouble."

"And before I forget," Eve said, "speaking of ol' fuck-face, his secretary called while you were out."

"Whatever for?"

Eve shrugged. "Wanted our address. Brett had something he needed to send you. Scared me, though, when the phone rang. I had forgotten the cottage had one. By the way, why'd you give him our phone number? This is supposed to be a holiday."

"I didn't," Maggie said, her stomach in knots. "He must have gotten it from someone at the office."

Seventeen

"*R*elax your fist now," the lab technician said as she untied the tourniquet around Maggie's bicep.

Maggie uncurled her fingers and watched as the glass vial began to fill with her blood. "So this will do it?" she asked. "Cover the whole kit and caboodle?"

"Yes," the lab technician replied. "Along with the urine sample and swab. And … we're all done," she said, easing the needle out.

"When will I get the results?"

"Since you haven't been sexually active for several months, we should be able to have answers for you Wednesday, or Thursday at the latest, depending on how busy the lab is."

Maggie tried not to think about it. She had done the necessary blood work. They had a urine sample and a swab from the inside of her mouth and from her cervix. Now it was out of her hands.

She kept herself busy: cozy teas and long talks with her sister, shopping excursions in town, ambles along the beach. Eve drove them by a couple houses for rent, just for fun. They picked up a Solace Studio Tour map and visited wineries, cheese makers, and artists who had galleries tucked into outbuildings behind their houses: some of them were talented, some of them not. "I could do this," Eve would whisper as the two of them walked down the driveway to their car. They checked out bakers and sampled their wares; visited jewelry makers and sculptors, too. But whenever there was a lull in their activities, Maggie's thoughts veered to the tests she had taken and the call that refused to come—and her stomach tightened in knots.

Thursday afternoon, Maggie and Eve were hiking through Hobbs Park. The trail followed the rugged coastline, with lookout peaks of land where the ancient fir and cedar trees gave way to bedrock. There, the trees thinned out, only an occasional scrawny evergreen or arbutus managing to force its way through cracks in the slabs of sandstone, compound rocks, or sheets of granite. *It must be hard*, Maggie thought, *to subsist on the meager portions of nutrients that these solitary trees have access to.*

Eve was bent over, studying the gnarled root structure that held one arbutus tree dangling over the cliff, the ocean crashing below, when Maggie's phone rang, startling them both.

Usually, they had their phones switched off on their nature walks, but for the last three days, they had made an exception. Maggie knew it was probably a lost cause. A good portion of the island didn't seem to be covered by her cell phone provider, but she was not going to waste several days of her vacation rigidly sticking only to the areas where a service bar showed on her phone.

"Don't move," said Eve, grabbing Maggie's arm. Good advice, because literally two steps forward or backward on Solace Island could mean the difference between having a connection or not.

Maggie pulled her phone out of her pocket and looked at the screen. It was a local number. She said a hasty prayer and pressed *answer*, feeling shaky inside.

"Hello?"

"Hi. May I speak with Margaret Harris, please?"

"This is she," Maggie said, biting her lip, glancing at her sister, who was standing stock-still, eyes wide.

"I'm from the clinic, and we just got your test results in. You are all clear."

"All clear?" Maggie said, suddenly feeling weak in the knees.

"Yes. Not an STD in sight," the woman said. "Have a nice day now."

"Thank you. Thank you so much," Maggie said, hanging up the phone. "I'm good," she said to her sister. "I'm clear." A huge smile spread across her face, mirroring the one Eve was wearing.

They did a happy jubilation dance right there on that bluff of land, whooping and hollering, legs and arms flinging out in all directions. "Let's go to The Tree House to celebrate," Eve said, her arm slung around Maggie's shoulder as they turned to follow the trail that led back to the parking lot. "My treat."

The replacement UV lightbulb Luke had ordered for his well purification system was in at Morgan's Hardware Store. He drove into town to pick it up.

He was heading back to his truck when something made him glance to the right. A surge of satisfaction coursed through him. Maggie and her sister were just settling into a booth at The Tree House.

He decided he was ravenously hungry, and a late-afternoon snack at The Tree House would satiate that need.

By the time he had deposited the bulb in his truck and entered the café, the women's beverages were being placed on their table. He started to walk over to greet them, but was waylaid by a table of people leaving, gathering their sweaters, hugging and kissing each other good-bye.

"To fresh starts and new beginnings," Luke heard Maggie's sister say as she lifted a steaming mug of what looked like some kind of latte.

Maggie looked so happy. Practically glowing. If there was a way to harness and bottle the pure, sweet essence that was quintessentially Maggie, he'd be a very wealthy man. *You already are, you idiot.* Okay, then, a wealthier man.

Maggie clunked her mug against her sister's. "To fresh starts, new beginnings, *and ...*" she added, laughing, "*no* STDs!"

"Yes!" Eve said, pumping her free fist into the air in a victory celebration.

"Ahhh," Luke said, casual as rain, as he stepped up to the table. "That explains why you ran out of my house Sunday night."

Maggie swung around, choking on her drink. Eve looked up at him, merriment dancing in her eyes.

"Mind if I join you?" he asked.

"Sure," Eve said, gesturing to Maggie's bench.

He slid in and patted Maggie on the back. "You okay there, sport?" he asked, jauntily.

She nodded, eyes watery; she was still unable to speak, but otherwise she seemed fine.

"What were you talking about? Oh, yes, STDs. Hmm." He nodded wisely. "That would explain the long string of condoms you brought over the other night. I've been thinking about that for the last few days. I aim to please, and I don't think I'm a slouch in the sack, but... *ten*? I don't think even a superhero could manage that in one night. I didn't want my silence on the matter to misrepresent my ... uh ... abilities. But then, thank goodness, I figured it out. You prefer perhaps a layered approach?"

Eve was laughing now.

"I know," he said, taking full advantage of Maggie's inability to speak. "It seems like it would be safer to throw a couple on, but actually, research shows that more than one condom at a time compromises protection. Rips and tears can occur from the added friction." He was enjoying himself mightily.

"All right," Maggie croaked, holding up a hand. "Enough."

"Okay," he said. "No worries." He paused, then leaned forward in a confidential manner. "Just one last question to appease my curiosity: why were we—"

"Maggie just got her test results back," Eve said, despite her sister's violent gestures from the other side of the table. "And, happily, she found out she's STD-free."

"You say that like I've been running around bonking everything that walks," Maggie said indignantly, her cheeks flaming.

"No, darling," Eve said, dryly. "But your fiancé was." She turned to Luke. "Our Maggie here is the unfortunate recipient of only one man's inept labors."

That statement hit him like a ton of bricks. "Seriously?"

"Jeeesus, Eve!" Maggie sputtered. "That's private!"

He tried to wrap his mind around it. She was a twenty-seven-year-old woman, the founder of a successful business—he'd thought. Well, he'd been wrong. "One guy? One?"

Eve nodded.

He glanced over at Maggie, who was shrinking down in her seat, her neck disappearing into her shoulders. Not just her cheeks, but her neck and forehead were beet red as well.

"Hey," he said, tipping down so she could see his face and know the teasing was over. "It's nothing to be ashamed of. If anything, it shows good judgment. You don't leap into things lightly."

"No," Eve drawled. "She sure as hell doesn't. I actually think it would do her some good to leap once in a while." She flinched. "Oww!" she said loudly. "Stop kicking me under the table, Maggs."

"Maggie," Luke continued, knowing she must be embarrassed as hell. "Everyone is nervous going in for that kind of test. You should have seen me. I was a wreck, waiting for my results to come in."

"Really?" Maggie said.

She looked so tentative. He wanted the Maggie he knew, expansive, and happy again.

"It was a year and a half ago, but just thinking about that time in my life makes me break out in a cold sweat." His brain flashed to the last time he had seen Adyna, red silk, a cloud of dark hair, a blur through the glass, rain pounding down. He forced his mind back to the present.

"See," he said, keeping his voice steady, "you aren't the only person to misjudge. To think you were in a monogamous relationship when you weren't." He wasn't one for personal revelations, but some rules needed to be broken.

"And," Eve interrupted, standing up, "I find I have a sudden need to check out the sales rack at Twang & Pearl." She glanced at her watch. "You've got fifteen minutes, max. Then I'm gonna be back, because our food should be ready by then. We skipped lunch and I'm starving."

"You don't have to …" Maggie trailed off, because Eve was already halfway to the door. She looked at her hands twisting in her lap.

The waitress came by and took Luke's order.

"Chicken Thai salad with peanut sauce. Coffee, black. Thanks."

The waitress left.

Silence.

"You okay?" he asked.

She nodded, her gaze still glued to her hands.

"Sorry I embarrassed you."

She looked at him now, a shy smile on her face, and he could see all was forgiven. "You guys were just having fun."

Still, he felt the need to acknowledge his part in her discomfort. "At your expense, and I'm sorry for that."

She waved him off. "Nah, I'm easy to embarrass." Her gaze softened. "I'm sorry someone you loved wasn't trustworthy as well."

And hearing it put into those particular words somehow eased the perpetual knot in his gut.

He had lambasted himself countless times for being so gullible, for failing to run even the most basic security check on "Adyna" and her "brother," Jasper, because *"he had been in love."* All the signs of a sophisticated con had been there; he'd just refused to see them. A toxic cocktail of guilt and anger at himself, but at them, too, for playing him for a fool, for what happened afterward. The aftermath.

And always, on the heels of that anger, came concern, almost to the point of nausea. His whole business had been founded on his ability to run massive, complex security checks and clearances, physical and personal. Every possible speck of minutia was inspected, nothing left to chance. His business had boomed because of his uncanny ability to find the unfindable and keep heads of state, government VIPs, members of Fortune 500 companies, and their families safe. He was counted on to know more, to see more, to have hyper-tuned instincts and reflexes. And yet in his personal life, he had failed colossally.

It was one of the reasons he'd passed the reins of the business over to his brother. He no longer had that cocky confidence and trust in the impeccability of his gut instincts. He'd let his personal life infect his professional life. As a result, in the field, he second-guessed himself and his decisions at every turn. He could no longer be in a line of work where a few seconds could mean the difference between life and death: for himself, for his clients, or for the men and women on his team. It had been clear he had to step down.

He remembered how difficult it had been to walk away from the company he'd built from the ground up. The early days had been tough. A high-wire juggling act of keeping the creditors at bay while trying to rustle up work. He'd felt responsible for the men who'd left secure jobs because they believed in him and what he was trying to do. Men who had wives and children to support. And there he was, flying by the seat of his pants, held afloat by sheer guts and duct tape, gambling with all of their lives. But he'd pulled it off. His company and the men who had been there from the start flourished. Everything had been going his way, and then he had slipped up.

There'd been times when he'd thought the stress and darkness would consume him.

But now, as he sat in the café, shielded by the leafy boughs of an ancient plum tree, he felt a weight lift, a lightness growing inside.

Someone I loved wasn't trustworthy.

It was as simple as that.

"Thank you," he said, bringing her hand to his lips. A light brush of his lips, as the scent of her skin, honeysuckle and tea, surrounded him like a benediction. "Thank you."

What Adyna, the woman he had trusted, had chosen, and the consequences of her actions, was not solely his doing. It was a burden he should no longer carry.

"**W**hat a charming place," Maggie said, as the three of them left The Tree House.

She had an urge to reach out and take Luke's hand in hers, to feel the comfort and intimacy of walking hand in hand. He had beautiful hands. Lying in bed last night, she hadn't been able to stop thinking about them. How they had felt on hers. They were the way a man's hands should be. Not soft and pampered like Brett's. What would it feel like to have those hands on her body? The night had been restless. She wanted, longed for the heat of those strong, sure hands, with their slight calluses. Restless legs tangled in hot sheets. She had kicked off the duvet, wet and slippery between her legs.

"Yeah," Luke replied. "The café's one of those crossover creatures. The tourists like the whimsy of it. The locals continue to come because the food is good, and the portions are generous and fairly priced. In the summer, it's harder to get a table, especially on weekends and in the evenings, too. They have more tables set up along the walk, and live music."

"Really?" Maggie said, trying to pull her thoughts back to the present, hoping like hell he wasn't a mind reader. "It doesn't seem big enough to hold a band."

"I've been," Eve said. "A really good bluegrass band was playing. It was lovely. Starlight overhead, a cold glass of chardonnay."

"They extend a little out that way," Luke said, gesturing toward the rear of the café.

The three of them crossed the road to their cars.

Maggie opened her mouth to invite him for dinner, but it was five o'clock and they had just eaten. *Invite him for drinks, then,* she thought, but quickly discarded that invitation as well. If she invited him over for drinks, he might think it was a blatant invitation to start using all those condoms.

"See you around," Maggie said, cheeks heating up as she hastily hopped into Eve's car, strapped in, and gave him what she hoped was a nonchalant little wave through the glass window.

He didn't follow suit. Just stayed there, looking at her with a bemused expression on his face. Then he leaned forward and rapped on her window.

Maggie lowered the window.

"We on for Saturday market?" he asked, bending down slightly, his arm on the roof of the car.

Maggie's fingers ached to smooth back the dark lock of hair that'd tumbled over his forehead, to trace the laugh lines that crinkled outward from the corners of his lusciously thick lashes framing beautiful, soulful eyes.

"Absolutely!" Maggie heard Eve say from over her shoulder. "We really appreciate it."

"Do you need me to swing by Saturday morning and help load up?" he asked.

"No, thanks," Maggie said, a feeling of gratitude filling the empty cavities in her chest. "A generous offer, but we're already taking advantage of your kindness. I know Saturday mornings are very busy for you as well— "

"If he wants to—" Eve started to say, but Maggie cut her off.

If she and Eve were seriously considering making this a business, then the two of them had to do as much of the work as possible. A true trial run was the only way to know whether their plan was even viable.

"We know the drill now," Maggie said. "Where to go, what to do. And hopefully we'll be able to improve on what we accomplished last week."

"Okay, then," Luke said, a gleam in his eyes that Maggie thought might be approval. Then he leaned forward and brushed a light kiss on her cheek. A light kiss, that was all. A kiss between friends, and yet the feeling of his warm breath fanning across her cheek, his lips making contact with her skin, shot through Maggie like liquid fire. Every nerve ending in her body tingled long after he'd shut the door and Eve had pulled out of the parking lot and driven them home.

Eighteen

A light rain was falling. Not enough for Luke to switch on the windshield wipers for the steady slap from side to side, but nor was it enough to ignore. No, the precipitation was the pain-in-the-ass kind that required personalized windshield wiper attention.

Rain on market day meant smaller crowds and a longer time spent at the stall before everything sold.

Normally, he preferred clear skies for Saturday market, but this morning, when he woke up, it was with pleasure that he had noticed the faint pitter-patter of the rain blowing up against the window. A slower market day meant more time with Maggie. She would be working, he would be working, there would be down time between customers where they could talk and get to know each other better. Perfect, really, since she was recently out of a long-term relationship and hesitant about testing the waters. The rain tapping on the roof of the tent would create a feeling of intimacy. Maybe she would get a little chilled. Standing outside on a rainy day for hours on end could cause the damp to settle into the bones. She might need to snuggle against him for warmth, and he would wrap his arms around her and breathe her in.

Luke smiled at the direction of his thoughts. He shook his head. "Jesus," he said, "you've got it bad." And hearing the words out loud made the smile on his face and in his chest expand.

He glanced in the rear-view mirror. Yup. The tarp covering his breads was securely in place. He knew it was. He had tied it. The tarp had never come loose, and yet, whenever there was rain and the tarp was called for, he would check more than once on the ride over. A puff of a voiceless laugh escaped his lips. Luke shook his head. *You're like a worried mother hen,* he thought. And in that moment, he flashed to an image of Maggie, round with his child growing inside.

Weird. Does she even want children?

A belly laugh erupted, filling the cab of his truck. *What the hell am I thinking? You're jumping the gun, buddy-boy. You aren't even dating yet, for Chrissakes, and even if you were, she might not even want kids—and I'm not sure I do, either.*

It was kind of a shock to the system, as if someone had dumped a bucket of water on his head. A shock. But the water was warm and oddly pleasing.

What was it about her that called to him so deeply? *Yes, she's beautiful, and smart, and sexy as hell,* he thought as he swung the trunk onto Rainbow Road, *but she's more than just that.* It was a gradual process of getting her to let her guard down, like the slow unfurling of a flower.

He glanced at his watch. 7:32 a.m.: he was running a little early. Hadn't planned it that way, but perhaps it was for the best. It took a bit of spatial creativity to organize the usual number of breads and such in half the stall space. Everything needed to be displayed, but in smaller quantities. Asiago cheese buns and sourdough-pesto-Parmesan twists would have to share a basket, instead of each having their own. Rustic French and the multi-grain round would need to co-exist as well.

Luke approached the school zone and shifted down. It was Saturday and school was out, but there was sports practice on the field. *Wonder what time Maggie and Eve will show up?* If last Saturday had been any indication, they'd trundle up around ten or ten-thirty in the morning. Maybe even eleven, without him helping with the loading.

Maggie enjoyed the surprised expression on Luke's face when he pulled into the parking at 7:36 a.m. and saw that she and Eve were already there. "Hey, there, sleepyhead," she called, as she got out of her car and headed over to his, "'bout time."

Eve stayed put in her rental car. She had an Adele CD playing full blast. Adele was singing about love lost and mistakes made and Eve was singing along full tilt as well. Adele had just finished the first chorus, and Maggie knew for a fact that Eve would never, ever shut Adele off mid-song. "She's an artist," Eve would say, "and I'd never disrespect her that way." She didn't have that compunction with any other songwriter that Maggie knew of. Just Adele.

Luke got out of his truck and she suddenly felt shy. Like she was in high school standing against the gym wall, hoping Robbie Zuckerman would ask her to dance. He never had. Of course, he had been two grades above her and not aware of her existence.

Sometimes she'd felt as if she were a ghost drifting through the school halls, lonely and invisible to most. Every once in a while, Eve would pass with a group of her friends, laughing and joking and surrounded by boys. Her sister would wave or blow Maggie a kiss. Sometimes, one of Eve's friends would smile as well, or pat her on the head as if she were a cute but awkward puppy with overly large feet. Then they'd whoosh past, smelling of lip-gloss, secrets, and after-school plans.

Luke didn't walk around to open the tailgate right away. Maggie couldn't tell for sure, with the truck between them, but he was holding onto the doorframe and appeared to be stretching his leg.

"Are you okay?" she asked, heading around the truck where she could see him clearly. He *was* stretching.

"Yeah," he replied, straightening, his voice gruff.

"What happened to your leg?"

"Old injury," he said, with a shrug. "Acts up when there's a shift in the weather." He made his way to the back of the truck with a barely noticeable hitch to his stride, but it was there, and a concern.

He unlatched the tailgate and started to unload the vending canopy. He was definitely favoring his leg. Maggie grabbed the back end of the carryall bag that contained the tent and poles and helped slide it out.

"I can manage," he said.

"I know you can," Maggie replied, "but so can I. I'm stronger than I look."

He opened his mouth to argue, but she cut in. "Please. Let me. It's important that I do my fair share."

They carried the canopy to his allocated site. Luke had been right: it wasn't that heavy and was easy to assemble, but Maggie was glad she had insisted. She enjoyed the cozy camaraderie of working with him, side by side.

Eve showed up and started staking the ties down, while Luke and Maggie returned to the truck and got the folding tables. As they returned to their site with the tables, she noticed that he was walking easier. No hitch now, so that was good.

"You looked surprised to see us this morning," she said.

"I knew you were coming," Luke said. "Just didn't expect to see you this early."

"Early?" Maggie glanced at her sister, and they both started laughing.

"What's so funny?"

"Oh …" Maggie bent and unlatched the metal table legs. "When we were teenagers, working part-time at our parents' construction business, our dad was a great believer in the early wake-up call."

"Five a.m.," Eve chimed in. "Now *that's* early. Dad marching into our bedroom, blowing that damned bugle!"

"Was in the military when he was younger," Maggie told Luke with a grin. "We'd get the long reveille version if we were slow getting up—"

"— If *I* was slow getting up. Maggs was the goody-two-shoes and would always leap out of bed, whereas I —"

"—That's because you had a social life," Maggie said with a chuckle. She turned to Luke. "We'd get the short version if Eve managed to stagger out of bed."

Eve flung an affectionate arm around her shoulder. "She was such a little suck-up."

"I liked going to work with them. It was exciting."

Eve rolled her eyes and grinned. "I rest my case."

Luke watched the two sisters, their heads thrown back, laughing and talking. He could feel the closeness, the love they had for each other and their parents. It was radiating off them like a force field. And he found his teenage-self leaning toward them, longing for that stability and warmth. Wishing he'd been able to provide that for his little brother: a normal home, with a mom and dad, and the opportunity to learn a family business inside and out.

He and Jake had managed to survive the steady stream of dysfunctional men their mom paraded through their apartment in her "hunt for a man." They'd looked out for each other and kept the wackadoodles at bay. It was a full-time job, but they had managed to craft a family of two out of the chaos of their broken home.

Maggie turned and looked at him, her smile like sunshine. "You look so serious. What's on your mind?" she asked.

"Nothing much," he replied, stuffing down memories of the past. They had no relevance to his life now. "Let's get set up, then we can grab some coffee before the hordes arrive."

Nineteen

*M*aggie dropped a lump of butter into the hot pan and swirled it around, then added two chicken breasts, dragging them through the melted butter so they wouldn't stick before she released them. She was cooking, but she was thinking of Luke, too. How his slow-blooming smile transformed the stern features of his face, and pushed back the traces of sadness that lingered just below the surface. At the market, she had found herself trying to find ways to call his smile forward, with amusing stories from her past, observations about people passing by.

Her feet ached a little, from running around baking late into the night. Was feeling a little sleepy, too. She had needed to get up a few hours later and bake some more, then stood in the damp and sold their goods. She was tired, but deeply content.

She now understood why Luke had fallen asleep and missed their first not-a-date. Bed was definitely calling.

However, her sister had a craving for Maggie's chicken with mushrooms, cream and Madeira sauce. It tasted fancy, but was relatively easy to make and always made Eve so darn happy.

"That was so frigging amazing!" Eve crowed, uncorking a chilled California chardonnay. "You baked more than you did the first week and we sold out an hour earlier!"

Eve poured the wine and handed Maggie a glass. "There were people who bought from us last week. I recognized a few faces, didn't you? Repeat customers!" She clinked her glass against Maggie's and took a long sip. "Yum. Nice and crisp. Can taste undertones of apple and honey."

Maggie took a sip.

"Good, huh?" Eve said.

Maggie nodded, smiling at her sister, loving her so much. "Thanks for insisting I come here," Maggie said. "It's been wonderful." She reached over and clinked her wine glass against her sister's. "To Solace Island and sisters."

They took another sip. Maggie could feel herself unwinding and yet, for a second, wistful sadness crept in. Two weeks of their vacation were already gone. Only one remained.

"To staying," Eve said, lifting a questioning eyebrow. "To never going back."

Maggie laughed. Her sister sometimes had this freaky ability to know what she was thinking. "That's crazy," she said, sprinkling some salt and pepper over the sizzling chicken breasts and then taking another sip of her wine. "Even if we did decide to stay, we'd have to go back." She picked up the halved lemon from the cutting board and squeezed the juice into the pan. "Our stuff's back home, our apartments—"

"Actually, it's more cost effective not to go back. Would be wasting a good plane ticket, *and* we'd have to spring for another ticket to fly here again. Trust me," Eve said, "if you return, that old life will suck you back in. I know. I've wanted to stay here before. But I dutifully go back to do the right thing. Wrap things up. Give notice at my job. And what happens?"

"I don't know—what?" Maggie said, because clearly Eve was waiting for a response.

"Absolutely nothing," Eve said, smacking her hand down on the counter. "I'm gonna have Carmen box up my stuff and ship it out, because if I go back to Brooklyn, suddenly that's the reality. This becomes a misty, pleasant dream that recedes as time passes and loses its importance. I get caught up with busyness and pointless things, and before I know it, another five years have flown by, and I have nothing, *nothing* to show for it." She plucked her wine glass off the counter, walked over to the window, and stared out. "No," she said shaking her head, still staring out the window. "I'm not going back." As if she were taking a vow. Eve turned and looked at her. "What about you?"

Maggie was tempted to keep her mouth shut. Would prefer to just enjoy the evening, a glass of wine and a job well done.

However, silence might be taken for acquiescence, and she wasn't sure what she wanted to do. "I haven't decided," she said.

"What's to decide?" her sister said, slight impatience creeping into her tone. "It's a no-brainer."

"I'm different from you, Eve. Solace Island might seem like the answer, but it's important for me to be pragmatic. I need to think through things logically before leaping in with both feet. I admire that about you. I *do*. But it doesn't work for me. I did that once before, dropped out of university, moved to Phoenix with Brett, and started our business. Look how that turned out—"

"You did the right thing, Maggie. Look at me: got my stupid degree, and for what?" Eve said, her face alive with passion. "You took a chance on yourself and built a thriving business. That's an amazing thing, Maggs. I'm sure no one in your graduating class has been able to accomplish what you have. You are twenty-seven years old—"

"—And what do I have to show for it?" Maggie said, cutting her sister off. "A business that I poured everything into, that I care about and now need to walk away from, because to stay would be untenable. A failed relationship—"

"You were with the man for over five years! The longest I've ever lasted with anyone was three—"

"He *cheated* on me and *bailed* the *night* before our *wedding*!" Maggie bellowed.

Silence dropped over the kitchen as the two sisters stared at each other, breathing hard.

"There is that," Eve said. She dropped into a chair and sighed. "I'm sorry, Maggie. I'm being selfish. I shouldn't have pressured you."

"It's okay," Maggie said. "I shouldn't have yelled. It's just … I don't feel very good about myself right now, and when you started painting me as a success—"

"I know, poppet," Eve said, "I'm sorry. I was so wrapped up in what I wanted. Whatever you decide to do is fine with me. Although, for the record, I do think that moving here and working together could turn out to be a very positive thing for both of us."

"I think it could, too," Maggie said, "but I need to make sure. And, Eve, I need to know that if I decide it's not for me, that you'll still love me. Won't hold it against me."

"Oh, Maggie," Eve said, rising and going to her. "Nothing in the world will *ever* stop me loving you. You're my little sister and I'll love you 'til the day I die."

Twenty

*E*ve was out painting. The cottage was quiet, so Maggie decided to use the time and try to sort out how she felt.

She sat down at the small Victorian desk in the living room, removed a piece of paper and a pen, and placed it on the desktop.

"Okay," she said, and puffed out a breath. The paper was so white and blank and empty.

"Right." She uncapped the pen and wrote: Move to Solace.

She underlined it.

Maybe she needed a cup of tea.

She went into the kitchen and brewed one up, and then returned to the living room. She took a sip of her tea. There was something so warm and comforting about a nice mug of tea. She took another sip, placed the mug down and began to write.

Pros:

-It would be fun to start a business with Eve.

-I've missed my sister, and this way, we would get to see each other all the time.

-I love it here.

-I love baking, and one of the key things you should look for when starting a business is something you love and are good at.

-I'm a good baker.

-Luke

Maggie paused. Just looking at his name written down on her paper caused a little tremor of warm to pool low in her body. *No*, she told herself. *You've done this before. Luke should not come into the equation. You either want to move or you don't. Having the hots for a man should not be a part of your decision-making process.*

~~Luke~~

-A fresh start

-I love the topography of the Pacific Northwest.

-Seasons! Clearly delineated seasons. Winter, spring, summer and fall.

-Great hikes.

-The market.

-The ability to purchase locally grown, organic produce and free-range, antibiotic and hormone-free eggs, chicken, etc.

-It would be nice to have Luke as a friend. He's smart and funny and generous and kind and I like his dog, Samson, too.

-I think Eve and I would make good friends here. Real friends.

-Solace has that small-town feel, but the grocery stores are stocked with gourmet items, etc.

Maggie read over her list as she took another sip of tea. "Oh!"

-There are no rattlesnakes, mountain lions, bobcats, tarantulas, scorpions, or Gila monsters on Solace Island.

-I won't have to fall asleep at night serenaded by the howls and yips of coyotes closing in on some poor, hapless cat or stray dog.

-Brett doesn't live on Solace Island.

-If I moved here, I wouldn't have to worry about running into mutual friends and business acquaintances and dealing with the awkwardness and sympathetic looks.

A tidal wave of embarrassment and humiliation at the whole wedding fiasco engulfed her. Maggie dropped her head into her hands and tried to catch her breath. How could she have been so stupid, so blind? Clearly, several people at the office had known what was going on between Brett and Kristal. *Why didn't anyone say something? Did his friends know, too?*

She straightened slowly. *His friends. Not ours. Not really.*

She leaned back in her chair, her mind flipping through the last three weeks of voice messages, texts, emails—none of them from the Phoenix crowd.

Maggie took a sip of her tea, then bent over her list.

Cons:

she wrote.

She waited for the deluge of possible negatives to descend on her, but they weren't forthcoming, so she decided to take a walk.

Twenty-One

Samson lifted his nose, his ears pricking forward, his body quivering. *Must have caught the scent of a deer nearby.* "Okay," Luke said, and Samson took off like a rocket up the bank and disappeared into the woods.

Luke returned his attention to his task, digging his hands into the gritty sand, turning it over and sorting through it. Seven littleneck clams. A couple of the clams were too small, so he tossed them back into the hole. The others joined the ones already in his bucket of seawater. A slight breeze was coming off the ocean. He could taste the tang of salt on his lips. *This is satisfying,* Luke thought as he dug into the wet sand again. *To be able to go out the door and, within minutes, be gathering food for dinner.*

"Hey there."

Luke looked up and saw Maggie coming toward him on the beach. She was wearing an oatmeal-colored, cable-knit sweater, jeans and hiking boots. Her hair was pulled back, but the wind had tugged a few tendrils free. He was envious of the strands of glorious hair for their right to caress her face at will.

"Hi," he said, straightening.

"Whatcha doing?" she asked.

"Clamming."

Her eyes widened. "Wow. I mean, I know clams come from the ocean and all, but ..." She peeked into his bucket. "Wow! There they are."

He knew the clams were the excitement, but still, the expression on her face made him feel as if he'd given her a wonderful gift.

"Can I help?"

"Sure," he said, "if you don't mind getting mucky."

"Are you kidding?" she said, grinning at him. "I love getting mucky." She pushed up her sleeves. "What do I do?"

"Just dig in," he said, bending over and scooping up a handful of sand, "and then sort through it and ..."

"Holy cow!" Maggie said, her eyes sparkling. "You've got some." She squatted down and dug through the sand. "Look at this! There are tons of them. This is a really great spot. Are the clams all over the beach?" she asked, digging with one hand and gathering clams in the other.

"Some places seem to be more fruitful than others. This particular strip of beach is really good. Oh, that one's too little. We need to throw back any that are smaller than one and a half inches."

"Look at this. Oh my goodness." In the palm of her hand, Maggie was cradling a baby clam that was around the size of the tip of her pinky. "It's so tiny."

"We'll cover the little ones up with sand before we leave, to make it harder for the seagulls to get them," he said, rinsing off a few more clams and tossing them into his bucket.

"I'll bury this one now," she said, poking the little clam into the sand with her finger. "Have a good life."

"Yeah, until you grow big enough, and then we'll eat you," he said.

"It's terrible, but true," Maggie said, shaking her head, ruefully. "And to think, I used to be vegetarian."

"Really?"

"Yeah," Maggie said, rinsing the larger clams off and dropping them in his bucket. "Seven years of no meat, poultry, seafood, and then last Christmas, I just snapped. Eve and I were staying with our parents for the holidays. They'd just retired to Florida. Needed to for Mom's arthritis. Took a little while for them to adjust to living there. Mom was feeling a little blue, missing our old family home. So, Eve and I hopped on a plane. We wanted her to know that her health was way more important to us than an old house full of memories, and a white Christmas.

"Brett wasn't pleased with the change of plans. He's always hated Florida with a passion. So, he decided to go skiing with a couple of his buddies." Maggie paused, scrubbed her nose with the back of her wrist. "Actually, now that I think about it, perhaps he wasn't skiing with his 'buddies'—more likely boffing his brains out with Kristal." She contemplated that for a moment, then shrugged. "Whatever."

That's progress, Luke thought. *She's talking about Brett, and not crying anymore.*

He watched her squat down and dig in the sand, enjoying the delight on her face when she discovered more clams.

"I think," she continued, "if Brett had come to Florida with me, I probably wouldn't have fallen off the herbivore wagon."

"He was vegetarian?"

She laughed. "Hell, no. He was always complaining about what a pain in the ass vegetarians are." She gathered the littlenecks up. "I wouldn't have caved because I wouldn't have wanted to give him the satisfaction. Actually," a mischievous look danced across her face, "he still doesn't know."

"That you're eating meat?"

"Uh-uh." She shook her head, looking very pleased with herself. "I probably shouldn't be admitting this." She chuckled. "What kind of person pretends to their fiancé that they are still vegetarian—January, February, March," she counted out on her fingers, "for almost three months?" Maggie started laughing. "A bad person. A *very* bad person." Big belly laughs were tumbling out of her now.

"He didn't notice?"

"No," she chortled. "In the beginning, I hid it. If I was staying over at his place, I'd still cook a vegetarian meal, and he'd poke at the tofu and complain." She had to wipe her eyes, she was laughing so hard. "And sometimes, I would be racked with such ravenous cravings for meat, I'd offer to pick him up some beer and then I'd zip into a hamburger joint and chow down." Her laughter started to subside. "After a while, I didn't even bother hiding it. I didn't tell him, mind you, but I didn't hide it, either." She shook her head, quiet now. "I even ate a salami and provolone sandwich during a lunchtime office meeting. I was sitting *right* beside him."

"What did he say?"

"Nada." A flicker of sadness crossed her face. "In hindsight, I think we didn't know each other very well. Weird, huh? To spend all that time in a supposed relationship and not really know," she softly thumped her chest with her fist, looking up at him, muted anguish in her eyes, "who that person is."

Luke started to step forward, wanting to wrap her in his arms and extinguish the sorrow that had risen up, but stopped his forward momentum. She needed a friend in this moment. If he hugged her, she would become aware of the raging erection that her full-body laughter had called forth. He, who had always taken pride in his self-control, apparently had none over that particular appendage, as far as she was concerned. Thankfully, his hard-on was hidden underneath his fisherman's sweater. He would stay where he was, and listen, and let her sort through the wreckage at her own pace. He could do that. He knew what she was going through. He'd been through a version of it himself. Time was what she needed. Time to heal. Time to replenish.

"So, what was the trigger?" he asked, hoping to change the trajectory of her thoughts. "What did you eat first? Give me the blow-by-blow."

Her expression lightened, and she nodded like she knew what he was trying to do and had decided it was the best course of action. "Well, Dad was showing off his new grill. He had some juicy T-bone steaks sizzling and the aroma was absolutely intoxicating." She rinsed the clams and added them to his bucket. "He also had the usual array of marinated veggies on the grill. My parents were real supportive that way: bell peppers, asparagus, cauliflowers, et cetera. Mom had baked potatoes roasting in a bed of salt and she'd set out cheese and crackers."

Luke could envision the scene: outdoor barbecue, family, smiling faces in the Florida winter sunshine.

"A delicious dinner," Maggie continued, "for any vegetarian, and yet, all I could see were those steaks. The next thing I knew, I'd bypassed all the veggies, thrown a huge honking steak onto my plate and devoured the whole thing in around five seconds flat. My family was shocked."

Luke started laughing. "How was it?" he asked.

"Best damned thing I'd ever tasted in my life," she said, looking up at him, her amazing, almond-shaped eyes twinkling again with humor. Their color seemed different today: the emerald green was even deeper, and there was a touch of blue. Was that bluish tinge always there, or a reflection off the ocean?

"And that was that," she said. "I feel a little guilty sometimes, but I've never gone back. If anything, I'm more carnivorous than I ever was before. Go figure."

They clammed for a while in companionable silence, each of them deep in their own thoughts, the seagulls circling overhead.

Samson came back, the tide came in, they gathered the clams and headed home.

"Can I ask you something?" Maggie said, as they started up the switchbacks that led to the bluffs above.

"Sure, anything."

"What made you decide to move here?"

A million things flew through his mind. Adyna, the explosion, regret, lying in that hospital bed, day after day, with nothing to do but watch the clouds drift by. "You've gotta stop blaming yourself," Jake had told him when Luke stepped away from his business, from the life he'd built in Washington, DC. "You've had too much time confined to your bed, obsessing with 'should-of's and 'could-of's. It's messed with your mind."

"Or sorted it out," he'd replied.

Samson nudged Luke with his wet nose, bringing him back to the present. "I needed a change," he said, shifting the clam bucket to his other hand. "I traveled for a few months, not sure where, or what I was looking for. Then I arrived here and ..." He hadn't really thought about the reasons why he'd chosen Solace Island, or put them into words. "It's hard to explain, really. It just—" He paused and looked at her. "The place felt right. When I drove off the ferry that very first time, I had a sense of coming home."

She nodded, staring down at the dirt path, clearly deep in thought.

"So," he continued, "two days later, I made an offer on my house."

"Just like that?" She looked at him now.

"Yeah."

"Were you scared?"

He laughed. "Hell, no. Look, if it didn't work out, at least I gave it a go. I've found regret only visits when I chicken out and don't take a risk."

"Did you know what you were going to do, work-wise?" she asked, a slight furrow in her brow.

"No, that came later," he said. "Why all the questions?"

She looked back out at the water. Was quiet for a moment. He wasn't sure she was going to answer.

"Eve and I are talking about maybe making our stay permanent. Eve's pretty much made up her mind, but I still have questions. Practical ones. Solace is a beautiful place to vacation, but will we be able to support ourselves? Where would we live? You know, that kind of thing."

"You could make a list of pros and cons——"

"I just did!" she said, swinging back to face him, her expression lightening. She pulled a folded piece of paper out of her pocket and waved it at him. "My list," she said. "So, you do that, too?"

"I do." As the words left his mouth, he felt as if he was acknowledging something much deeper that was occurring between them. Like a chord had been struck, back at the ferry, when he first laid eyes on her. And ever since that time, the sound had been quietly resonating, and realigning all his molecules to hers.

Twenty-Two

*M*aggie hesitated for a second outside her sister's bedroom, and listened. She hadn't bothered to turn on the hall light. The moon through the skylight was enough. She couldn't hear any noises coming from Eve's room that would indicate her sister was awake, but the warm illumination that spilled out from under her door meant that her bedside lamp was on.

She tapped softly on the door. "Eve? You awake?"

There was a rustling noise. "Huh? What?" Eve said loudly. "Everything okay?" Her sister's voice had that groggy urgency of someone who'd woken abruptly and was trying to pretend they hadn't been asleep.

Damn. "Sorry," Maggie said, keeping her voice low, as if that would help her sister go back to sleep. "Your light was on, so I thought—"

"I'm awake. I'm awake. I was just," Eve opened the door, "resting my eyes for a second." She stifled a yawn, and plopped a companionable arm around Maggie's shoulders. "Are you all right, honey? Do you need to talk?"

"I just—I wanted to let you know …" Maggie took a deep breath and then made the leap. "I've decided I want to stay on Solace Island, too."

Twenty-Three

Maggie hung up the phone. She was shaking. Literally shaking, from a potent cocktail of emotions that were surging through her. Frustration and anger were leading the charge.

"What did Brett say?" Eve asked.

Maggie blew out a puff of air. A headache was threatening to take up residence behind her eyes. She rubbed her face and then turned.

Her sister was waiting expectantly on the sofa, her legs tucked up under her.

"He said I was a vindictive, ball-busting bitch—"

"What a dickhead!" Eve said, rocketing to her feet.

The outrage on her sister's face helped defrost some of the numbness that seemed to have descended on Maggie.

"And this was because?"

Eve's expression reminded Maggie of the stray black-and-white kitten their mother had brought home from the pound when they were kids. Wide-eyed, arched back, bristling fur, claws extended. Maggie had a brief image of her sister flying through the air with a bloodcurdling screech and landing on Brett's shoulders, all teeth and claws, spitting with rage and ready to do damage.

"He was unable to secure a loan."

"That's weird. Comfort Homes would be collateral, so you think it would be a no-brainer. Maybe he's bluffing, trying to grind you on price."

"That's what I thought, but apparently he has a terrible FICO score—a lot of outstanding debt—and they won't give him a loan without me attached."

"Are you kidding?" Eve said, shaking her head in disbelief. "You didn't check his FICO score before you moved to Arizona with him?"

"Why would I do that? He was my boyfriend and we were in love. I trusted him."

"Wow." Eve sat back down. "That blows my mind. If I date a guy and we're starting to get serious? I check his credit rating, because how a man handles his debt, whether he pays people and businesses what they are owed, will tell you a lot about his moral character." She was gearing up to full-throttle, big-sister mode. "You are so lucky he bailed on you! You want to know why?"

"Because he's a cheater and a creep?"

"Ha!" Eve said, batting her answer aside. "That's peanuts compared to the pain-in-the-ass pickle you would have found yourself in if you'd actually *married* the guy! If you'd married him, and filed joint taxes—which most married couples do— then *all* of his debt would've become *your* debt. Wouldn't matter if you divorced one year later. You would still have to pay off everything that he owed. Everything. As it stands now, you are tied business-wise. You need to cut ties with this loser and cut them fast."

Maggie sank into the desk chair, suddenly feeling a little weak-kneed. "I had no idea." Her mind spun through an alternate reality of what her life would now have been like if she'd actually married the guy.

"You okay?" she heard Eve ask.

"Yeah. I'm great," she said. And she was. "Better than great. *Lucky* is what I am. Can I borrow your computer for a second?"

"Sure." Eve picked up her computer and handed it to Maggie, who booted up a search engine and started typing. "What are you looking up?"

"The phone number for Pondstone Inc. Here it is."

She picked up the phone and punched in the number. She had slight butterflies in her stomach, but that was to be expected.

The receptionist picked up on the second ring.

"I'd like to speak with Gerry Pondstone, please."

"Who's calling?" the male voice on the other end asked.

"Margaret Harris, from Comfort Homes."

"One moment, please." Some tinny music began to filter through the earpiece. *No need to be nervous,* she told herself. *He'll either want to, or not.*

"Hello, Maggie?" His gruff voice reminded her of her dad.

"Hi, Gerry. How you doing?"

"Good. Good. How're your parents?"

"Enjoying retirement."

"Give them my best," he said.

"I will. Look, Gerry, you mentioned that you and your cousin were thinking about expanding your operations to Phoenix. I'm going to be selling my portion of Comfort Homes and wanted to give you first dibs. Heads up: the situation's a little complicated."

"This have anything to do with that punk that dumped you?"

"That's right. I've decided to move and want to sell. I do own sixty percent of the company, however—"

"Well, then, we have no problem. I'll need to talk it over with Larry, but it's just a formality. We'll make you a fair offer. Who's your lawyer?"

"Robert Sheffman."

"He's a good man."

"Yeah, my dad hooked me up with him. I'll let Sarah Johnson—who handles our accounting—know that it's okay to give you access to the books, et cetera."

"All right," he said. "Let's get this party started. Should be able to get something drawn up fairly quickly."

"Sounds good. Thanks, Gerry. Bye." Maggie hung up.

Again she was shaking, but in a good way this time. And there was Eve, leaping around the living room, pumping her fists into the air and doing high-fives with imaginary fellow celebrators. When she noticed Maggie had hung up the phone, her silent celebration became a vocal one.

"Whoo-hoo! Go get 'em, girl!" Eve crowed. "So, what'd Gerry Pondstone say?"

"He wants to go for it—going to talk it over with his cousin, but assured me it was just a formality. They've had their eye on our company for some time now. Will need a few days for their lawyers to draw up an offer. If it's a clean and fair one, I'll pass it on to my lawyer to hash out the details, and hopefully we'll have a nice chunk of change to plow into our new business."

"Brett's going to shit himself," Eve said with relish.

"Yeah. He won't be pleased," Maggie said, remembering how much he'd screamed at her over the phone. Acting as if his inability to get a loan was her fault. No telling what kind of rage he'd fly into when he realized she hadn't been bluffing about selling to Pondstone Inc.

She rolled her shoulders to try and dissipate the prickling tension that was building there. Brett was behind her now. She was on Solace Island with her sister, and the future stretched out before them like a promise shimmering on the horizon.

Twenty-Four

*M*aggie curled her hands around her coffee mug, trying to warm her chilled fingers. The tide was out so Maggie had convinced Eve to take a break from their number-crunching, list-making, and brainstorming, and go for a walk along the bay's edge. And if Luke happened to be collecting oysters or digging clams or out for a seaside run himself, so much the better.

The walk had been gorgeous. A heron had been standing motionless on a rock outcropping, patiently awaiting the arrival of an unsuspecting meal. The harbor seal surfaced, its sleek brown head idly turning in their direction, giving them a full-on view of dark eyes, huge in its whiskered face. Then, *sploosh* and it was gone.

They came upon a half-eaten fish, and a jellyfish the size of a dinner plate, stranded by the outgoing tide. Tiny sand crabs scuttled away as they approached, slipping under rocks, along with glistening seaweed, and broken shells.

But there was no Luke to be seen.

Maggie had glanced over as they passed his house. All she could see was the upper portion of the peaked roof and part of the stone chimney.

They had walked a bit further, and then headed home. She smiled. *Home.*

Something had brought Luke out of his house and onto the cliff. And once he got there, he knew what it was. He saw the slight figures of Maggie and her sister walking back toward their cottage. They stopped to pick up a shell or rock, ooh and aah, and release it again.

Samson poked his wet nose into Luke's hand. *Perfect!* he thought. "Go on, boy," Luke said, pointing at the women, who were just about to disappear around the outcropping of rocks he called the Three Sisters.

Samson looked at him, cocking his head.

"Go get 'em," Luke said, encouragingly.

Samson gave an excited sideways hop and lowered his chest toward the ground, his butt in the air, his tail going a mile a minute.

"No," Luke moaned. "It's not wrestling time. I want you to find Maggie and Eve—come on, boy. Where's Maggie and Eve?" Even as Luke said it, he knew it was probably hopeless. It wasn't a command they'd ever worked on.

Samson did another sideways hop. "*Woof!*" he barked happily, his tongue lolling out of the side of his mouth.

Luke sighed.

Well, he knew where the women were headed. He returned to his house. He grabbed his keys and wallet from the kitchen counter and a beef chew from a drawer in the mudroom, and then snapped a leash on Samson's collar.

"Let's go, boy," he said. "I have important work for you to do."

"**I** highlighted the best of the bunch in yellow," Eve said, sliding some rental listings across the kitchen table to Maggie with one hand and taking a sip of her jasmine green tea with the other. "The three with red stars? Those are my favorites, and I think we should look at them first. Although you never know, sometimes something sounds wonderful and turns out to be a steaming pile of—"

Maggie quirked an eyebrow. "A steaming pile of Brett, perhaps?"

"Yeah," Eve chuckled, shaking her fingertips. "Yucky. We're gonna run from those."

Thunk!

"What was that?" Maggie said, getting up and heading for the door. "Hope a bird didn't fly into the window." She opened the door and looked down. There was some sort of … *what is that? A dried-up stick or*—

With a sharp *woof* and the thunder of paws, Samson burst out of the woods and raced toward her at a dead gallop.

"What the hell?" Eve said, looking over Maggie's shoulder.

"Hey, Samson," Maggie called, her heart lifting, because if Samson was here, Luke must not be far off. "Whatcha doing, boy?"

Samson skidded to a stop in front of her and picked up the stick thing from the welcome mat.

"What do you have there?" she asked, as the large dog grinned at her around the thing in his mouth. "Is that for me?" She reached out, and he dropped it in her hand. It was a bit slimy from drool.

Samson turned, woofed proudly, ran toward the woods, then returned and sat looking up at her, his tail thumping on the porch floor.

"Samson."

Maggie looked up. She could feel heat flushing her face. Luke was ambling down the path, looking ten times more handsome than the last time she'd seen him.

"Hi, Luke."

"Hi there. Sorry, is he bothering you?" He clapped his hands and Samson bounded to his side.

"No. Not at all," Maggie said. "He brought me his …" She bent her head to look at it closer. "What is this thing?" She heard Eve snort from behind her. "What?" she said, turning to her sister. "What's so funny?"

"Here, I'll take that," Luke said, plucking it from her hand. He drew his arm back and hurled the thing way off into the field. Samson spun and charged after it, a gray blur in motion. "It's a … uh … beef chew."

"Come on, Luke," Eve said. "Tell her the truth."

"That is the truth," Luke said, looking slightly embarrassed. "It's a beef ch—"

"It's a bull penis," Eve said, her voice dropping to a lower register as if she were the fount of all knowledge.

"What?" Maggie said, looking from Eve to Luke and back to Eve again. "Eww," she said, wiping her hand on her jeans.

"You," Eve came around Maggie and poked a finger into Luke's chest, "threw an old, dried bull penis on our doorstep as a way to get to see Maggie. Great romantic opening move, dude."

"A dried-up bull penis?" Maggie said, torn between the urge to remove Eve's finger from Luke's chest and to race to the sink and deep-scrub her hand.

Since she didn't actually have a claim on Luke's chest, Maggie walked over to the kitchen sink and washed up.

"Yup," she heard Luke say. "You caught me out."

She didn't turn her head, but she could see the two of them out of the corner of her eye. Eve stepped back into the kitchen and sat down at the table, and started shuffling through their papers.

Luke leaned his rangy body up against the doorjamb. "I had a craving for Becca's," he said. "Was wondering if you guys would like to come along."

"What's Becca's?" Maggie asked, turning to face him.

He had that little half-smile on his face and was looking right at her. "The best Italian gelato ever. We can drop the dog off and head on over."

"Okay," Maggie said. "I'd like that."

"The best decision you ever made," Luke said. "She makes it locally, using top-quality ingredients, and small batches means it's always fresh. No preservatives."

Maggie smiled. "You sound like an advertisement."

"I suppose I do," he said with a laugh.

It was the first time she had seen him with a no-holds-barred smile, all the shadows in his eyes momentarily vanquished. The effect was breathtaking. Made something lurch almost painfully in the region of her heart.

"Guys," Eve said, "would you mind terribly if I don't come?"

"Of course not, but Eve, we can keep working if you like," Maggie said. "I don't need ice cream. I just thought—"

"No. You two go, eat, have fun," Eve said. "And don't worry about hurrying back. I started a painting that's calling to me. This will be the perfect opportunity for me to dive back in."

"Okay, then," Maggie said, giving her sister a quick hug. "You're the best," she whispered in her sister's ear, and then a bit louder, "See you later."

Twenty-Five

I wanted to thank you," Maggie said, shifting to face him on his truck's worn leather seat. "For Sunday, for our talk on the beach. It really helped."

"Any progress on your decision?" Luke said, acting casual, as if he hadn't spent the last forty-eight hours on tenterhooks, wondering what she was going to decide. He swung his truck onto the main road.

A multitude of possibilities had been unspooling before him ever since they'd gone clamming on the beach: the sisters moving to Solace; Maggie, her sunshine smile, her mouthwatering baking.

"We're going to stay," Maggie said.

Luke glanced over. She looked lighter, as if a burden had been lifted.

She's staying!

"That's wonderful news," he said. He felt like his heart was doing backflips in his chest. "I'm so glad."

"Me, too!" Maggie beamed at him happily. "I know it seems impetuous, crazy almost, but we love it here."

"Hey." He settled into the backrest, relaxing muscles he didn't know had been tensed. "You're preaching to the converted. At least you took a couple of weeks to decide, whereas I ...?"

"Two days, two weeks? Big dif,'" Maggie said with a laugh. "And, it looks like I might have a buyer for my part of Comfort Homes, so next," the giddy sparks of energy streaming out of Maggie were so tangible Luke could almost see and taste them, "we have to find a cozy place to rent and figure out the work situation. Although the Saturday market was profitable, I don't know if it would be enough to sustain the both of us. I think it's better suited as a supplemental type of income."

Luke nodded. "You're right about that. You can make enough to live on, but it just depends on *how* you want to live."

Maggie grinned. "Point well taken. I enjoy the occasional camping expedition; however, I'd prefer not to dwell in a tent permanently."

Luke and Maggie stepped out onto the sidewalk, the screen door at Becca's swinging shut behind them.

"Here goes," Maggie said, sliding a spoonful of salted caramel gelato into her mouth. "Oh my God," her voice a husky murmur, rather how he imagined she'd sound in the throes of passion. "You're right. *So* good."

"You should try the two together," Luke said, tipping his cup of Belgian chocolate in her direction.

"Okay."

He watched her spoon dip, first into his and then hers. There was something so intimate in this simple act of sharing. He felt something more than just an erotic pull as he watched her lips close around the little pink plastic spoon of combined gelato. There was a tenderness, a longing in his chest.

Her eyes closed as she savored the taste of the two together. "Oh boy." She sighed, happily. "Now you're in trouble. You better guard your ice cream. Otherwise I'll be all over it." She opened her eyes and smiled at him. The strands of her hair glittered gold and copper in the sun. "Hey, I just had a great idea! What if we open a little café? I cook, Eve manages, and we can display her gorgeous art on the walls."

It was a beautiful sunny day, but suddenly something didn't feel right. Luke scanned the area. The place looked clear.

"She's such a talented artist," Maggie continued, reaching over for another spoonful of his gelato. "When you see her paintings, you'll know what I'm talking about. She's truly gifted. And I'm not just saying that because I'm her sister."

He was jumping at ghosts again. "Yeah," he said, forcing his attention back to Maggie, who was looking at him a little quizzically. "I think the café is a good idea …"

No. Something was off.

"Is something wrong, Luke?" she asked.

"Hang on." The feeling was getting stronger. He did a three-sixty.

Bingo. There it was. A black Cadillac Escalade tearing out from behind the gas station, burning rubber. It slammed its way across the road, dodging the oncoming traffic.

Not a second to lose.

He grabbed Maggie, yanking her close, tucking his body tightly around hers. He could hear the loud roar of an eight-cylinder motor pushed to the limit, a sharp, panicked cry from the rotund, gray-haired woman in the purple muumuu who had been exiting the optometrist's, the squeal of tires as the Escalade SUV jumped the curb.

In situations like this, it was as if the world slowed— every second stretching into twenty. He dived for the protected space between the building next door, felt the air rushing past them, saw her gelato fly from her hand. Mid-roll he clocked the SUV's premium-painted wheels with chrome inserts, the privacy glass, the four-wheel drive, the lack of a license plate.

"What …?" Maggie seemed to be having difficulty forming words. That was to be expected. The landing would have knocked the wind out of her. "The hell was that?"

The woman in the purple muumuu ran over. "Sweet heavens to Betsy! Are you okay? Oh, my goodness!"

A crowd was forming. Not good.

"I was so scared!" the woman continued. "That truck went roaring right up onto the sidewalk. It was almost as if it was *trying* to run you over!" She shook her fist at the SUV, her dozen bangles jangling. "Some people," she shouted, as the SUV skidded around the corner on two wheels and vanished from sight, "should not be allowed on the road!"

"Did you see inside?" Luke gritted out. "See the driver?"

"No," the woman said, squatting down. "Those windows were darker than shit. Are you okay, dear?" she asked, helping Maggie up.

"Yes …" She looked pretty shaken. "Thank you."

Hell, he was feeling pretty shaky himself. Luke managed to get to his feet, using the wall for support. Once he was upright, he leaned against the wall, trying to look casual, as if his leg wasn't hurting like hell.

"Your boyfriend, he's a keeper," the woman was saying sotto voce, patting Maggie comfortingly on her shoulder.

"Oh," Maggie started to say, "he's not my—"

"Well, if he isn't," the woman interrupted, "you should snap him up, pronto. That quick-thinking young man saved your life."

If he hadn't been in so much pain, he would have laughed out loud at the expression on Maggie's face, but laughter wasn't an option. His leg was cramping bad. Real bad. Controlling his breathing wasn't working. He could feel a trickle of sweat slide down the side of his face as he prayed he wouldn't humiliate himself by passing out.

The woman is right. Luke saved me. Maggie turned to thank him, but the words caught in her throat. He looked terrible. Sweat beaded on his forehead; the color was gone from his face, leaving it deathly white with a hint of green around his nose. Deep lines of pain bracketed his mouth.

She instinctively knew that he needed space, and he needed privacy, and he needed it now.

She turned back to the people who were crowding around; she kept a calm smile on her face as she blocked their view of Luke. "Thank you so much, everyone, for your kindness and concern. We're fine. Just need a little space and privacy to process what just happened."

"Well," the aging lovechild in purple said, "I can tell you what happened. I saw the whole thing! You were walking down the street—"

"I mean, process it in a deep, fundamental way, on the spiritual plane," Maggie said, attempting to phrase it in a way the woman would empathize with, as she gently steered her away from Luke. "And for that, we need to be alone. We're quite shaken, as you can imagine, and need a little quiet and calm."

"Oh," the woman said, her wrinkled face beaming at Maggie. "I understand completely, bless your little heart. You're taking my good advice, aren't you? I guarantee you," the woman said, waggling her bushy eyebrows at Maggie and giving her a sturdy nudge in the ribs with her elbow, "you won't regret it. He looks like he's very good in the sack, and mark my words, I'm never wrong about these things." She gestured for Maggie to lean closer. "And," she said in a hoarse whisper, "I took a quick look at the bulge in his pants. The man's got a long dong. So you enjoy, honey. I would be all over that, if he would have me." She cackled and started shooing bystanders away. "Move along," she hollered. "Everybody, show's over! Nothing to see here." She glanced back at Maggie like a happy cocker spaniel, as if to say, *how am I doing?*

"Thank you," Maggie mouthed, then turned back to deal with Luke.

Twenty-Six

*H*e had expected her to hand him the gel ice pack. He was just grateful that he hadn't had to take the extra steps to the kitchen and his freezer. However, she bent over him and wrapped it around his thigh, her long, wavy hair falling forward, first caressing his cheek, then his shoulder.

He didn't know what surprised him more: the fact that the simple touch of her silky hair could cause such an intense erection, especially given the pain he was in, or that the heat emanating from his cock didn't cause his jeans to burst into flames.

He gritted his teeth while she secured the ice pack with a kitchen towel. The initial bite of cold made him inhale. *Yeah, she still smells like sweet tea and honeysuckle.* Being this close to her without reaching out was killing him.

"Are you okay?" she said, her eyes dark with concern. "Did I hurt you?"

"No," he said. "I'm fine. Thanks. I really appreciate your help."

"Your color's better. How are you feeling?"

"So much better. Thanks." Luke sighed, uncurling his fists, forcing himself to sink back into his sofa rather than lean forward to taste her lips. He shut his eyes, tried to wrestle his body into some semblance of control. Tried to focus on letting the numbing cold of the large gel ice pack sink into his thigh. "And thanks for driving, too."

"No problem. It was the least I could do." She paused. "You know, I was wondering if maybe that woman was right. That car looked like it was intent on mowing us down. Crazy, huh? I've read about that kind of thing in the paper, but never expected a random act of violence to almost happen to me."

The jury was out on whether it had been random or not. He'd be going back to Becca's once he dropped Maggie off. If it had been an attempted hit, the SUV would've been waiting nearby for them to come out of the shop. He'd ask around, might find tire-track marks, as the vehicle was moving fast; he could take an imprint—

The slide of fabric as Maggie shifted distracted him from his thoughts. He wished he were that fabric, sliding across her skin.

"Anyway," she whispered, "thank you for saving me," and then her warm lips brushed against his mouth, soft, tentative, barely there. Luke froze. His heart kicked up to a gallop in his chest. A brief caress, but sweet mother of God, it was the most erotic thing that had happened to him in a very long time.

He held still, hoping, praying, and yes, there she was again. He could feel her hovering an inch or so from his mouth, her sweet, warm breath mingling with his.

And then she was there, bolder this time, more warmth, more hunger. Her hand caressed his cheek, slid up to tangle in his hair, the tip of her tongue tasting his lips, a slight moan against his mouth, and he was undone.

She was drowning in sensations. *This*, she thought triumphantly, deepening the kiss. *This is what the magazines were talking about!* She was tingling all over, liquid warmth pulsing through her limbs, making them feel languorous, heavy, and alive all at once. *Good God,* she thought. *If a kiss can be this good, imagine what this man could make you feel in bed.* He tasted so good, so right. Another moan escaped, and a far-off part of her brain marveled, *This is really interesting. I never make noise. Ever.*

She had made that mistake only once. Brett had got angry, said she was acting like a slut. So she had learned to lie on the bed, quiet and unmoving, him working in and out, on top and inside her. And with that memory came defiance and an idea. A wonderful, daring, thrilling idea. *I'm going to seize that word back*, she thought gleefully. *If enjoying the sensations in my body means I'm a slut, then count me in! I'm going to* revel and delight *in being a slut, because this is* my *body, and I am going to* do *what I want*, taste *what I want, and* touch *what I want!*

Holy shit! Luke's eyes snapped open. She had moved from his mouth to the side of his neck, little licks and bites and kisses. But her hand—her hand seemed to be journeying downward to—*holy fuck*!

She was stroking now. Jesus Christ. He arched up, breath coming like a freight train. He was going to lose it like a green schoolboy. "Honey … Maggie …" He grabbed her hand, stilled it.

"What?" she murmured, her voice low and husky. She caught her plump lower lip between her teeth, and her pelvis moved, undulating slightly as if she was trying to find release.

"I understand how you're feeling. I'm feeling it, too. But you need to be aware of the reason why." His throbbing dick was cursing the fact that he had chosen this moment to be honorable. "Having a near-death experience can affect people in different ways. One of those aftereffects is heightened sexual arousal. Being in a car accident, at a funeral, the grief of losing someone important to you: all of these can act as a powerful aphrodisiac—"

"I don't care," she said, with a sexy-as-fuck, breathy moan. He could feel her breasts against his chest and his shoulder.

"But you will care, Maggie. It's just your body and mind's way of trying to counteract what just happened," it was getting increasingly difficult to focus, to get through what needed to be said, "not only nearly being run down this afternoon, but—"

Her other hand was starting a slow, teasing, downward descent.

He grabbed it, looked her in the face.

"Maggie, Maggie, listen to me. You're also processing the sudden and unexpected loss of your fiancé, and the pain and stress and grief that that brings."

"No, I'm not." But pain and embarrassment flickered across her face.

"You are."

"Oh," she said, shrinking into herself like a wounded animal, the color draining from her face. "You don't want me," she said in a barely-there whisper.

"No," he said, hastily. Vehemently. "That's not it. One hundred percent, I want you." He slapped her hand back on the hard mass in his jeans. "Feel that. That is a man who desperately wants you. But you're vulnerable. And I don't want to take advantage of you."

He could see the color seep back into her face.

"So you do want me?"

"Baby, I'm burning for you."

"Well, then," she said, a smile blooming, "first, with regard to my ex, I am *so* over him." She lifted his hand to her mouth and gently kissed his knuckles, then placed his hand along the back of the sofa. "But so sweet of you to worry about it." She picked up his other hand, tenderly kissed it and placed it, too, along the back of the sofa.

"Stay there, okay?" she said, leaning in and taking possession of his mouth. "I just want to touch you," she breathed against his lips. "That's all. Don't be scared."

"I'm not scared—"

"Oh, good. Then you'll stay. I'm so glad." She slid her hand down his body until she was cupping him again. "And you don't have to worry about taking advantage of me, okay?" She was stroking him now through his jeans, tracing the shape of his erection. "You can erase that worry from your mind, because right now ... I'm the one who's taking advantage of you."

Luke had never in his life shot off in his pants, but he was getting damned close. "Baby ..." he ground out, frantic now with need, struggling to keep his cock in line. "Maggie, honey. You can't keep this up."

"Sure, I can."

"No. You gotta … stop now, hon … I'm gonna come …" Hands fisted, tendons in his neck straining, every cell in his body screaming for release.

"Oh," her voice a breathy whisper. "I wanna see," her hands, fumbling with the buttons on his Levis, "I wanna see what it looks like. Will you let me?" She looked up at him, face flushed, her pupils so enormous they almost obliterated her irises. All shyness, all caution, all sorrow totally gone. "Please … please let me," she pleaded. "I've never seen a cock come before."

Hearing that plea come out of her mouth just about did him in. "But," he managed to croak, "I thought … you weren't," so hard to bring enough blood back to his brain to form coherent sentences, "looking for … a relationship. Wanted," he felt like he was running a marathon, "just to … be friends." He was trying so hard to be honorable, to do the right thing.

"I know," she said, smiling at him, looking totally adorable and impish. "And we will be just friends." A sly, mischievous expression danced across her face. "But maybe you could be a friend who lets me see his cock come? Just this once, okay? You'd be doing me a *huge* favor."

The incongruity of that statement forced a choked laugh out of him.

"Okay," he said, surprising himself. He might burn in hell for this, but at this point, he was willing to pay the price. "If you're certain you want to, but for the record, I'm not sure who is … doing the favor for whom."

She had his fly open now and was peeling his jeans back. She shoved his jeans and his briefs down to reveal his thick, throbbing boner.

"Oh my …" She wasn't looking at his face anymore. All her attention was focused on what she held in her hands. She ran her fingers lightly along the swollen, engorged shaft that was straining toward her. She laughed softly. "I didn't expect it to be quite so massive." She looked up at him. "Would it be all right if I …?"

He wasn't sure what her question was about, but she must have taken his moan for ascent, because she bent over and placed a soft kiss on hot head of his cock, her hair draped forward, brushing against his exposed hips and balls.

"Oh, look," she said, delight in her voice. Her pink tongue darted out to capture a droplet of moisture that had formed.

His hips jolted upward. "Jesus, Maggie," he groaned.

"Hold still," she said pushing his hips back down to the sofa. "When you move around like that it makes it hard to see everything, up close and personal." She knelt between his legs, the look on her face a mix of innocence and hunger.

Then she wrapped her fingers around him, and the sight of his engorged, ruddy dick in her beautiful hand was so damn sexy it nearly blew the roof off his head.

And then—dear holy mother of God—her hand started to move. "Show me," she said. "Show me what to do, what feels nice." And unprincipled bastard that he was, he placed his hand over hers, tightening her grip, moving their hands in tandem, up and down. It felt so damned good that he took the torture a step further, and slid her hand up over the swollen head, with a little rotating movement. Almost died from the pleasure that created, her hand gliding easily, wet from his juice.

"Okay," she said, her voice husky. "I think I've got it. Put your hand back on the sofa and don't move." With a moan, he removed his hand and watched her stroking him, a slight smile curving the corners of her lips upward.

Maggie felt so powerful. Liberated and humbled all at once. He was letting her do what she liked. He was letting her look at his most intimate parts. The masculine scent of his arousal surrounded her. The salty taste of him on her lips, on her tongue, flooded her senses.

He was trying not to move, as instructed. Whenever his hips lurched forward, she stopped moving her hands and raised her mouth from his cock where she was indulging in the occasional lick, kiss, or suck until he was forced to sink back into the sofa. His body shook, his breath coming hard and fast, his groans guttural.

"You're killing me … Maggie," he gasped.

And she felt proud, like a quick study, like she was getting really good at this.

Her panties were soaking wet. She was slippery, aching between her legs. She wanted to yank off her clothes, climb onto him, straddle and ride him to completion. Wouldn't he be surprised if she did that!

But she wanted to see the come shoot out of his swollen cock more.

And then it happened.

She'd thought he might be close. He'd been clenching and unclenching his hands, head thrown back, strain on his face and in the cords of his neck. He was so hard and hot and wet in her hand.

And then it happened. It actually happened.

A choked roar erupted from his mouth, his hips jutted forward, his cock swelling even more. Then it spurted, then again, and again, and again. Creamy cum shot out from the tip, arcing into the air, then splattering across the chest of his charcoal-gray T-shirt like a Jackson Pollock painting.

And it was so beautiful, so intimate, that it made her feel like weeping.

Twenty-Seven

*T*he cabin of the truck was quiet, neither of them talking, just the thrum of the engine and crunch of the tires spitting gravel off the road. Maggie's gaze was glued to the side window as if the scenery streaming past was beyond fascinating. But even though she was turned away, every molecule of her body was inhaling Luke.

He swung into her driveway. Luckily, she was holding on to the grab handle, so she didn't end up on his lap. No seatbelts. One long, smooth seat. The truck had been built before seat belts were required. She had ridden in his truck only a couple times, but already she loved it, the simplicity of the dashboard. Not a lot of whistles and bells.

The driveway to Rosemary & Time had a lot of potholes, and Luke didn't take them at the snail's pace she usually did. The sturdy wheels of his truck charged right over them, the vibrations massaging her nether regions.

Luke stopped the truck, shifted into park and turned to Maggie. "We need to talk about what happened."

She flushed and fiddled with the straps of her purse

"About the near-accident," he said drily. He must have read her mind. "Outside Becca's."

Oh, jeez. "Yes. Absolutely.

"Do you know," he asked, his face serious, focused, "anyone who drives a black, four-wheel-drive Cadillac Escalade? Privacy glass, painted wheels, chrome inserts?"

Her mouth went dry. "You think someone was trying to hurt me."

"Maybe," he said, "maybe not," but it was like a shutter had come down over his eyes, and she couldn't tell what he was thinking. "Could be I was the one who was targeted, of course; there's always the possibility it was a random freak accident. Maybe someone was having a stroke or was high on drugs. But it's wise to explore all possible scenarios—cover all bases."

"I see," she said, thinking about his question. "I know a couple people who have black cars. Black SUVs? It's possible. What brand their cars are? I wouldn't have a clue. I'm sorry. I just don't notice such things."

"No worries," he said, reaching over and patting her hand; his brow furrowed, he stared out the windshield, deep in thought.

She could tell he wasn't seeing the meadow or the woods beyond.

"Is there anyone in your life you're afraid of?" he asked. "Or who wishes you harm?"

She flashed to Brett momentarily, screaming at her over the phone. Yeah, she had been shaken, but Brett was a self-absorbed narcissist—he wasn't violent. "No," she answered. "I can't think of anyone who wishes me harm."

"What's this Brett guy like? Is he hot-tempered? A poor loser? Has he ever hurt you in any way, Maggie?"

"He has a bad temper, yes. Always had, but he's more verbally abusive. Never hit me, or anything like that."

"Good," he replied, under his breath. So quietly she almost didn't hear him.

They sat like that for a moment. Still. Just the soft sound of their breathing.

"Well, then," Maggie said, reaching for the door handle, "thanks for the ice cream and the ride."

He turned to her, his face clearing. "You're welcome," he said, quirking an eyebrow, a slight smile on his face. "Anytime."

Maggie could feel her face growing hot, because they both knew what he was referencing. *Anytime? She thought. Like now? I could just reach and grab ahold of it?* She hopped out of the truck, and headed for the cottage.

"**Hello**," Maggie called, swinging the cottage door open, pleased with how normal and natural her voice sounded. As if it was just a standard, old, ordinary afternoon and she hadn't just had her hands wrapped around … Maggie yanked sharply back on the reins of her thoughts. *None of that! Thank you very much.*

"Eve, I'm back." Maggie listened.

Nothing.

The teasing expression vanished from Luke's face. "Would you mind if I took a quick spin around the cottage? Make sure everything's okay?"

"Sure," she said. "Good idea. Thank you."

He was back a few minutes later, a note in his hand. "Apparently, Eve's painting in the lower field. I'll swing by there and make sure she's fine."

"That would be wonderful," she said, relief rushing over her. *So kind, how he's looking out for us.* "I really appreciate you doing that."

He turned to go.

"But," she said, her hand alighting on his forearm, causing a surge of heat to momentarily befuddle her brain. *It is so intense. Does he feel it too?* She dropped her hand to her side, but even with the connection broken, her skin still tingled. "If you could do it surreptitiously, because Eve gets really pissed if she's interrupted while painting."

"She won't even know I've checked on her," Luke said, handing Maggie the note as he headed for the door. "Everything looks fine. I've secured the doors and windows; just a precaution until we know what we're dealing with. Keep your cell phone with you at all times, and if you hear anything out of the ordinary, don't check it out. Leave the house immediately. Go to Ethelwyn and Lavina's, and then call me and 911."

"Okay. Thanks, Luke."

"Lock the door behind me," he said, and then he was gone.

Maggie slid the deadbolt into place and glanced down at the note in her hand.

Out painting. Don't hold dinner for me. Love you. Hope you had fun!

— Eve xo

She was grateful to have a chance to get her thoughts in order before her sister arrived home. There wasn't a lot of time, as dusk was fast approaching and her sister would be unable to paint outdoors much longer.

What to do, Maggie thought. *Something soothing and indulgent to counterbalance the very unusual afternoon.*

She headed to the kitchen. She'd bake a cake and then start dinner. She lifted the apron off its brass hook and slipped it over her head; was starting to tie it when the phone in the living room rang.

The loud, shrill jangle made her jump.

She went back into the living room and picked up the receiver, as the surge of adrenaline started to recede. "Hello?"

No one answered.

"Hello?"

Still no answer, but someone was there. She was sure of it.

"I can hear you breathing," Maggie said, torn between irritation and unease.

There was a clunk on the other end and the phone went dead.

She froze for a second, her mind spinning. *Was that important, or just a prank call?* She exhaled slowly, released her grip on the receiver, and placed it back on its base. She made a mental note to tell Luke about the call when they next spoke.

She returned to the kitchen and turned on the old radio. Fiddled with the dial until she found some nice, mellow music to cook by. She poured herself a glass of chardonnay and settled in to cook.

By the time Eve came home, Maggie was taking the chocolate cake with caramelized pecan topping out of the oven. She had chicken fricassee simmering on the stove, green beans almondine prepped, and buttery mashed potatoes keeping warm in a pot.

"The smells coming out of this house are amazing," Eve said, pouring herself a glass of wine, then collapsing with a satisfied sigh into a kitchen chair. "I could smell your cooking as I tromped across the field, and I thought to myself, 'how lucky am I?'" She took a healthy sip of wine. "I paint all afternoon, then come home to this." She stretched her arms out exuberantly. "My sister, a cozy, warm home, delicious food cooking, beautiful nature surrounding us—a feast for the eyes, for the soul, for the belly. Life truly doesn't get any better than this."

"I take it," Maggie said, tasting the sauce, adding a bit more salt, "painting went well."

"How did you guess?" Eve said with a grin. "I was on a rampage. Couldn't stop. Finally it got too dark, and I had to stop. Didn't want to, though, I can tell you that. If I had a way to keep that sun up in the sky, I would have done it. But hopefully, the muse will return tomorrow, and I can finish the painting. You don't mind, do you? I promise after that we can start sorting out housing and whatnot."

"Absolutely not," Maggie said, tasting the mashed potatoes. "Hmm …" They were almost where she wanted them. She added a glug of buttermilk and a handful of freshly grated Parmesan.

"How was your afternoon?" Eve asked, ambling over to the counter. "Hey, you've got a couple texts. Must have your sound off. Want me to read them?"

"Sure." She dropped another slice of butter into the potatoes.

Eve picked up Maggie's cell. "First one's from Brett. *What the fuck? Call me.*"

"Guess Gerry Pondstone's gotten in touch," Maggie said, stirring the melting butter in, feeling slightly nauseated. She would be glad when everything was sorted out and they could both move on.

"Next one's from—ha!— Gerry Pondstone. So, yes, your supposition was correct. *Things are moving along nicely. Should have something for you to look over in the next day or two.* Wow! That's fast." Eve took another sip of her wine and scrolled down. "And then we have one from Luke. Ho, ho, ho! *Eve's fine. Will talk later. Keep your doors locked.*" She looked at Maggie. "What the hell?"

"There was an incident ..." So weird. Just saying it caused her body to start trembling. "Outside the gelato store."

"Oh, sweetie. Are you all right?" Her sister rounded the counter and put a comforting arm around her shoulders. "What kind of incident?"

"A car almost ran us over."

"Jesus ..."

"It could have been random, but just in case ..." She exhaled, trying to dissipate the nerves that were jangling through her.

"We need to be aware, and lock the doors." Eve nodded.

"Yeah," Maggie said.

Luke leaned back from his desk, phone against his ear. "There's none?"

"That's correct," Jake said. "I ran our programs, cross-checked. There are zero Escalades with those pimped upgrades, black or any other color, registered in Solace."

Luke drummed his fingers on the polished wood surface of his desk. "What about part-timers?"

"I checked that as well. I found two black, extended models owned by part-time residents. One lives on Morningside Road and the other on Sunset. I've emailed you their addresses, copies of vehicle registrations, and driving records. Although, F-Y-I, both owners are senior citizens, so fancy maneuvering like you described is probably not in their wheelhouse, and neither vehicle has the upgrades you mentioned."

"Thanks, Jake."

"No prob. Let me know if there's anything else you need."

"Will do," Luke said and hung up.

He sat for a moment longer. Then picked up the phone and hit redial.

"Yep?" Jake said.

"Can you spare a couple guys?"

"You're that concerned?" his brother asked.

"I don't know." Luke shook his head. "It's a feeling. It could be nothing, but ..."

"Ah, yes. The old feelings. I'll send them out tonight."

"Thanks, Jake. I appreciate it."

"Who do you want?"

"Gunner and Colt available?"

"If you want them to be," Jake replied.

"Yeah," Luke said. "I want the best for Maggie and Eve, just in case."

Twenty-Eight

*L*uke set up camp in the woods, directly behind the cottage. That way, he had a clear view of the driveway, the front entrance and the back kitchen door, as well as the field, in case someone decided on a more stealthy approach. He and Samson were tucked down, nice and discreet, when Samson's nose started twitching.

"What's that, ol' boy?" Luke asked.

Samson let out a soft, mournful *woof.*

"You seeing something?" Luke flipped his night-vision goggles down over his eyes and scanned the area. All was quiet. Then he realized what Samson was moaning about—the delicious aroma of comfort-cooking drifting out of the cottage windows.

Samson nudged him with his snout as if to say, *come on, let's go get some.*

"No," Luke replied. "We've got a job to do."

Samson sighed heavily, looking at Luke from under his shaggy brows, his head cocked to one side.

"I know, I'm hungry, too," Luke said, his stomach growling. "Odds are the driver of the tricked-out Escalade has a contract to take me out, not her. However, on the off chance …" Luke trailed off, shook his head. "A career low. Now I'm explaining my actions to a dog." He reached into his pack and pulled out a handful of nuts, gave a couple to Samson and ate the rest.

There had been heavy rain the night before, which had blown out to sea by the morning. They had enjoyed a glorious day of sunshine, but now the moisture from the night's downpour was seeping from the ground into the seat of Luke's jeans. The damp cold and the drop in temperature weren't doing his injury any favors.

He slowed his breathing, focused inward, and opened his senses. He leaned back against the thick bark of a Douglas fir, drawing strength from it and from the earth as he hunkered down to wait out the long night.

2:18 a.m. He heard the low rumble of an engine, the sound of tires crunching as the vehicle slowly made its way down the gravel driveway. Luke sat up, every sense on high alert. The engine went quiet. But Luke could tell the car was still moving. Must have killed it and shifted to neutral, using the downward grade of the driveway to propel the SUV closer. Now he could see the dark shape of it gliding closer through the trees, the headlights off.

Damn, he thought, standing and shaking his leg to alleviate some of the stiffness that had set in. *They are after Maggie. I'd hoped it was me.*

The SUV rolled to a stop. The right shape and size for the Escalade. Hard to confirm, since it was partially obscured by the trees. His night-vision system was good, but it couldn't penetrate the dense foliage. Two large men got out. Anger surged, bright and hot; a predatory growl threatened to erupt. Only years of discipline kept him silent.

They were packing.

Shit.

"Okay, Samson," he whispered, removing his goggles and stuffing them in his backpack. "Let's go, boy."

Maggie had been unable to fall asleep. Her mind was spinning a mile a minute, playing and replaying the events of the last few weeks. *Well,* she thought, *at least no one can say my life is boring.* She fluffed her pillow and flipped onto her other side.

Maybe she should get out of bed. She had learned, in the days after Brett's betrayal, different tools recommended by articles on sleep health. If she couldn't sleep, she needed to get out of bed, go into another room, do something peaceful until she got drowsy.

What was that?

Some noise outside the cottage. It sounded like a scuffle.

Maggie got out of bed, tiptoed to the window, pulled back a corner of the curtain, and peeked out. She saw bodies lunging, heard fists hitting flesh. The unmistakable sound of Samson's ferocious growling. Which meant Luke was out there. She had to help!

Maggie slammed her feet into her shoes and grabbed the first weapon she could find. She bolted through the kitchen and out the back door, the hefty John Fitzstien *Stone on Steel* sculpture firmly in hand.

Luke was grateful he'd had the element of surprise on his side. He had disarmed the first assailant and was struggling for control of the second assailant's gun, while Samson kept the first one at bay. Luke hoped he could disarm the bastard without resorting to his Glock. Safer that way, with the sisters asleep in the house.

The first assailant screamed as Samson knocked him to the ground. The thug Luke was wrestling glanced over, and that was the split-second opening Luke had been waiting for. He grabbed the gun and twisted it down, snapping the assailant's trigger finger.

"Who sent you?" he growled.

"Fuck you," the guy spat out.

"Suit yourself," Luke said, as he systematically broke another bone in the assailant's hand. However, the tough son of a bitch still didn't release his grip on his gun.

"No paycheck's worth the kind of pain I can put you through," Luke said, watching a trickle of sweat drip down the side of the guy's face. "Drop the gun, and I'll let you go."

"Go to hell."

Suddenly, a third figure leaped from the shadows to join the fray.

A jolt of added adrenaline shot through Luke. He'd seen only two men getting out of the SUV, and then he realized—

Shit! It's Maggie.

The guy had a gun and was trying to shoot Luke. *Over my dead body,* Maggie thought, swinging the sculpture with all her might and smashing it over the guy's head. It worked pretty well, because he let go of the gun right quick and crumpled to the ground.

"And Brett called you a useless piece of junk," Maggie said to the sculpture. "Well, we showed him."

"Watch out!" Luke yelled.

Maggie whirled. The other man was charging at her. He had a nasty-looking knife. She could see the blade of it glinting in the moonlight. *Holy mother of God. Okay. No problem. Don't freak out. It's only a knife.*

She hoisted her trusty *Stone on Steel* art piece to her shoulder like a bat, scared shitless but ready to rumble.

There was a loud crack, a faint smell of sulfur. "Get back! Get back!" Luke was yelling. She felt Luke grab the back of her nightgown and drag her backward.

In her peripheral vision, she could see the creep she had bashed over the head staggering to his feet. "Luke—" she called out, but instead of charging toward the two of them, the man tore down the driveway, hand clutched to his bleeding head.

The other guy was still advancing, his face contorted in bloodlust and rage. There was another loud crack, which seemed to jerk the guy back. He shook it off and continued to stagger forward, thick, dark blood blossoming outward on his chest. Luke shoved her behind him. In the distance she could hear a vehicle door slam, an engine roar to life, the sound of the SUV speeding off.

"That fucker," the guy choked out, more breath than voice, a slight sneer flickering across his face. He managed to lurch another step forward and then crashed to the ground like a felled oak tree.

Maggie and Luke stood there, the night quiet around them. Then gradually the frogs started up: first one, then two, and then a chorus of them.

"Do you think he's going to be okay?" Maggie asked. She was shaking; couldn't stop shaking.

"I doubt it," Luke said. He wrapped his arm around her tightly, the other arm hanging at his side, the gun in his hand. "If anything had happened to you—" He exhaled, dropped a gentle kiss on her head. "You all right?"

"Yeah. I'm fine." But she most definitely wasn't.

"You handled yourself well, but in the future, I would prefer it if you stayed out of it. Keep yourself safe. I know how to handle this type of situation."

Maggie managed a wan smile. "First of all, for the record, I am hoping we don't run into this type of situation ever again. And second, I'd never leave you to face an unfair fight on your own, two against one. Luke, I had no choice but to jump in. My mom didn't raise wimps. It was important to her that Eve and I learned how to defend ourselves in case of an emergency."

"You were a ferocious warrior woman tonight," Luke said, giving her shoulders a squeeze. "Thanks for coming to my ..." he cleared his throat, "um ... rescue." He rested his cheek on the top of her head for a moment.

She wrapped her arms around his waist. The faint ringing in her ears was lessening. "You're welcome," she said. She could smell blood. She didn't want to look. "What do we do about—" She swallowed. Her throat felt thick, like its walls were closing in.

Luke gave her shoulders another squeeze, then walked over to the guy, flipped him onto his back, and squatted down to check for vitals.

"Is he ..." Maggie swallowed again, "...dead?"

"'Fraid so." Luke straightened. "Guess he won't be answering any questions."

"What about the other guy?" Maggie asked. She was trying to act all calm, grateful for the dark so he couldn't see how badly she was shaking, her teeth clattering like it was thirty below outside. "Will he be back?"

"Don't know," he said, returning to her side, wrapping her in his arms. "We'll have to wait and see."

"Okay," the beefy, bald-headed cop said. He put away his pen, gathered his papers. "We're all done here."

"Do you need us to follow you to the station?" Luke asked. He looked exhausted. The morning sun was just starting to peek over the horizon.

The cop shook his head. "We'll call if we have more questions. Might need you to swing by the station later. I doubt this will go to court. The vehicle parked up the driveway matches the description from the report you filed yesterday afternoon."

Luke filed a report. Oh my God, I never would have thought to do that.

"My neighbor, Dorothy Whidbee, mid-sixties, a ..." the cop cleared his throat, "unique personality, apparently was an eye witness. Barged into my house while the wife and me were sitting down to dinner. Helped herself to a healthy portion of pot roast, and then treated us to a detailed reenactment of the incident," the cop's eye flicked down to Luke's crotch for a millisecond and then snapped back up to his face, "before she headed to her belly-dance class. Her version of the events corroborated with yours."

Thank heavens for Luke, Maggie thought. *Eve and I would probably be dead right now if it weren't for him. Why did those men want to harm me? I've never seen them before in my life.* Her eyes felt like sandpaper. She was dog-tired. Needed sleep.

The skinny, sandy-haired cop gulped down the last swig of his coffee. *Two sugars and cream,* Maggie thought. She felt removed from the situation, like she was floating around on the kitchen ceiling, watching herself interact, answer questions, and every once in a while race off to the bathroom to dry heave over the toilet again when last night's images and memories rose up and overwhelmed her.

"It was a real honor to meet you, Mr. Benson," the fresh-faced cop said, grasping Luke's hand and pumping it enthusiastically. He looked around twenty-two or twenty-three. "A real hero. Didn't know you were *the* Luke Benson. And living right here on Solace Island."

"A pleasure meeting both of you, as well," Luke said. "I'm hoping we can keep my previous line of work on the down-low. I've retired from that and—"

"Yes, sir, Mr. Benson, sir. Not a word. You can count on us."

"Let me know if anything else comes up," the beefy cop said as they pushed back from the table.

"Will do," Luke said, walking them to the door.

"You have a nice day now," the cop said, tipping his hat. And then they were gone.

Eve stood at the window until the cop car disappeared from view and then turned toward Luke and Maggie. "All right, you two," Eve demanded, her face tense, pale, "what the hell is going on?" She pointed a finger at Luke. "And you, Mr. Bread Baker! What was all that hero-worship business from the cop? Retired? From what? If you've gotten my sister mixed up in some kind of scheme … so help me, God!"

"Eve!" Maggie pried the front of Luke's shirt out of her sister's grip. "Stop yelling at him. He's not the enemy—"

"How the hell do you know that? You're so damn trusting." She thrust her finger over Maggie's shoulder and jabbed it into his chest. "Well, I'm not, buddy-boy! Are you running from a drug deal gone bad?" She shook her head. "Nah, couldn't be a drug dealer, if he's friendly with the cops," she muttered. She jerked her head back up to glare at him. "You a snitch? Huh? Huh!" She tried to shove him, but Maggie held her off. "Look, I didn't live in New York and learn nothing. You mess with my little sister? I *will*. Take. You. OUT!"

"Eve—"

"It's okay, Maggie," he said, his voice radiating calm, strength. "She's right to be concerned. I am as well." He turned to her sister. "To answer your questions, I am a baker—Let me continue," he said to Eve, holding up his hand. "Before that, I worked in security, and prior to that, I was in the Armed Forces."

"See, Eve," Maggie said, as if this wasn't news to her as well. "He was in the Armed Forces, just like Daddy."

"Where were you based?" Eve asked, her chin jutted out, her eyes narrow.

"Fort Campbell, Kentucky."

"What division?"

"The Fifth Special Forces Group Airborne."

Maggie watched the suspicion leave her sister's eyes.

"Okay," Eve said, giving a short nod.

"I've been trained to handle dangerous situations. I was hoping that I was the intended target, but after last night's events—" He broke off, glanced at Maggie, almost apologetically. "It's clear to me that someone has taken out a contract on your sister. It's possible that you're included in the hit order. There's a lot of information I don't have yet, but I swear to you, I will get to the bottom of this. And I will do my damnedest to keep the two of you safe."

"A contract ..." Eve said, her eyes huge, "as in ... someone has been hired to kill my sister—and maybe me?" Her voice was getting progressively higher, ending on a squeak. Eve grabbed hold of her arm. "Come on, Maggs. We're leaving—"

"No," said Maggie. "We're going to live here. Remember?"

"Fuck that," Eve said, with a half-laugh-half-cry. "I don't care how *pretty* Solace Island is. If you aren't safe, we aren't staying—"

"It doesn't matter where you go. They'll find you," Luke cut in, his voice calm. Maggie was aware of a regretful sadness in his eyes. "This has the markings of a professional, outside job. Yes, one of the hitmen from last night is dead. But the other is still out there, and his buddy is easily replaced. Your safest bet is to move to my house. Immediately."

"Your house?" Maggie said faintly.

He nodded. "I can protect you better there. I have a state-of-the-art security system, for both the house and the exterior. The driveway gate has reinforced hinges and a steel core. There is a six-foot wall around the perimeter of the property that is equipped with cameras. I made a call to my brother last night. He works at a security company and is sending two of his best men down. Men I have worked with, and would trust with my life. Finally, Samson is not only a damned fine pet, he's a trained guard dog as well."

Maggie's mind was spinning with this information overload. "But ... why do you have so much security?" she asked.

He shrugged, looked a little embarrassed. "Habit, I guess."

"Right," Eve said, all business, as she steered a dazed Maggie out of the kitchen. "Let's go pack."

Maggie sat on the bed, watching her sister race around the bedroom, throwing their belongings into suitcases. "Eve," she protested, "I was thinking ... I'm not sure if this is necessary, moving in with Luke." She was so tired. "Maybe we're overreacting."

"Overreacting?" Eve screeched. "*Overreacting?*" Maggie could almost see the fireworks exploding from the top of her sister's head. "First, someone tried to mow you down in broad daylight. And then two assailants arrive in the dead of night armed with guns and knives and God knows what else. There's a fight. One of the *hired hitmen* is *dead*, the other on the loose! And, by the way, you appear to be their *target* ... This is in *no* way 'OVERREACTING'!" Eve yanked open a dresser drawer, scooped out the socks, underwear, and bras, marched the armload of stuff over to the suitcase, and dumped it in. "And ... for the record—I am worried! I am very worried, and I don't care if I have to drag you by the hair, but we are going to stay with Luke until this whole thing can be sorted out. No ifs, ands, or buts!"

Twenty-Nine

When Maggie came into the kitchen, dragging a large suitcase, Luke was able to breathe a little more easily. He hadn't been sure if she was going to agree to the move. He had clearly heard Eve's bellowing—it was impossible not to—but had been unable to make out the words of Maggie's quiet murmur. His instinct had been to march in there, throw her over his shoulder, and not stop running until he had her safely at his house.

He hadn't.

He'd paced the kitchen like a caged animal, instead.

She looked pale and drawn, and Luke wanted to wrap his arms around her and never let go. She had flown to his rescue like a possessed she-devil. Not that he'd needed rescuing. Her appearing on the scene had frightened the hell out of him, and at the same time moved him deeply.

"Can I help with anything?" he asked.

"Sure," she said, swiping her hair back from her face with her forearm, as she gazed around the kitchen blearily. "We've got to pack up the kitchen, all our food in the cupboards and fridge. Some of the measuring spoons and cups are ours, as well as the mixing bowls—" She paused mid-sentence and looked at him, concern filling her eyes. "How are you holding up? You must be tired, too. Look, you've already gone above and beyond, and I really appreciate everything you've done. Go home and get some rest. We'll follow as soon as—"

"Maggie," he said, walking over to her and pulling her gently into his arms. "We're in this together." He could feel her relax against his body, her hand on his chest. He was tired, but the mere fact that she was nestled, so trustingly, in his arms ... hell, he'd have happily stayed up another twenty-four hours. "I'm not going to leave here without you," he murmured, "so tell me what you'd like me to pack?"

Maggie wasn't supposed to let anyone drive her rental car. However, in trying to unlock the vehicle, she accidentally set off the alarm, then the trunk release. Too tired.

"Maybe I should drive," Luke had said.

She didn't argue, just handed him the key-fob, let him figure out how to turn the damned alarm off. Which took him all of one second.

The rental company would probably prefer a fully intact vehicle to be returned to them, she thought as she rounded the car.

"Good move, Luke," Eve called out the window of her car. "Maggs is a mediocre driver at the best of times—"

"Am not," Maggie said, but there was no heat behind it, because Eve was right.

"—But when she hasn't slept ..." Eve shook her head.

"Whatever," Maggie said, getting in the passenger side and shutting the door.

"Duly noted." Luke opened the rear door. "Up," he said. Samson leaped into the backseat, folding his huge body like an origami paper until he managed to cram himself in with all of her stuff.

A couple minutes later, they were at his gate. She was glad he lived so close. Sleep was beckoning.

Luke lowered the window and punched a security code into the keypad and the gates slowly swung inward. Interesting, Maggie thought. Hadn't noticed the keypad, or fancy gate. Must've been open the other night and I whizzed past. She also hadn't noticed the cameras before. There was one on the top of the gatepost, and she'd seen another camera attached to a Douglas fir at the top of the drive. Were there more? Probably. She hadn't known that Samson was a trained guard dog, either.

She felt safer already.

"Thanks, Luke," she said, wanting to reach over, touch him, hold his hand, make some kind of physical contact, but she kept her hands stowed in her lap. "I'm glad we're here."

"Me, too." He drove past the gates, Eve's car following close behind. He stopped and waited for the doors to swing shut behind them, then continued on.

As they approached the house, she noticed two men— long, lanky and powerfully built—lounging on the front-porch steps. They looked like a couple of mountain lions basking in the sun, pretending to be domesticated.

"Luke," she said, placing a cautionary hand on his forearm, a jolt of adrenaline coursing through her veins.

"Don't worry," he said, expressions of gladness and relief flashing in quick succession across his face. "They're my friends, Gunner and Colt. They've come to help me keep an eye on things, make sure you and Eve are protected."

The men rose to their feet, grace in motion. *That must have been how Luke used to move, before his injury.* She glanced back at him. Just looking at his profile calmed her somehow. Soothed, healed, like aloe gel poured on a burn.

He shifted to park, engaged the brake, switched the ignition off, and got out. "Hey, there," he called, opening the rear door of the car, because Samson was making his desires known. The wolfhound catapulted from the car with a jubilant *woof,* bounded to Gunner and Colt, and then morphed into an overgrown puppy, all whines and wiggles and wet, sloppy licks.

"That was fast," Luke said, stepping forward. "Colt, good to see you."

"Hopped on a red-eye," Colt said, pulling Luke in for a hug and a couple of back thumps.

The other one must be Gunner, Maggie thought. He had a broad smile on his face, his arms wrapped around Samson. "You're such a good boy. Yes, you are," he said, giving the wolfhound a final pat. He rose, wiped the dog slobber off his face, and joined the back-thumping-hug-fest.

Good friends, she thought. The warmth and affection for each other was radiating off them. She could feel the strength of their bond. It was a beautiful thing to witness.

"Aren't you supposed to be 'back on the block,' living the peaceful good life now?" Gunner asked, stepping back. He gave a low whistle. "Must not agree with you, Luke. You look like shit warmed over."

Colt laughed. Maggie could hear Eve's chuckle from behind her.

"It was going just great until twenty-four hours ago," Luke said, reaching out, snagging her hand and tugging her forward to his side. It felt like he was making a claim, but she didn't mind. "Then it turned into a soup sandwich. I appreciate you taking a bite of it." He turned and smiled down at her. "This is Maggie," he said. "And her sister, Eve." She loved the feeling of her hand enclosed in his; wanted to sink into the warmth and strength of him. It was as if, in connecting their hands, she was plugged into him and could feel his energy source pouring through and replenishing her body. *Who needs sleep?* she thought.

He tipped his head down. "What's the secret smile for?" he murmured, his voice barely discernible.

She shook her head, unsure whether it was disconcerting or thrilling that he could read her so well.

"Hello there," she heard her sister say. Eve stepped forward and shook their hands. "So nice to meet you. Thank you so much for coming to help out." Her back was to Maggie, so she couldn't see her face, but she didn't need to. Maggie knew what it meant when her sister's voice shifted to that low purr. *Must be intrigued by one, or both of the men. Good. Hopefully, that will help distract her from worrying obsessively about me.*

"How about we go inside," Luke said. "Maggie desperately needs some sleep—"

"You do too," she said, as they headed toward the front door.

"True," he said. She loved the warmth in his eyes, the way the tension in his face seemed to soften when his gaze landed on her. She felt like she mattered. "And I will. Promise. But first I want to get you settled and bring Colt and Gunner up to speed with the situation. They know the ins-and-outs of my security system, since they helped me set it up when I moved in. However, I've made a few tweaks in the meantime, and I'd like to run through them with them."

"Oh," she said, stifling a yawn. "I guess that's how they managed to get past the gate."

"Yup," Gunner said. "If he hadn't futzed with the interior alarm system, Colt and I would be lounging in the living room, finishing our second cup of coffee."

Luke carried Maggie's suitcase inside. She was too tired to argue. Felt a little guilty, leaving the unloading of the cars to Eve and Luke's friends, but her sister had insisted she go to bed. Luke had, too.

She followed him through the living room, down a hall. *Skylights, alcoves, gorgeous artwork,* Maggie thought. *Eve's going to love staying here.*

He swung open a door at the end of the hall. She entered and her breath caught in her throat. It was a stunning, expansive corner room with tons of natural light streaming in the floor-to-ceiling windows, which overlooked the cliffs and the sparkling blue bay beyond. Other windows faced an outgrowth of slate-gray rock with lush, emerald-green moss covering most of its surface. An arbutus tree, its roots embedded in the rock, balancing the undulating, tan-and-rust-streaked trunk and limbs that curved upward, embracing the sky.

"It's beautiful," Maggie said. She must have swayed slightly on her feet because Luke's hand was suddenly steadying her elbow. And as tired as she was, she couldn't help the frisson that always rippled through her whenever her body came into contact with him.

"You okay?" he murmured in her ear.

She could feel his concern, but something else was there, too, woven through and shimmering like a promise. And the memory on her hands around the firm length of him, the taste of him on her tongue ...

"I'm fine," she said, straightening and taking a step away, her cheeks hot.

He laughed low and husky, as if he could read her mind.

Luke turned away from Maggie, and made an adjustment, trying to make the enormous erection—which seemed to spring forth at the slightest contact with her—less apparent. "Extra linens are in there," Luke said, pointing to the closet, stalling for time, trying to get his unruly body under control. "There's a spare toothbrush, toothpaste, soap, et cetera, in the top right-hand drawer in the cabinet under the sink. If you need anything, or get scared, don't hesitate to call. I'm right across the hall from you."

"Thank you," she said, standing in the middle of the room.

She looked so small and lost. Again, he had the urge to go to her and wrap his arms around her, simply to give comfort. But maybe she would misconstrue his intent. Maybe his body would misconstrue his intent. Especially given the boner he was wielding. They were both in a vulnerable state. What had arisen after a mere car incident was peanuts compared with what could possibly occur after last night.

His less-than-honorable self was encouraging him to stay, but he managed to force his body to turn around, walk out of the room, and close the door softly behind him.

They'd unloaded the cars. Luke had shown everyone their rooms and the lay of the kitchen, and stored Maggie and Eve's boxes of kitchen goods in the spare pantry. He'd brought Colt and Gunner up to date on the security system, and now they were doing a sweep of the property. There was something about the mossy bluff in front of the house that Eve needed to sketch, wanting to grab it before the light shifted. Samson had been given the command to remain at her side. She would be safe.

Everyone was settled. Thank God, because he was running on fumes.

Luke gathered Eve's suitcases from the living room floor, where she had dropped them in an artistic passion.

"I'll get them later," she'd said, plunging her hand into the canvas bag and yanking out a sketchbook and a metal box that rattled. Pencils or charcoal or something like that. Then she'd dropped the canvas bag as well and dashed outside, Samson on her heels.

Luke placed Eve's things inside her bedroom and continued down the hall. So damned tired. He paused outside Maggie's door. It was quiet. Good. She must be sleeping.

He walked further down the hall and entered his bedroom. On his way through to the bathroom, he tapped the control panel on the wall. The overhead lights started dimming, and the bedside lamp switched on. The blackout blinds had almost completely lowered by the time he reached the bathroom.

Luke turned on the shower, stripped off his clothes, and stepped inside, letting the hot, steaming water flow over him. He lathered up with locally made lemongrass and lime soap, breathing in the fresh, clean scent, visualizing the night's violence running off his body along with the water and soap and disappearing down the drain.

He rolled his shoulders, his head, trying to release the accumulated tension. He turned the knob to make the water even hotter and dug his fingers into the aching flesh around his old wound. He hoped the massage would cajole the spasm—which had been tormenting him all day—into letting go of its grip. Then he turned off the water, stepped out, ambled over to the sink and brushed his teeth, even though he was planning on raiding the fridge before collapsing into bed. He was flirting with the idea of a shave when he heard a tentative knock on his bedroom door. "Yeah, be right there," he called. Hopefully, whoever it was, it wouldn't take long. His stomach was growling like an angry lion's. He grabbed a thick Turkish towel as he left the bathroom, wrapped it around his hips, and tucked in the end at his waist.

Had he heard her? Maggie stood in the hall outside his door. Should she knock again? Or maybe she should return to her room? She wished she could stop the shakes that were coursing through her. Stop the violent images of last night, which were lurking in the shadows, ready to pounce every time she shut her eyes.

This was stupid. She was a grown woman, not a child scared of the dark. *Turn around*, she told herself sternly. *And go back to your—*

His bedroom door swung open, and there he was, lounging in the doorway in all his masculine magnificence.

"Oh my," Maggie said her mouth suddenly dry. She took an involuntary step backward. Needed to. Clothed Luke was impressive; nearly naked Luke was heart-stopping. His hair was wet and slicked back, and droplets of water were clinging to his beautiful shoulders. She had no idea he had such sculpted pecs. *Forget the gym,* she thought in a daze. *He could give classes. Knead Bread as a Workout and Look Like a God.* Tiny rivulets of water were making their way through the sprinkling of golden-brown hair on his chest, trickling downward over the ripped, lean muscles of his body. She wanted to follow their path with her tongue. Journey across his taut, chiseled abs, his belly button, with her mouth licking, nibbling, kissing until she reached the pristine white towel slung low around his narrow hips. She would remove that with her teeth and explore to her heart's content.

"Maggie, are you okay?"

Maggie snapped her head up. *Jeez. You're ogling his body like a sex-crazed maniac. That is so disrespectful. Keep your eyes on his face.*

"Yes. Um …"

He waited patiently.

It was so hard to think, to form sentences, with him standing there like that. It was everything she could do not to lean forward and breathe in his sexy, clean scent. She shut her eyes to block the view of him, but that just heightened her other senses. She could feel the heat and male pheromones coming off his body in waves.

She opened her eyes and stared at his knees. Sheesh. She even found his knees sexy. She linked her hands so they wouldn't be tempted to reach out and touch him, and turned her gaze to the doorknob under his hand. He had beautiful hands, strong and capable, with long fingers and clean, neatly trimmed nails.

"Maggie, honey. What is it?"

She wasn't looking at his face, but she didn't need to. She could hear the tenderness, the caring and warmth in his voice. Brett hadn't spoken to her like that for years. Had he ever spoken to her like that? If he had, she couldn't remember. It had seemed there was always an underlying impatience and condescension thrumming through him when he spoke or looked at her. And the thought that she had wasted all those years on someone who valued her so little ...

"Maggie, why are you crying?"

She hadn't known she was. "I ... just ..." She dashed the unexpected tears from her eyes, but more appeared to take their place. "I'm tired. I'm so damned tired, Luke, but I can't seem to sleep. When I shut my eyes, I see that guy, hear the sound of the sculpture making contact with his skull. See the dark blood streaming over his hand as he ran away, clutching his head. I think I might have hurt him bad. Didn't mean to—just wanted to stop him from killing you." She must have been tired, because she was crying in earnest now. And that was odd, because in her regular life, she wasn't a crier, but she had cried more in the last month than she had in the rest of her whole life. "And it makes me really mad that I'm even worrying about him, and his stupid, bleeding head." She wiped angry tears from her face. "He's a creep, wanted to hurt me, doesn't deserve my concern—"

"I know how you feel," he murmured, and she could feel the truth of it resonating through her. Somehow, the distance between them had been closed, and she was being held in the safety of his arms—his scent, his warmth, his strength surrounding her.

"So I pry my mind away from the guy I injured, but then the other guy takes his place, charging for me, knife in his hand, blood spurting out of his chest, eyes blazing..."

"There, now." His voice was a comforting rumble, his lips in her hair. "It's been an extremely trying time. You're tired. You need sleep ..."

"But I can't. I've tried, but I can't ..."

"Come on," Luke said, scooping her up in his arms. "I'm going to lie down with you—"

"But—" Maggie said. Weary. So weary. And yet, pressed up to his naked, freshly showered chest, she wanted to sneak a taste.

He carried her toward his bed, limping slightly. "Platonic," he said, placing her down gently.

A slight mist of disappointment settled over her, but in the next breath it dissipated. Tired. So tired.

"Just friends." He pulled the covers up over her and stepped away.

"Don't leave," she said, suddenly panicked.

"I won't," he said. "I'm just going to put on some sweats and a T-shirt. I'll stay with you while you sleep."

"Promise?" Maggie said, sleep waves crashing over her.

"Promise."

She must have drifted off for a second, because the next thing she was aware of, the bed was shifting as he climbed in and gathered her in his arms. "You are safe now." His voice and the steady thump of his heart so soothing. "I am here. Go to sleep, sweetheart ... Go to sleep ..."

Luke woke suddenly, dragged out of a deep sleep and unsure why. And then he knew. Maggie was whimpering and moaning in her sleep, breathing rapidly. Her head was flailing from side to side. Her legs, tangled in the sheets, were twitching as if attempting to run.

"Maggie," he said, soft and low, his hand alighting on her shoulder. "You're having a bad dream, Maggie. Honey, wake up."

Her eyes fluttered open, and he watched the night terrors fade from them.

"You're here," she whispered.

"Yes, I'm here."

"Good," she replied, her hand rising briefly to cup his cheek, and then she drifted back to sleep.

He watched her for a while. Listening to the tempo of her breath, hoping that her sleep was peaceful or dreamless. Her breath slowed and deepened. A slight smile flickered across her face. Reassured, he, too, gave in to the night's calm embrace.

Thirty

*M*aritza Vásquez closed the front door behind him, keeping her gaze lowered, her expression blank, impassive. Just like she would if she had met a rabid dog.

"This way, please," she said, making sure to stay out of reach as she led him down the hall to the study. This was his third visit to the house, and she could smell death all around him.

She stayed for a moment in the hall, after the study door had closed behind him. There was a low murmur of voices, too quiet to make out the words. Just as well, she thought. The less she knew, the better.

She turned to see to her duties. Yes, there were duties even at 10:15 at night. Sometimes it was a twenty-four-hour-a-day job. No overtime pay, but at least it was a job—a means to an end. Living on the premises meant she didn't have to pay for rent, utilities, or food. She could send the bulk of her salary to her *madre* to pay for the expenses of her children, José and Alejandra, who were growing up, so quickly, in El Salvador without her. Her babies, already four and six. How she missed holding their warm little bodies.

"What do you mean, she isn't dead?" the voice exploded from behind the closed doors.

Maritza froze mid-step, fear coursing through her. Not wanting to hear. Wanting to run. Unable to move.

"I paid top dollar to take care of the problem."

There was a low, controlled murmur in response. Maritza couldn't hear the words, but the ice-cold, flat tone sent shivers up her spine.

"Then double up. I've had it with this fucking incompetence. Matter of fact, I'll come, too. Haven't had a holiday in a while and," a crazy laugh rising, building, and then snapping abruptly off, "it'll be amusing," the voice dripping with venom, "to take care of her personally. And *no more* mistakes. Understand?"

The low murmur again.

Santa María, Madre de Dios—footsteps coming toward the door. Maritza forced movement into her legs, whirled, and ran. Not quick enough … Not quick enough … She heard the blast before she felt it. Loud, so loud. Falling, falling down. Heat, pain in her chest spreading outward. Vision blurring. Her sweet babies, her sweet, blessed babies, holding their faces in her mind. "Dios te salve, María, llena eres de gracia … el Señor es contigo … Bendita tú eres entre todas las mujeres … y bendito es el fruto de tu vientre … Jesús …"

Footsteps approaching.

"Santa María, Madre de Dios …"

Voices.

"Why did you shoot her?"

"She heard."

Someone kicked her hard in the stomach. "Ruega por nosotros pecadores … ahora y …"

"Make her stop praying."

Another kick, forcing blood and vomit upward and out. For a second, she worried about the mess. *No importa qué.* "En la ... hora de ..."

"Shut up! Shut the fuck up!"

"Nuestra muerte."

Another loud blast.

"Amén," Maritza Elena Vásquez breathed out, and then darkness—blessed, sweet darkness—took her.

Thirty-One

*M*aggie woke discombobulated, not knowing where she was and why. She wasn't alone in the darkness. She was wrapped around a large, male body, one leg flung over his thighs, her head on his chest. Her hand tightly gripped a fistful of his T-shirt, as if to keep him from leaving while she slept. The fresh, clean scent of him surrounded her.

Luke.

She was in Luke's bed.

She was safe.

"Good morning."

She could hear him, but she could feel his voice, too, in a visceral, tactile way, through muscle, sinew, and bone. Vibrations of his rumbling baritone made their way through his body to merge with the parts of her body in contact with his.

He was awake.

How long had he been lying there, letting her sleep in his arms? "What time is it?" Maggie asked.

"Mm ..." He shifted slightly to look at a bedside clock, still keeping her tucked in the crook of his arm. "It's three twenty-two in the morning."

"Wow. We slept for ..."

"Almost thirteen hours."

"I've never slept so long in my life," Maggie said. It was remarkable how comfortable she felt, lying in his arms.

Actually, she was comfortable, except for the pressure in her bladder. "Um," she said, reluctantly shifting from the warmth of his arms to a sitting position. "I need to use the … uh …"

"Facilities?" he asked with a grin.

"Yeah," she said. "You want me to use the one in my room?"

"Nah," he said, waving a magnanimous hand. "Feel free to defile mine."

"I don't have to do *that*," Maggie said, hopping off the bed and heading toward the bathroom, his warm chuckle following in her wake.

When she returned, he got up and went in.

Maggie stood by the bed. What should she do? She felt well rested. He knew how long they had been sleeping, so if she got back into his warm, comfy bed, he might think it was an invitation to continue what she had started on his sofa yesterday. It was weird how time had morphed. Yesterday on his sofa felt like a long time ago. So much had happened in the last twenty-four hours. Her mind flashed to Luke flipping the dead man onto his back, his arm flopping outward from his body, fingers curling gently upward.

She blew out a long, slow breath. A tremor ran through her. *Let it go. It's over and done with.*

She heard the toilet flush. If she left and went back to her room, would it seem rude? Or would it be a relief for him to get her out of his hair?

Now the water running in the sink. *What to do? What to do?* She heard the water being shut off, his footsteps approaching the door. And then he was there. His long, lean, muscled body silhouetted in the bathroom doorway.

"I was wondering," he said, running a hand through his tousled, dark hair, "if I could ask you for a favor?"

"Anything," Maggie said, and just saying the word *anything* to this virile, strong, sexy man caused heat to pool in her breasts, her abdomen, and lower.

"I am ravenously hungry," he said, "and have been lusting after a slice of your chocolate cake for what seems like an eternity."

"**Life**," Luke said, carefully scraping the last crumbs of chocolate cake off his plate with the back of his fork, "doesn't get any better than this,"

"You can have another piece," Maggie said, biting into a ripped-off hunk of one of his baguettes, slathered with locally churned organic butter, a wedge of four-year-aged cheddar in her other hand. She hadn't wanted to eat, but once Luke got her to force down the first couple of mouthfuls, her nausea seemed to calm. Her body's survival mechanisms had kicked in and she was now eating with relish while Luke watched with quiet satisfaction.

"I want more cake, believe me," Luke said, "but I am trying to muster up a little restraint, seeing as how I've already had seconds. It's time for something savory." He slid the chopping board closer, cut a length of baguette, and slit it down the middle. He smeared on a thin layer of butter, then some truly decadent French triple-crème

Pierre Robert, and finished off his creation with paper-thin slices of prosciutto.

"Ah," she said, "I see you are going the multicultural route. I, however, am a purist and am sticking with locally produced goods."

She was still a bit pale, but he was relieved she was feeling up to a little lighthearted banter.

"Don't knock it till you've tried it," Luke said, handing over his sandwich to her.

It was only a sandwich, but there was something so erotic about watching her hold it, two-handed, fitting her mouth around the end. Even the action of her teeth biting down turned him on, which didn't make any kind of sense.

"Mmm …" Maggie moaned. "So good."

Luke shifted in his seat, needing to make a discreet adjustment. "Finish it off," he said, mesmerized. "I'll make another."

"Twist my arm," Maggie said, oblivious to the effect she was having on his nether regions. She took another bite. "Best thing *ever*."

He enjoyed the view as she chewed and swallowed. She lifted the loaded baguette up to her mouth again and then paused, a look of consternation on her face. "What?" she asked.

"What, what?" Luke replied, startled out of his reverie.

"Do I have something on my face?" She put the baguette down and wiped her napkin across the corners of her mouth.

"No," Luke said, forcing himself to look away. "I was just daydreaming." He broke off another length of baguette and started slicing it open.

"Luke," Maggie said, her voice hesitant, "can I ask you something?"

"Sure." He scooped up a dollop of butter.

"I've been thinking about what you said this morning. When Eve asked about that police officer acting so star-struck, you mentioned being in the Special Forces, based out of Fort Campbell. But that wouldn't explain why he was yes-sir-ing you all over the place, unless he'd been stationed at Fort Campbell at the same time. Then I thought, no, he's too young. Maybe his dad was, and the young cop met you that way." She paused and took another bite of her sandwich. Tipped her head, thinking it through. "But that explanation didn't make sense because he didn't know you. He said, 'it was an honor to meet you.'"

Luke shrugged and started spreading the butter, aware of her studying him.

"And another thing. Last night, as I was drifting off, I had an image flash before me. I was going to ask you about it, but I must have fallen asleep. When that guy was rushing toward me with the knife, I thought you must have shot him with the other guy's gun. Picked it up or something. But you couldn't have, because you didn't bend over. You were dragging me backward."

Maggie was speaking in a calm and logical manner, but Luke could see the slight tremor running through her body, the paleness and strain on her face, as she sorted through memories.

"And then I thought, well, maybe Luke had a gun? But that didn't make sense. Even if you owned a gun, you were out on a peaceful evening stroll. Why on earth would you bring a gun along for that? And then Eve came charging out of the house, freaking out, and the cops came and we had to move here and I forgot all about it ..."

"Until now," Luke said, quietly.

"Yes, until now."

Luke placed his butter knife carefully on the table. "All good observations and questions."

"Did you have a gun?" Maggie asked, her eyes dark, face serious.

Luke nodded.

Maggie sank slightly back in her chair. She turned her head to look toward the windows, even though there was nothing to see out there, just the reflection of them inside. Beyond that, dark night surrounded them.

What is she thinking?

"I have an authorization to carry," Luke said, both hands on the table, palms down.

"Um ... hm ..." Maggie said, with a nod but still not looking at him.

The room was silent. Just the barely-there hum of the refrigerator and the sound of their breathing.

"I didn't point out the discrepancies, because my sister was already extremely upset this morning, but there is more to the story than you told us."

"Maggie, I am a baker."

She shook her head. "I should have known. So many signs—this home, for one. Baking bread isn't that lucrative. So how did you earn the money? And yes, I know you were in the Special Forces, but that is hardly lucrative enough to afford all of this." Her voice starting to rise, as was the color in her cheeks. "I hope to hell you weren't involved in anything illegal, but I have to tell you, the more I think about it, the more worried I get. Why, Luke, is there the need for over-the-top security around this place? 'Habit,' you said. But this is not a mere choice of whether you like catsup with your eggs! This kind of setup takes a great deal of effort—"

He started to open his mouth, but she cut him off.

"—Don't you blame it on your military background. My dad was in the Army and all my parents have is a good, old-fashioned lock on the door. This is Solace Island, and yet you have a six-foot-high fence around the perimeter, cameras at the gate and at the doors …"

"Maggie …"

She whirled to face him. "Don't 'Maggie' me," she said, eyes blazing.

"I didn't think it was relevant. That was my life before; this is now—"

"Excuse me," she interrupted, "but from my point of view? There is a *big* difference between deciding to date a cozy, albeit sexy-as-hell, bread baker and a … a … gun-packing …" She waved her hands around in frustration, and then threw them up in the air. "This is ridiculous. I know nothing about you. Is Luke Benson even your real name? Or is it some alias—"

"It's my name—"

She gave a short, brittle laugh. "No need to act like that's such a stretch. If you want me to trust you, if you want to build on the friendship," *friendship?* Definitely not the direction he was hoping to steer things toward, "then you need to stop being so damned secretive. Who are you really? Huh? How did you injure your leg?"

"Gunshot wound—"

"Gunshot wound?" she squeaked, her eyebrows levitating.

He nodded.

"Terrific." Clearly she did *not* think it was terrific. "So that's why there's all this security. You're in some kind of trouble." She shook her head, then sighed as if she was suddenly weary. "Is there a tie to the men who were after me?"

"No," he said. "That was a one-off and the shooter's dead."

She studied his face, intently, as if she knew there was more to the story. "And the shooter was?"

"My fiancée's boyfriend."

She digested that comment. Squared her shoulders. "Did you kill him?" she asked.

He looked into her clear-eyed gaze. "Indirectly," he replied. He could hear the sharp intake of her breath. "Didn't mean to. After Jasper shot me, he ran, yanked Adyna out of the room."

"Adyna was your ex?"

"Yeah. Should have let them go. Blockheaded stupidity on my part. Didn't have all the information. Was convinced he'd forced himself on her physically and was making her run against her will. So I followed them in my truck."

"Had he?" Maggie said, concern in her eyes, but she hadn't heard the rest of the story. How it ended.

He made himself continue. "No. It had been an elaborate con from the start and I was the dupe. She wasn't in love with me. Didn't even like me, according to the journals that I found." He shrugged, trying to keep the mask of indifference from slipping. He was just reciting a story—nothing to do with him—even though the telling of it was causing adrenaline to ricochet through his veins. "Anyway, they took off; I followed. The roads were slick, rain thundering down, visibility was poor. Jasper's Porsche skidded out of control, smashed through the guardrail."

Luke could still hear Adyna's ear-piercing scream as the vehicle spun out of control, into the oncoming traffic. The Porsche had slammed head on into a fully loaded fuel truck, and her scream cut off.

"By the time I jumped out of my truck and ran across the freeway, it was too late—the explosion was too big, the flames too intense. Nothing anyone could do. Adyna, her lover, the driver of the truck: all dead." Luke blew out a breath. "The man had two kids ..." He broke off. He'd helped the man's family financially, but how does one compensate for the death of a father?

"That wasn't your fault," Maggie said, such certainty in her voice.

"If I hadn't chased them—"

"Not your fault," she repeated firmly. The icemaker in the freezer dumped a load of ice into the bin, the noise loud in the silent kitchen. "So, why'd you end up on Solace?"

He didn't answer.

"Luke," she said, her voice soft, persuasive.

Luke looked at her, this strong, beautiful woman he hoped would become part of his future, and made a decision. "All right," he said. "Where should I start?"

"The beginning," she said, an encouraging smile curving the corners of her lips.

He paused. It was an unfamiliar situation he was navigating, revealing his past. "I graduated from high school and enlisted in the Army, served for three years, and was in the SF pipeline for another two," Luke said.

"Special Forces." Maggie nodded. "Go on."

"As you know, I was based at Fort Campbell, Kentucky. I was part of the Fifth Special Forces Group Airborne. It was ..." He reached for a word that would be true, but not overwhelm her. "... Intense." His voice was even, calm. He was in control, even though images, smells, sounds from that time were rising up to bombard him. He took a moment, focused on his breath.

She was watching him closely, compassion on her face. "I can't even imagine," she said.

He was glad she couldn't.

"I was proud to serve my country. When I was deployed, it became even clearer to me, the necessity of the fight, the need to keep America strong. To keep in place the everyday freedoms and privileges that so many civilians take for granted."

"So why did you stop?"

More memories assailed him. "A member of our team, Teddy, slipped up." He had never spoken those words. To anyone. Ever. "And the ODA is only as strong as the weakest link."

"ODA?"

"Sorry. Stands for Operational Detachment Alpha— consists of twelve Special Forces soldiers, all cross-trained in different skills and languages. Two officers, ten sergeants. He was an officer. A good man."

"What happened to him?"

"Dead. Along with nine other members of our team."

"Oh, Luke."

He felt her hand cover his. The coolness of her fingers soothed.

"He'd been in the field seven years longer than me and was starting to buckle under the strain. Nonstop deployment. We all noticed the strain, the fraying around the edges. He'd just found out the week prior that his wife had filed for divorce. Had two small children that he adored. Needless to say, he was gutted. No way for him to go back and sort things out. His focus was off, and he accidentally triggered an improvised explosive device. Boom. Colt, Gunner, and I were left standing. Ian was in pieces, but still alive. He didn't make it through the night, though." He let out a shaky breath.

Maggie got up and walked around the table, wrapped her arms around him. Her scent, sweet tea with the tinge of honeysuckle, surrounded and comforted him.

"Ah," she said. "That explains the bond I felt between you all."

"Yeah, well, ODA does that. The twelve of us thrown together, working so closely for months on end in isolated circumstances. And when you aren't on deployment, you're together in garrison, training and training and training some more. You get close. They are your blood brothers."

"And that day you lost three-quarters of your family."

Luke felt an unaccustomed thickness in his throat. "Yeah." He nodded. "It was …" Words failed him.

"Beyond rough," she said, her hand soothing his hair back.

He nodded.

He had spent so much energy over the last few years, trying to suppress, shut out that time. To forget the things he had had to do and the things he had seen. But tonight, the past and present collided. Maggie was here, warm and caring, sexy as hell, and yet with an untouched innocence, too. Gunner and Colt outside, who had dropped everything and come, no questions asked. True friends. Loyal.

He was alive. And so fortunate. He had so many blessings. It was his task now to acknowledge and embrace them. Luke turned in his seat and wrapped his arms around Maggie's waist, breathing her in, her worn flannel nightgown soft against his cheek.

They stayed like that for a long time, just holding each other in the darkened kitchen.

He felt her shift and step away, and instantly missed the warmth of her surrounding him. She stooped down and took his hands. "Come on," she said softly, tugging him to his feet.

He didn't know what she had in mind, but it didn't matter, because he realized, in that moment, that he would follow her to the ends of the Earth and back.

Thirty-Two

*M*aggie's heart was beating triple time as she led Luke out of the kitchen, through the living room, down the hall, and into her bedroom.

She closed the door behind them and locked it for good measure.

Moonlight was streaming in through the floor-to-ceiling windows, illuminating the room. The rain that had been thundering down while they were eating had abated. Fast-moving clouds traveled across the sky so the moon appeared and disappeared, shimmering its magical light on the wet limbs of the arbutus tree and gleaming off the slick, wet rock formation beyond. There was no need to lower the blinds, as the enormous embedded rock offered the occupants of the room absolute privacy from all directions.

"I want to …" She paused. Her mouth suddenly dry. "That is, if you do," she continued. "No pressure." She felt a nervous giggle rising up. *No pressure? I just locked the poor man in my room and I'm not planning on releasing him.* She stuffed the giggle down deep and gathered her courage. "I would like to make love with you," she said. "If you're willing."

Luke's pupils darkened, and a surge of heat flared in his eyes. "If I want to?" he said, an eyebrow lifting, a slight smile starting to form. "Woman, I have been ravenous for you since the day we met. You still have those condoms you were packing?"

"Mm-hm." Maggie nodded. "I put them in the bedside table—not that I thought ..." She trailed off, because the rest of what she was about to say would have been a lie.

"Good thinking," he said, stepping toward her.

Nothing passive about him. This was a six-foot-three, hot, aroused male. She could practically taste the ramped-up testosterone that was pulsing through the air.

"But," Maggie said. She was in his arms now, his hard body around her, his warm lips nuzzling her neck, sending shivery tingles dancing over her skin. Maggie moaned, trying to keep her head, her logical mind wrestling with the wave of desire pouring through her.

"Wait." She managed to get her hand between them to his chest. She was longing to explore the broad expanse of warm muscle and bone, but she pressed her hand firmly against him to create a modicum of space between their hungry bodies.

It was necessary. There was something that needed to be said, and with him so close, his warm lips and the caress of his breath working their way up her throat to the soft hollow right below her ear, it was impossible for her to think, to form words.

"I need to tell you something," Maggie made herself say.

Luke pulled back, his eyes dark with passion. "Okay," he said, his hand rising, his work-callused fingers skimming her face, light as a butterfly's wing, as he traced the slight hollow at her temple, her cheekbone, the curve of her cheek. That this big, strong man could be so tender and gentle filled her heart to overflowing. But she was scared, too—scared to tell him this.

"I ..." Maggie said. She looked down, unable to hold his gaze. She could feel the thump of his heart, heat radiating outward, warming her hand, which was still spread, palm down, on the worn T-shirt covering his chest. "I want ... to make love with you." *Bomp ... bomp ... bomp* ... went his heart. "But I don't want to mislead you." Maggie took a deep breath, gathering her courage, exhaled slowly. "I'm not good at it," she said.

"What are y—" he started to say, but she cut him off.

"I don't want you to take it personally." Now that she had started down this road, there was no going back. It was scary, but a relief too. "There's something defective with me," she said, her eyes suddenly hot, making her have to shut them for a moment. "I read the romance novels, the magazines. I know fireworks are supposed to happen, but they just ... don't with me."

She could feel Luke looking at her, but she couldn't make her gaze rise up to meet his. She smoothed out his T-shirt beneath her hand, felt the texture of hair underneath. "For years, I thought maybe the magazines were lying—all this talk about 'the Big O.' I figured it was written by a few sadists who had nothing better to do with their time than to dream up ways to make the rest of womankind feel defective. But then one night, I was out with Eve. She'd stayed up the whole night before, finishing a painting, had a tiny nap during the day but hadn't eaten much. Basically, she was running on fumes, but you know Eve. She wanted to go celebrate.

"Well, the two Long Island Iced Teas she indulged in hit her like a ton of bricks, and she started talking about things we had never discussed before. Ever. Experiences she had had. How good certain ex-boyfriends were. The things they would do. How wonderful making love was. I was embarrassed, so I pretended I was having those kinds of experiences, too. But I wasn't." Maggie let out a shaky breath. "I never have."

Maggie was glad she had told him. Got it out in the open so he wouldn't have expectations.

"Never?"

Maggie shook her head.

"And your ex?" Luke asked, his hand gently tilting up her chin. Her gaze slid to the side. "Maggie," he said.

She made herself look at him. "Everything was fine on his side. No problem," she said. "The problem was me. After that evening out with Eve, I asked Brett if maybe we could try some of the things that Eve had mentioned, but Brett explained to me that it would be pointless. That I was frigid and some people are just born that way." Maggie shrugged apologetically. "But if you don't mind going to bed with someone like me, I'd really like to, because I think it would be cozy and nice to be intimate with you."

A flare of anger flashed across Luke's face. It was so strong and potent that Maggie backed away from him, even though her body instantly longed to return.

"It is fortunate," Luke gritted out, his hands clenching, "that your bastard of an ex isn't nearby. Otherwise he'd be spitting out teeth." He glared out the window for a moment or two. Then he took a deep breath, and gradually the tension left his body. It seemed to melt away like an ice cube spilled to the pavement on a hot summer day.

He turned toward her, the hardness in his eyes softening. "You are," he said, "a wonderful, sexy, luscious woman. You are not defective in any way. 'Frigid' is a word that was made up by men to justify and excuse the fact that they suck in the sack."

"You don't know that," Maggie said, trying to tamp down the tiny spark of hope that was rising in her chest.

"I know," he said, an implacable expression on his face. "You're going to have to trust me on this one, Maggie."

The spark of hope rose to a flame in her belly.

He took a step toward her. "Will you do that?"

Maggie nodded, energy building, swirling around them like an electrical force field.

"Now I know you mentioned something about cozy and nice?" He took another step toward her, all ambling, lazy grace, but she could feel the hungry predator lurking inside, wanting to feast ...

On her.

He wanted her. She could see it in his eyes, in the hardened lines of his body. Luke was holding himself in control, but he was primed to pounce. The knowledge of that made her feel tingly and nervous and full of liquid heat.

He took another step toward her. Still not touching, but almost, mere inches away. The fresh, clean, male scent of him surrounded her, making it hard for Maggie to think. A throbbing warmth pooled in her abdomen, and lower.

"But there," Luke murmured, his baritone rumbling through her, weakening her knees, "I have to draw the line.

I have nothing against cozy and nice." She was in his arms now. His work-roughened hands slid up her back, leaving trails of heat and sensation in their wake. "You're welcome to classify afternoon tea served on dainty grandma china, complete with miniature sandwiches and an array of desserts, as cozy and nice. No problem there." His hands were in her hair. He looped the long strands around his knuckles and tipped her head back. "But I'll be damned if those are the words you'll use to describe what happens here tonight."

His mouth descended on hers, passion-filled and demanding a response.

Her arms rose of their own volition and twined around his neck, her fingers buried deep in the silky strands of his dark hair.

A breathy moan escaped her lips, and he took full advantage of the slight opening and dipped his tongue in, to taste her more completely. Maggie's knees felt weak, a low whimper building in her throat, *take me ... take me ... take me ...*

"Good God, Maggie," he growled, his voice husky. "You are many things, but frigid is not one of them." He scooped her into his arms, and the next thing Maggie knew, she was lying spread out on her bed, Luke's hard body kneeling over her. "So beautiful," he murmured, and then his mouth was back devouring hers, and she thought she would die from the pleasure of it. She felt restless, slippery and wet between her legs.

More. She wanted more.

She could feel his fierce, hot erection, thick and hard, through their clothes. She was undulating against him, wanting, needing to get closer—to him, to life, to being alive; filled with a desperate need to replace last night's images with something better.

Luke lifted his head with a husky groan. "Maggie ..." he breathed, his eyes dark with passion and something more.

She could feel his heart pounding like a runaway horse. Feminine triumph surged through her like a high-octane cocktail, setting fire to all her senses.

"Off," she said. "Everything off." She felt hungry, greedy, the tip of her tongue gathering the taste of his kiss from her lips. "I want to see you naked."

"Far be it from me to deny you," he said, a faint smile on his lips. He rolled off and in one fluid movement was standing by the bed. He grasped his T-shirt, pulled it over his head, and tossed it to the side, the moonlight playing over his sleek, muscled shoulders, his sinewy arms, the washboard abs, and narrow waist, his sweats hanging on his slim hips.

Maggie's breath caught in her throat. She knew she was staring, and she didn't care.

His hands went to his sweats, pushing them down, stepping out of them.

Magnificent, she thought, or maybe she said it; nothing mattered but the fact that she was here, with him.

"Your turn," he murmured, returning to the bed. As he approached, she noticed he was favoring his left leg slightly.

"Oh," she said, seeing the nickel-sized, star-shaped scar on his inner left thigh, but then the weight of him was on her. His warm mouth kissing her again, tugging her lower lip gently between his teeth, then soothing the slight swelling of her lip with his tongue.

She had never much liked kissing. Found it kind of gross, the way Brett would thrust his whole tongue in her mouth and leave it there, a thick, slimy, fat, wiggling slug. It always made her feel like gagging.

But this? What Luke was doing was so damned erotic. She found she was craving the fresh taste of him, the possession of his lips, the sensuous dance of his tongue that made it impossible not to join in. *I like kissing*, she thought, dazed. *I really, really like it.*

He rose, kneeling above her, the strong muscles of his legs straddling her thighs. She wanted to trace his scar with her fingers, kiss it tenderly, but perhaps he was self-conscious about it, so she didn't. *That can come later*, she thought, as his fingers deftly unbuttoned her nightgown and started to peel it back.

"Oh, goodness," Maggie said, a flash of shyness. Were her breasts too small? She grabbed her nightgown to keep it in place, but his hands captured hers.

"Uh-uh," he said, shaking his head, amusement in his voice. "That wasn't the deal." He slid her hands up over her head, his hand securing hers. Holding her there. His mouth returned to hers, driving her wild, but only for a moment. Then he was making his way down the slope of her neck, dropping kisses in his wake.

Maggie, half-crazed with desire, wanted to move, touch, taste, but was pinned in place by his hands and his thighs.

He nuzzled the hollow of her throat, the slight scrape of roughness from the sandpaper texture of his cheek, another erotic sensation, highlighting the differences between his body and hers. She moaned, her hips undulating of their own volition.

He continued his torturously languorous trek downward. The neckline of her nightgown was now open. A lick on bare skin, then the scrape of his teeth dragging against her downward, grasping her nightgown and yanking first one side, and then the other, open with his teeth.

She was splayed out like a feast, her small breasts jutting upward, her pale-pink nipples taut and straining toward his mouth. *Too small,* she thought, *I'm too small.* Held in place, unable to move or cover up, she was both embarrassed and turned on as hell. His heated gaze was on her. *Is he disappointed? Brett always was.*

She was about to squeeze her eyes shut when she heard an approving growl of satisfaction deep in Luke's throat. "Perfection," he said, his voice husky with need, and then his hot mouth lowered to her breast. A lick of his tongue, and then she felt him blow gently, the cool air causing her nipple to tighten even more, her back arching. Aroused, and wanting, all her thoughts and worries of not being enough vanished into the night.

He repeated the butterfly-light caress. And then, without warning, his mouth latched on. Suction, tongue, the barest tease of teeth. The sensations were overwhelming, not just on her breast, but as if his mouth suckling there was sending a direct channel of pleasure to throb between the crux of her legs: wet, swollen, pulsating heat.

"I need ... I need ..." she was whimpering. "Please ..." Her breath ragged, her heart racing, a caged bird in her chest.

He was lavishing attention on her other breast now. Tremors building, a mini-earthquake rising.

"Please ... please ..."

Both her hands now held in one of his, the freed hand sliding down her body, caressing, stroking, a hard pinch on her nipple that jolted her body upward, and then a kiss to soothe. She could feel the hot, hard length of him against her thigh, clear evidence that he was fiercely aroused. She felt dizzy with need. "Please ..."

But he didn't enter her. He pressed her wrists into the bed. "Don't move," he whispered, and then released them.

Both his hands were on her now. One lavishing attention on her breasts, the other journeying down, spreading her nightgown on the way. Down, past her abdomen, past the slippery, wet heat between her legs.

"I like you like this," he murmured, sliding the last bit of her nightgown off her body. He shifted his weight as he nudged her thighs open. "Completely exposed." He was kneeling now between her legs, spreading her further, his hand traveling down to cup her intimately. "You're killing me ..." he groaned, lowering himself, half on her, half on the bed, one leg flung over hers, keeping her open. The weight and warmth of him was a welcome relief.

He slid his hand up from her breast to tangle in her hair. Turning her face toward him, his mouth took possession of hers while his fingers started a slow, sensuous dance. Dipping one finger, then two, inside her most private and intimate place; a long, slow stroke, and then another, before his slickened fingers slid out and circled over her secret, hidden bud. Again and again. Winding her tighter and tighter, making her dizzy with need.

Maggie heard a low, desperate moaning, rising in intensity and volume. Was she making those noises? Wild, unconstrained sounds that he was wrenching from her body, taking from her lips. Sensations building, building until, finally, she flew over the edge into the earthquake that roared through her, tremor upon tremor of unimaginable pleasure, as if a rainbow had exploded inside her and was sending shimmering molecules coursing through every cell in her body.

She heard the rip of a foil pack, and then Luke was over her, his weight on his elbows, his hard, hot erection nudging the pulsing entrance of her body. His gaze locked on hers, fierce desire and something else. "More than friends."

He said it like a statement, but she could see the question in his eyes.

"More than friends," she answered, her hands rising to cup his beautiful face.

He surged forward, watching her with a burning intensity as he buried himself to the hilt, filling Maggie completely, stretching her past what she had known she could accommodate.

"Oh my ..." she whispered. "Oh my ... I never knew ..."

Emotions flooding her, sensations building, the two of them spiraled upward together, gazing deep into each other's eyes. Each stroke, each slide, each rasp of breath felt like a sacred promise, a vow. Momentum built as they soared higher and higher, and then an orgasm tore through her, more powerful and intense than the one before.

Luke lifted her hips, thrusting hard, and then he followed her off the cliff, his exultant, satisfied roar filling all the empty spaces in her heart.

Every millimeter of Luke's body was satiated and utterly content. Maggie was tucked up beside him, warm and cozy. His arm was around her, her fingers gently ruffling and then smoothing the hair on his chest. It was a nice, peaceful feeling.

"Well," Maggie said, her voice drowsy, like she was about to drift away on a sleep wave. "I'm glad you," she yawned, "cleared that up."

"What's that?" Luke asked.

"Well, two things, really. First, Brett was wrong, and …" She nuzzled into him like a warm puppy.

Luke waited for the rest of the sentence, but it didn't come. He gave her a little nudge. "And what?"

"Oh …" she said, sleepy satisfaction in her voice. "The magazines … they were telling the truth."

He felt her body give in to sleep, her breath slowing: silent on the inhale, faint puffs of air on the exhale. Deeper and deeper she sank into sleep.

"Well, what do you know," Luke whispered, dropping a kiss on top of her head, her hair silky against his lips. "Seems I've fallen in love with you, Maggie."

Thirty-Three

*M*aggie was wearing a white tank top and a flowing wraparound skirt. Her hair was still damp from their morning shower and pulled back in a ponytail. The color had gradually returned to her cheeks. That was good. Hopefully the aftereffects of shock and trauma were receding.

What a shower it had been.

Luke had planned on giving her a break. They'd made love three times during what was left of the night, but instead of scratching the itch, each encounter had only seemed to heighten his hunger for her. However, he needed to be sensible. Enough was enough.

It had been torture lying on the bed, watching her shower through the partially open door, but he had managed to stay put. Until she lifted her arms to wash her hair, causing her back to arch. Her pert, pink-tipped breasts, which he had licked and suckled less than an hour before, caused his gentlemanly intentions to fly out the window. He had descended on her like a ravenous beast.

Not that she had complained, Luke thought with a smile, watching her pad barefoot around his kitchen.

It felt so good. So right.

"What are you thinking?" she said, tipping her head to look up at him. The trust and warmth emanating from her hit him like a blow to the solar plexus.

"You have cute feet," he replied.

"Weirdo." Maggie grinned at him.

"And you're only discovering this now?" he asked, quirking an eyebrow. He was standing before his beloved stainless-steel espresso machine, capturing the last drips of an Americano in a mug.

Maggie laughed, flipping open the egg carton. "Do you think Gunner and Colt will be wanting some breakfast?"

"Oh, yeah," Luke said. "I'm sure they would love some, but they can tend to themselves. You are in no way obligated."

"It's no problem at all," Maggie said, cracking some eggs into a mixing bowl. "I like feeding people." She swung open the fridge, got out some cream, and poured a couple of glugs into the bowl. "So we got a little sidetracked last
night ..."

"Sidetracked, or on track, depending how you look at it," Luke said, stepping in behind her, nuzzling her neck as he removed the cream from her hand and added a drizzle to her coffee.

"You know what I mean," Maggie said, a becoming blush streaking her cheeks. Seeing the effect his nearness had on her was a powerful aphrodisiac. His cock started to swell, rebelling against the constraints of his jeans.

"Physically impossible," Luke murmured, leaning into her, the swollen evidence of his desire rubbing between the cheeks of her buttocks. "And yet, there it is. I want you again."

"Again," she squeaked, growing even redder.

He reached around her. So what if his hand, on the way to the sugar bowl, brushed against the side of her sweet, upturned breast. Her sharp intake of breath threw gasoline on the fire. His cock surged to an almost painfully rock-hard state.

"I need you," he said, his hands traveling up her legs, her silk skirt gathering at his wrists. Up over her thighs, over her sweetly curved ass. "Jesus, Maggie, no underwear? You're killing me."

He groaned as she leaned forward, laying her elbows and chest flat on the marble countertop and grinding her bare ass against his erection. He could feel her wet heat through his jeans.

"Take me, then," she ordered, her smoky whiskey-and-honey voice even huskier than usual. "But do it fast," she said, tossing him a siren smile over her shoulder; her eyes, almost slumberous in their arousal, watching him through dark, sooty lashes; a brief peek of her tongue moistened her kiss-swollen lips. "I have breakfast to make."

Jesus, Mary, mother of God ... The last vestiges of blood in his brain surged downward. His fingers shook with need, unable to rip the buttons of his jeans open fast enough.

"What are you waiting for?" she growled.

He grabbed a condom from his pocket, ripped it open with his teeth, reached inside to free his stiff, ruddy cock, and sheathed it.

"I'm wet," she panted, "I'm ready, I want you n—"

He slammed his cock into her wet, welcoming warmth.

"More," she moaned. "More ..."

And he gave her more, again, and again. His hands gripped her hips. Harder and faster, intensity built, slamming into her over and over. Maggie spread out on the counter, like a perp waiting to be cuffed.

Then she slid her hand off the cool, marble surface to the slippery, wet heat between her legs. She caressed her sweet, swollen clit, now him, his balls, encircling his shaft with her finger and thumb, feeling its thickness, its girth, its slick, throbbing length, as it entered and retreated from her body. "Mmm ..." she moaned, and then was back to her clit.

She was close, so close. He could feel her body clenching around him, drawing him up, in. His teeth clenched, trying, *trying* to hold off, to give her time.

"Faster," she growled. "Harder."

He reached up, wrapped her ponytail around his fist like reins and slammed his cock into her, all the way to the hilt. She screamed, her body convulsing around him, wrenching his orgasm out of him; fireworks exploded, knees weakened while the tremors of her body sucked every last drop out of his pulsating cock.

Maggie turned the oven dial to convection and the temperature to four hundred degrees.

"So, after you left the military?" she asked. Her knees were feeling a little wobbly, but she had the feeling that had more to do with their nocturnal and early-morning activities than any emotional hangover from that disturbing killing business ... *It's over and done with*, she told herself. *Let it go.*

"Started my own business," Luke said, handing her a coffee.

"Must have been scary," Maggie said, taking a sip. "Mmm … perfect." She sighed, allowing contentment to spill through her. "A bit of cream and one sugar. How did you know?"

"You were here for dinner."

"But I dressed my own cup."

Luke shrugged. "I must have noticed, clocked it subconsciously." He moved back to the coffee machine, slid his mug under the dispensing spout and pressed a button.

"Well, thank you," Maggie said, raising her voice slightly so he could hear it over the grinding of the coffee beans. She laid strips of local, hormone-free bacon on a baking sheet.

"It was scary," Luke said, "now that I look back on it. Plowing into it every penny I had, and even then, I had to negotiate an enormous loan from the bank. Canned tuna, peanut butter, and beans were my daily diet that first year." He shook his head. "Still can't eat them."

"Note to self," Maggie said, placing the bacon in the oven. "No peanut butter cookies for Luke."

Luke laughed. "Yeah, but you can make that killer chocolate cake anytime." He leaned against the counter and took a sip of coffee.

Maggie paused to enjoy the view of his long, lanky body.

Luke smiled warmly at her, relaxed. "Don't look at me like that, Maggie, my girl, or you'll find yourself bent over the counter again."

Maggie smiled back at him. "Oh no, you don't," she said. "No more of your distraction techniques. I want to know what happened next."

"Party pooper," he said, taking another sip of his coffee, his eyes twinkling over the rim of his mug.

Maggie opened the spice drawer, removed paprika, onion powder, salt and ground pepper, added them to the bowl, and then started beating the eggs.

"It was touch-and-go at the start," Luke said. "First year and a half was really hard. Small jobs. Low and sometimes no pay. I thought I might go belly up, but then I landed a big contract when an old buddy who knew my work recommended me to his uncle. I had two weeks to go from a two-man operation to needing ten fully trained men on the field."

"Wow."

"Tell me about it," Luke said, shaking his head. "It was a scramble. I knew a lot of good operators, but if you want good people, you have to pay well, and I didn't have the money. My buddies came through in a big way. They took a chance on me and showed up, knowing that they might or might not get paid. That it all depended on the client settling his account in a timely manner. If the client had bailed on the bill, I would have been bankrupt. As it was, I had to take out a second loan to pay the expenses for the team during the job."

"Sounds stressful."

"It was. I was popping Prilosec like it was penny candy. It was tough, but my guys—they did an amazing job. I owe them a lot." Luke tipped his head toward the oven. "Want me to flip the bacon?"

"Yes, thanks," Maggie said. "I forgot it was in there." She tossed a pat of butter into the frying pan; the aroma rose to her nose. Ah ... nothing better in the world than the smell of melted butter. "So, what happened next?" she asked, swirling the butter around so it covered the bottom of the pan; then she turned down the heat and poured in the egg mixture.

"Well, that was the turning point," Luke said, slipping his hand into an oven mitt and removing the sizzling bacon from the oven. "The client paid. He was so pleased with the job we'd done that he kept us on and recommended our services to other Fortune 500 companies. The thing snowballed. I kept the guys on, hired more, and so forth."

The kitchen door opened and Colt and Gunner entered, bringing the crisp morning air with them.

"Smells good," Colt said.

"We're making plenty," Maggie said. "Were hoping you'd join us."

Maggie had been too weary yesterday to notice, but Luke's friends were almost as impressive to look at as Luke. Both of them were tall, rugged men. Hard, lean bodies, handsome as hell, with chiseled cheekbones and tousled hair. They had soulful eyes with long lashes and a slightly bruised quality, as if they had seen too much.

She sometimes saw those shadows in Luke's eyes.

Maggie turned and studied Luke's face. "So then what happened?" she asked. "Did someone not pay? Did your business go under? Is that why you—"

"Go under?" Gunner whistled, low, between his teeth. "Whoo-hoo." He leaned back, hip against the table. "This is gonna be good."

Luke shot him a look.

"Would you mind letting my sister know that breakfast is ready?" Maggie said, stepping into the gap, "She's painting on the bluff out front."

"You do it, Colt," Gunner said, grinning. "I'm gonna stay and watch Luke squirm."

"There will be no squirming. You're both going," Luke growled. "Unless you prefer foraging in the woods for your food."

"Tyrant," Gunner tossed over his shoulder, and the two men exited the kitchen, the door swinging shut behind them.

"So?" Maggie said, turning back to face him.

Luke's posture didn't change. He appeared to be relaxed and comfortable—his face, too—but she could sense the coiled tension within him, feel the waves of wariness spreading outward from his body.

"Tell me," she said, moving the pan of eggs off the burner on her way to him. She wrapped her arms around his waist. "Whatever it is," she said, holding him tight, "we'll deal with it."

Luke stood, encircled by her arms, a beautiful ache in his chest. He felt humbled by her faith, her strength, and her courage.

He tipped her chin up, smoothed a strand of hair from her eyes. "Maggie," he said. "Don't look so worried. Everything's okay."

"Why was Gunner acting funny? There is still something you're hiding, isn't there?"

She was so frigging cute. Luke couldn't help it: a chuckle escaped—which did not help matters.

"Why are you laughing?" she said. "This might be funny to you, but it's not to me. I care for you. If you're in trouble, I need to know."

"I'm not in trouble," Luke said. "Gunner was teasing me because ..." Luke paused, unsure how to continue. He didn't want things to change, for her to regard him differently. Having money was a double-edged sword. He had strived so hard to earn and save, and to make the business grow, but after a certain point it was just more money. There was a weight that came with it. A responsibility. And people's reactions to it? Luke shook his head. Money could destroy relationships, wreck lives.

"Luke?" Maggie said, placing her hand on his arm. "Are you all right?"

Luke nodded. "Yeah," he puffed out a breath and dived in. "Look, the truth of it is ... I'm obscenely wealthy."

"Wealthy?"

"Yeah, and Gunner finds it amusing that I choose to live here, like this," he said, shrugging, feeling a little embarrassed; a little defiant too. "Baking bread."

"Oh," Maggie nodded. She looked a little dazed.

"I know it seems crazy. People think 'rich,' and they imagine owning huge mansions all over the world, a large staff, lots of bling, Bentleys, yachts ..." His voice trailed off.

"No." She shook her head. Thought about it for a moment. "I think if I were obscenely wealthy, I would do the same. Craft a peaceful life, do what I want in a beautiful environment. Take long walks, cook yummy food. Share good times with family and friends. I wouldn't want a big old mansion or staff. Although," she said, laughing, "your house is pretty damned nice."

Relief washed over Luke, and something that felt suspiciously like joy.

"So you made all this money ... how?" Maggie asked, her head tilting slightly to the side, eyes trusting.

"My business was security."

"Security. Yes, you mentioned it at the cottage, but I thought perhaps you'd snagged a job as a security guard in a mall or something. Didn't know you owned and ran a security company."

Luke nodded.

"What does that mean, 'security'? Did you install alarm systems, and monitoring, things like that?"

"That does fall under the 'security' umbrella. However, the types of security my company offered were advanced, comprehensive security solutions and highly trained operatives to assist organizations and allied governments worldwide manage security risks, sometimes in hostile and complex environments."

Although Luke rarely spoke of what he had done, he was, in a quiet way, rather proud of what he had accomplished.

However, Maggie didn't seem impressed. On the contrary, she looked aghast. "Jesus ... That sounds extremely dangerous."

Luke shrugged. "No more than the Special Forces."

222 · SARA FLYNN

She wrapped her arms even tighter around him and buried her head in his chest. "You could have been killed."

"But I wasn't."

"I'm glad you quit."

"Me too," he said. And he was. If he hadn't walked away from the job, he never would have met her.

They stayed like that, in each other's arms, with the kitchen quiet around them, until the back door opened. The hungry horde tramped into the kitchen, laughing, and talking, and eager to be fed.

Maggie leaned back in her chair. *So enjoyable, cooking for these big, strapping, hungry men,* she thought, watching Colt scoop a third serving of scrambled eggs onto his plate.

"So, Luke," Eve said, slathering local-made strawberry jam onto a slice of toasted sourdough bread, "tomorrow's Friday; Saturday's coming fast. You up for sharing your stall with us again?"

"Yes, he is," Maggie said, smiling at Luke. "Aren't you, honey?"

"Uh ... I guess I am," Luke said, looking amused.

"And I was thinking, Eve, that maybe we should consider opening a little eatery." Maggie's cell phone started singing from its perch on the counter. "Just a second." She held up a finger, scooting back from the table. "Don't let me forget what we were talking about, Eve. It's a really good idea." She rounded the counter and picked up her phone ... and saw the familiar number on the screen.

Damn.

Brett, again. She'd forgotten to switch off her phone after calling the police.

She did not want to talk to him. The jerk. Telling her she was frigid; treating her like his personal doormat for all those years.

She was tempted to shut it down and let it go to voicemail, as she had been doing. But continuing to avoid him meant she was allowing him to have power over her. It was best to deal with him and move on.

"Hello?" Her voice came out a little too high and cheery, as if she were hosting a children's morning show. She cleared her throat. "What can I do for you, Brett?" That was better. She sounded brusque and businesslike.

Luke looked less than pleased. His eyebrows shot up to his hairline, then lowered as storm clouds rolled across his face. He looked hard and dangerous—and sexy.

"Where the hell are you?" Brett sounded upset.

"I'm ... I'm ..." Maggie said, feeling a flush of guilt— and turning her back on the counter, the one where Luke had taken her so enthusiastically less than an hour ago. On the heels of feeling guilty came a surge of anger. "It's none of your business any longer," Maggie snapped, "where I am or what I'm doing."

She stalked into the living room, shutting the kitchen door behind her. No need for Luke to witness her being a virago. "Why are you calling me? We have nothing to say—"

"I'm calling because I traveled all the way down here to see you. Two flights and a fucking boat ride—"

"What?" Maggie squeaked. "You're ... you're here?" She couldn't wrap her mind around the concept. Why would he be here? Nothing on this island would appeal to Brett's sensibilities.

"—Only to discover that you aren't where you were supposed to—"

"Hey!" Maggie cut him off. "Don't you yell at me. I don't answer to you. I owe you nothing."

"I'm sorry, Maggs. You're right." He sounded terrible, his voice low and ragged, as if he hadn't been sleeping, or had been crying or something. "I'm in a terrible fix. I need to see you."

Wow. Brett had just admitted she was right? Things must be bad. "What's going on?" Maggie asked, a tinge of worry thrumming through her. "You don't sound good."

Yes, she was mad about the way he had handled things, and verbally castigating her over the phone on Monday hadn't helped. But that was the way he was. Brett always acted badly when his back was to the wall. It was important for her own healing to remember that he'd been her friend, too. They'd spent many years together, and there had been good times as well as bad.

"Look," Maggie said, her voice softening, "if you need another week or two to secure a loan, that's okay. I'll tell Pondstone Inc. to wait. You didn't have to travel all this way."

Maggie could hear Brett exhale heavily. She knew he was rubbing his face. He always did that when he was stressed or agitated. He was quiet for a moment.

"We need to talk," he said.

"Okay."

"Not on the phone, face to face." His voice was slightly muffled, as if he had his hand cupped around his mouth. "Where are you?" he asked.

"I'd rather not say." That was the last thing in the world she needed, Maggie thought, massaging a knot that was taking up residence in her stomach—for Brett to show up on Luke's doorstep. She couldn't imagine that ending well.

"You're with someone, aren't you?" Brett said, sounding slightly accusatory.

"Again," Maggie said, "none of your business."

The kitchen door swung open. "Everything okay?" Luke asked.

Maggie made shooing motions, but Luke didn't budge. Just parked himself more securely in the doorframe, his arm slung up, his hip bumping up against the wood like he was planning to stay there all day.

"Who's that?" Brett said.

"Nobody," Maggie said, turning her back on Luke.

Which was a mistake. He was there in two strides. "That's not the song you were singing bent over the counter this morning," Luke murmured in her ear, wrapping his arms around her waist, pulling her close so her butt was snug up against his seemingly ever-ready erection.

Jesus, Maggie thought with a mix of irritation and pleasure. *So frigging primitive.* "It's none of your business, Brett," she said, trying to maintain her cool, but it was hard. Luke was doing a barely discernible undulation of his hips, mirroring a more intimate act while she was on the phone, trying to be proper. Maggie pushed away from him, even though her body was already thrumming, readying itself for entry.

Luke laughed low in his throat, as if he knew how swollen and wet she was getting. *Stop it*, she mouthed, scowling at him. He flopped in a chair, grinning at her as he slowly undid the top button of his Levis.

Maggie made a fierce cease-and-desist movement with her free hand.

Luke just smiled like a hungry wolf and stroked strong, tanned fingers down the straining fabric of his worn jeans. She watched him undo another button while Brett sighed heavily over the phone.

"I really fucked things up, didn't I?" Brett said.

"Yeah." Maggie tore her eyes away from Luke. "You did." She made her way past the coffee table and sofa. She needed to give herself a little distance from Luke so she could think clearly.

"Will you see me, at least?"

"Brett—"

"Fifteen minutes. That's all I ask. Face to face. For old times' sake."

Maggie stared out the window. Sunlight was sparkling on the water, dancing prisms of silver light dappling the branches and the ground around tall evergreens that swayed slightly in the wind at the cliff's edge.

"Please, Maggie," Brett said. "It's important."

An eagle launched off a tall Douglas fir tree, plummeting down toward the water and, at the last second, swooping upward, a small fish caught in its talons.

"Okay," she heard herself say. "Where do you want to meet?"

Thirty-Four

*T*his really isn't necessary," Maggie said for the hundredth time, as she made the left-hand turn into the gravel parking lot of the Halfmoon Bay Motel.

"I, for one," Eve piped up from the back seat of the car, where she was wedged between Gunner and Colt, "am glad Luke insisted."

"Thank you," Luke said; his voice was casual, but his gaze was scanning the empty lot like it was a potential war zone.

Maggie glanced in the rear-view mirror. Gunner and Colt were doing the same.

"Guys, relax," Maggie said. "It's *just* Brett." She pulled in next to a navy-blue sedan with a rental company's name on the license-plate holder.

"Which, in my mind, is no reassurance at all," Luke replied. "Two attempts have been made on your life in the last twenty-four hours. In instances like this, one follows the money. Your money. And it leads right back to ol' Brett-baby."

"Not necessarily," Maggie said, as she shifted into park and switched off the ignition. Even to her own ears, she didn't sound very convincing. "Besides, Brett would never …" Her voice trailed off.

Luke was right. Brett had motive and was on the island. She got out of the car so she wouldn't have to finish her sentence.

Luke, Gunner, and Colt were out of the car in a flash, forming a circle around her and Eve, the men facing outward.

"Seriously?" Maggie said, trying to act cool, but her mouth was dry and her heart was banging against her chest.

Now that she was here, she was glad they had insisted on coming along. Even in daylight, the motel had a depressed, abandoned air about it. Not the type of place Brett usually liked to frequent. The paint was peeling; the windows were dark. The wind was tumbling an old, empty garbage can across the parking lot.

"Kind of spooky," Eve said, pulling her sweater up around her neck.

"Hello?" Maggie called.

No answer.

Eve took Maggie's hand and gave a reassuring squeeze, reminding Maggie of walking to school, her first day of kindergarten. She had been so scared, but she had managed because her big sister was there, holding her hand, giving her strength and courage.

"Brett?" Maggie called, a little louder this time.

Still nothing.

A shiver of foreboding rippled through her.

"Let's go," Luke said, taking her arm. "I don't like this."

She wanted to leave. Badly. "No," Maggie said. "I promised I'd meet him. He traveled all this way. I can't go back on my word."

"Then call and arrange to meet him in a more public location," Luke said, gently trying to usher her toward the car.

"Luke," she said, looking him square on, "I know you're concerned, and I appreciate your expertise, but I'm a grown woman and this is my decision to make. You didn't hear him on the phone. I did."

Luke opened his mouth to argue, but Maggie continued. "Yes, he treated me badly. Yes, he's a jerk. But that doesn't make him a killer. So he's not in the parking lot as agreed. Maybe he's stuck on the phone. He gave me his room number," Maggie said, letting go of Eve's hand so she could smooth out the scrap of paper she had clenched in her damp fist. It was crumpled, the ink slightly smeared, but it was still legible. "Room 204. I'm going up. You can come or you can stay."

"Jesus, Maggie." Luke ran his hand through his hair as he stared down at her in frustration.

She held her breath. Waited. Hoped he wouldn't call her bluff, because there was no way in hell she was going to go up there alone.

He huffed out a breath. "Okay," he said, "I'll come up with you. Eve, it's best if you stay here. Gunner, Colt, you know what to do."

"Do you want me to come with you, Maggs?" Eve asked, clearly concerned, her chin jutting out like she would take on the world if Maggie said yes.

"It's safer here," Luke said. "More possible escape routes, better visibility. Two of the finest men in the business guarding you."

"Just in case I'm colossally wrong about Brett," Maggie said, her mouth drier than chalk, "I'd rather you stay here." She gave her sister a quick hug. "I'd never forgive myself if anything happened to you."

"You sure?" Eve said, studying her face.

"I'm positive," Maggie said, then she straightened her shoulders, and headed for the metal stairs on the outside of the building that led to the second floor.

Luke lengthened his stride. "I'll go first," he said, as they reached the stairs. Amazingly, she didn't argue. "Until we see what we're dealing with, stay close, okay?"

Maggie opened her mouth.

"I know. It's just Brett," he said, keeping his voice calm, measured. "But I'm asking you to do this for me. As a precaution. That's all."

She studied his face, then gave a short nod.

He started up the stairs, keeping his footsteps quiet on the metal rungs. She followed his lead, her face pale, determined.

They reached the top and turned right. Luke glanced over the handrail to the parking lot, where Colt and Gunner were keeping watch. Gunner gave him a quick thumbs-up and continued scanning the area.

There was a noise at the opposite end of the walkway. Luke stepped in front of Maggie, reaching inside his jacket and closing his hand around the cool, smooth grip of his Glock 19. A middle-aged woman with rounded shoulders and graying hair appeared, wheeling a housekeeper's trolley out of a room. She looked tired and worn in her stained uniform. She disappeared into the next room, leaving the door ajar. He could hear the TV flip on. A daytime soap.

Maggie exhaled behind him. "Well, that answers that question," she whispered. "It's a functioning motel."

"Just barely, by the looks of it," Luke answered, keeping his voice low.

She smiled at him, and it caught him low in the gut.

"What?" she asked, tipping her head.

"Nothing," he replied. They continued on. Room 202 … 203 … and then they were there.

"I'm scared," Maggie whispered, her hand clutching the back of his jacket.

"Make sure to stay behind me. If I say run, then run. Get to Gunner and Colt. They'll keep you safe."

"And who will keep you safe?" she whispered, fiercely. "I'm scared, but I'm staying."

Figures, he thought, shaking his head. And yet it was one of the reasons he had fallen so hard for her.

He rapped on the door.

No answer.

Tried the doorknob.

It turned easily in his hand.

He paused, took a breath, and turned to her. "Maggie. I need you to go downstairs." Something in his face must have convinced her—or maybe she felt it, too. Whatever it was, he was grateful when she nodded, slowly turned, and retraced her steps.

Once she was in the stairwell, he swung the door open, already knowing what he was going to find. Death left a certain miasma, a certain taste and texture to the air around it.

Thirty-Five

*B*y the time they had finished giving their statements to the police and headed home, it was almost noon. Eve had taken over the wheel, and Luke had wedged himself into the back so he could keep his arms around Maggie, who was badly in shock.

"I can't believe he shot himself," she kept saying through chattering teeth, over and over, while uncontrollable shakes coursed through her. "And in the face, of all things. He was so vain. It just doesn't make sense."

Luke agreed with her assessment, although for entirely different reasons. The placement of the gun was off—seemed staged. Add to that, no serial number on the frame. The slight scent of perfume was almost indiscernible through the coppery smell of warm blood, but it was there, a lingering afternote.

Could be a plant. Could be a clue.

Didn't matter. The important thing was that the police had ruled it a suicide, at least initially, and Luke hadn't corrected their assumption. The fiscal reasons that had made him suspicious of Brett's motives could send unwanted attention in Maggie's direction.

Her shaking had lessened by the time they arrived back at his property, but she was still wringing her hands.

The small pebble he'd put on the gate was undisturbed. Luke checked the perimeter system. No evidence of anyone entering. That was good. He nodded to Colt and Gunner, and they loped off in opposite directions, disappearing quietly into the woods.

Once he had checked the perimeter of the house and the doors and windows, he disarmed the house security system and gave Samson the "release" command. Only then did the women enter the house. Luke booted the system back up, then went into the kitchen. He made coffee for Maggie, cream and one sugar, and a mug of peppermint tea with honey for Eve.

When he returned to the living room, the two sisters were ensconced on the sofa, Eve's arm around Maggie's shoulder, Samson lying at their feet. The sisters were talking quietly. Eve looked up when Luke entered, gratitude in her eyes.

"I'm thinking," Luke said, handing them the hot beverages, "that I should contact the Saturday market coordinator. It's late notice, but there might be a seasonal vendor who would like to take my spot."

Maggie's head snapped up. "Over my dead body," she said, eyes blazing, and then she flinched, the fire draining from her eyes. "What a terrible phrase that is. Never thought of it like that before."

She looked down at the mug of coffee cupped in her hands as if she was just now seeing it. She brought it to her mouth, her hands shaking slightly, pretended to take a sip, then placed it on the coffee table.

Luke knelt down so his face was level with hers. Her face was so pale. "You sure you're up to it? Might be a bit of a scramble to get everything ready. Especially with us sharing the kitchen."

"Your kitchen is enormous, Luke," Maggie said. "You've got your multi-deck oven for your breads, and I can commandeer your Viking Tuscany range, which," she attempted a smile, "I've been longing to do since I first laid eyes on it."

Eve laid her hand on Maggie's arm. "We could do it next week, honey. When all this craziness has been resolved and things have calmed down."

"I have to, Eve," Maggie said, her eyes darkening, her voice catching slightly. "I want to keep busy. Do something normal to ..." She swallowed hard. "To ... take my mind off ..." Maggie looked down, a shudder running through her. Luke could see she was struggling for control. "There will be a lot of people around who would be witnesses, so I doubt anyone would try something. Not to mention, Luke would be there, and Colt and Gunner."

Luke felt torn. Those were all good points, and yet he wanted to keep her locked up tight until he had eliminated the danger.

"Please ..." Maggie said, looking up at him.

Luke wanted to say no, but he nodded instead. Maggie was a grown woman. The decision was hers and hers alone to make. "All right," he said, extending a hand to her. "Let's draw up our grocery list, then."

Maggie smiled at him wanly. "Thanks," she said, her voice soft. She placed her hand in his and stood, her slender fingers cold as ice.

Thirty-Six

*M*aggie stretched and watched with satisfaction as Luke carried the final boxes of baked goods out to the truck. It had been a lot of hard work, but she was glad she had pushed for it. There was something about settling into the process of baking that calmed her. Putting ingredients together and creating something tasty had beaten back the darkness that threatened to close in on her like fast-moving fog. The warm, comforting smells surrounded her: apple, cinnamon, nutmeg, clove, and ginger, sugar and melting butter, roasting pecans, chocolate, and a tinge of brown sugar—these were the smells that filled a house and made it a home.

She'd called her parents while the final pies were baking. There was a three-hour time difference, so they were up. Maggie had wanted, needed the comfort of their familiar voices. Didn't tell them about Brett, or the attempts on her life. She would, eventually, when the danger had passed. No need for them to worry. There was nothing they could do, so far away. Although, knowing her parents, they'd probably hop on the first plane heading for the Pacific Northwest, which would put them in danger, too.

She dusted the lingering traces of flour off her hands. For the last couple nights, her sleep had been fractured, but every time she woke in a cold sweat and unable to breathe, Luke had been there, safe and steady, chasing the darkness away.

She took off her apron and hung it on a hook. She hitched her shoulders and circled them back, pulling her shoulder blades down and together. It felt good and helped ease the stiffness that had built up from rolling out copious amounts of pie dough and cookies on Luke's glorious marble counters.

It had been a pleasure to cook in his beautiful kitchen. She yawned and arched her back, her fingers digging into the lower lumbar vertebrae to help release the slight ache there.

"Maggie," she heard Eve call from outside.

"Coming," Maggie called back, downing a glass of cool, refreshing water, corralling the flyaway strands of hair back into her tortoiseshell clasp, and heading out the door into the bright, crisp morning sunshine.

The Saturday market was hopping. It seemed the number of market-goers had doubled from the week before. A bluegrass band was playing on the green; a few beribboned free spirits were twirling around, leaping and dancing. It was a joyous thing to watch and, oddly, made the attacks and finding Brett seem far in the past, almost as if Maggie were viewing the incidents through the reverse end of a telescope.

Maggie counted out change, then handed the boxed cherry-plum pie to the older woman, Dorothy Whidbee, who had helped her outside the ice cream store. "Enjoy," Maggie said.

"Hey," Dorothy said, an impish look on her weathered face. She tipped her head in Luke's direction. "Did you take my advice and try out the goods?" she asked in a stage whisper.

Maggie flushed, then leaned across the table. "I did," she whispered, feeling incredible risqué. "And am pleased to announce that the results were ..." She paused, searching for the right word. "Spectacular."

The woman cackled and nodded. "Good for you. Good for you, my girl." And then shuffled away, doing a little free-form boogie-woogie to the music that filled the air.

Maggie watched her gyrating body disappear into the crowd. "I love this place," she murmured, filled with sudden contentment. "That was the last of the pies," she told her sister.

Eve turned and looked at her, concern in her eyes.

"You okay?" she asked putting an arm around Eve.

"I'm just so worried, Maggie." She shook her head. "I barely slept last night, trying to make sense of everything. Twice someone tried to kill you. Brett's dead. Was he the one who hired those guys, then felt so ashamed that he did himself in? Or is there a whole other threat out there that we need to worry about?"

"I know," Maggie said, nodding. "Those are real concerns, but I'm so sick and tired of being worried. Yes, something bad might happen. If it does, I'll deal with it then. Right now, I'm going to try and focus on the positive. On the now. I'm alive. I'm in love. There are blue skies overhead."

"Oh, Maggie, seriously?" Eve said softly, looking at her with a mix of longing, hope, and worry. "You've only just met Luke."

"I know," Maggie said, glancing over her shoulder at him. He was tied up with an elderly female customer on the far side of the stall. The woman was counting out a mountain of pennies, nickels, and dimes from her coin jar and kept losing track of how much she had counted out. And Luke, bless his heart, was being so damned patient. "He—"

Gunner emerged from the crowd, moving fast, Colt on his heels. "Caught a partial view of a black SUV, tinted windows, southbound."

Maggie's heart accelerated.

Luke stilled. "Escalade?" he asked.

"Don't know," Gunner replied. "Going to check it out."

"Okay," Luke said, with a quick nod. "Keep me posted."

"Will do."

The two men jogged off.

Maggie let out her breath, slow and easy. They were on it. Luke was here. She was safe.

Luke must have felt her watching him, because he shot her a reassuring look over his shoulder, before turning back to his customer. "Here," she heard him say to the woman, "would you like me to …?" He gestured at the coins, and the woman shoved the pile over to him with a grateful look.

"He—?" Eve prompted.

Maggie pulled her gaze back to her sister. "He's just ... such a sweetheart. I know he seems all gruff and macho, but in private, he's so tender. Makes my heart sing, when I look at him, think about him, hear his voice. And he gets me, Eve. Do you know how rare that is?"

Eve nodded. "Unicorn rare."

"Tell me about it. Feel so lucky. He makes me laugh. Feel safe in his arms. Love the crinkles around his eyes when he smiles, and I ... Oh, Eve, I just love him so much." Maggie could feel her eyes get misty, much like her sister's appeared to be doing.

"I'm so happy for you, Maggie," Eve whispered fiercely, catching Maggie up in a deep, heartfelt hug. "*So* happy!"

"Um ... excuse me? Excuse me, ma'am?" Maggie felt a tug on her shirt. She looked down, and there was a freckle-faced, tow-haired little boy with a slightly grubby face, looking up at her.

"Yes?" Maggie said.

He seemed a little scared. There were dried tear-tracks on his face, so she knelt down to his level.

"Hey, kid," Eve said, "you aren't supposed to be back here. This area is only for the vendors."

"What's going on?" Maggie asked softly. "Are you okay? Where's your mom?"

The little boy swallowed, clearly trying not to cry.

"Are you lost?"

The boy nodded.

"Okay." Maggie put out her hand. "Come on. I'll help you find her."

The boy hastily put his hand behind his back and took a step backward, his brown eyes large in his face.

"It's all right," Maggie said. "You're safe with me. Come on." She reached out and took his hand in hers. "Are you hungry?"

The way his eyes flew hungrily to the apple tarts, she could tell that he was. She grabbed two and gave them to him, snagging a couple napkins as she rounded the table.

"Be right back," she said to Eve, and then Maggie and the boy plunged into the crowd.

The boy was too skinny. He wolfed down the two apple tarts in record time, barely taking time to breathe.

"Wow, you were hungry," Maggie said, reaching toward him to brush the traces of crust and dab of filling off his cheek, but he jumped back like a startled, wild thing, head ducking into his neck, flinching slightly as if expecting to be hit.

Maggie stilled, her heart aching. "You have some ..." she said, dabbing her finger at the side of her mouth.

The crowd adjusted its path, separating and streaming around the two of them like water flowing around a rock.

"Oh," the boy said, scrubbing the back of his grubby hand across his mouth, his cheeks turning red.

"It's nothing to be embarrassed about," Maggie said, acting nonchalant, even though a part of her wanted to scoop him in her arms, comfort him, take him home, feed him, and then pop him in a long, piping-hot bath. "It was my fault, really." She leaned closer, and this time he didn't leap away. "It's because of the special way," she lowered her voice, as if imparting a sacred secret, "my Great-Aunt Clare taught me to make her delectable crust. Super flaky.

A good pie or tart crust should always leave crumbs when devoured."

The boy nodded solemnly. "It was good," he said, reverently. "Best thing I ever ate in my whole life."

"Well, thank you," Maggie said, smiling down at him and taking his warm little hand in hers. "I'm glad you enjoyed it. Now, how about we go find your mom."

A countenance too weary, too sad, too mature for his age descended over his features. He shook his head, stared down at his hand in hers, like the weight of the world was on him. "Pretty lady," he said, his voice a barely-there whisper, shaky, urgent, "you shouldn't be with me ... you need to leave this place. Go far away and ... make pies and be happy and never, never, *never* come back."

What on earth? Maggie thought, trying to make sense of what he was saying. *And why is he crying like his heart is going to burst?*

"Come on," Maggie said, taking his hand, leading him away from the crowds, ducking through a gap that led to the back of the stalls.

It was quieter back there, private.

Maggie knelt down and wrapped her arms around his small, thin shoulders. "What's your name, sweetheart? Hmm?" she said, wiping away his tears, even though it was useless because more just followed. "Don't cry. We can sort this out. There's nothing that's unsolvable."

The boy's gaze shifted from her.

"What is it?" she asked, because he was staring over her shoulder as if the zombie apocalypse had just arrived.

"Run!" he choked out, half-bellow, half-cry, lurching backward and trying his hardest to drag her back the way they had come, but it was too late. His head snapped back from the force of a woman's hand striking him hard across the face.

The boy didn't even cry out, just crouched low, with his little arms trying to shelter his head from blows.

"Hey!" Maggie yelled, lunging forward to try to protect him, but an arm lashed around her, and she was jerked up short.

"Stupid brat!" the woman shrieked, backhanding the boy and sending him flying through the air. His small, flailing frame crashed into a straggly pink rhododendron bush, flower petals raining to the ground. "You are a fucking waste of space!" the woman screamed.

All Maggie could see was the back of the woman hunched over the boy, her arms slashing downward again and again.

"Stop it," Maggie cried, trying desperately to reach the boy, but she couldn't free herself from the enormous muscular hand that wrenched her arm behind her back in an incredibly painful manner.

"Let me go, you Neanderthal!" she yelled, flailing out with a kick behind her, but not making contact. Maggie lashed out again with her foot, hit something with a satisfying force, and was rewarded by his grunt of pain. But then he wrenched her arm higher. She felt tearing in her shoulder socket, and searing pain. Unwanted tears flooded her eyes. She opened her mouth to call for help, but all that came out was a gasp of pain as he yanked her arm even higher so her toes were barely skimming the ground.

"Shut the fuck up," he growled in her ear, giving another jerk upward for emphasis. His voice was raspy, as if he gargled daily with battery acid. She twisted her head around and managed to catch a glimpse of him, and immediately wished she hadn't. She knew in her gut that if she lived through this, she would have nightmares about those ice-cold, shark eyes for the rest of her life.

"You come with us quietly," he said, "or I kill the brat, too."

And that was when Maggie became aware of the cold metal gun barrel jammed against her ribs, and heard the snick of the safety catch being released. It was as if everything slowed to a dead stop.

"Nice and easy, like we're taking a Sunday walk in the park. Got it?"

"Okay," Maggie managed to say, amazed at how calm she made her voice sound. "I'll leave without a fuss, but the boy stays here."

Thirty-Seven

*F*inally, the transaction was completed. Luke had finished counting out the damned coins and the woman had departed with her eight croissants and sourdough round. He slid the coins off the table and into a plastic container. He'd sort it later.

Mr. Henderson was at the front of a line of customers waiting to be served. The line snaked around in front of the French patisseries booth as well as Cedar Hill Farm's booth.

The other vendors were not pleased.

"Mr. Henderson," Luke said, giving him a nod, "sorry for the wait." Luke started to bag Mr. Henderson's weekly order of two loaves—one multi-grain, one rye—when a sense of foreboding swept through him.

Luke whirled around.

Eve was on the other side of the stall, boxing up chocolate cupcakes.

"Where's Maggie?" he demanded.

"What?" Eve said, looking up.

"Where's Maggie?" The sense of urgency was rising. She was in danger. He could feel it. "She was right here two minutes ago. Where did she go?"

Eve glanced around.

"Oh dear. She's not back yet," Eve said, her face paling.

"Was she with anyone?" Luke said, keeping his voice measured and calm, even though everything inside him was bellowing like a gored bull.

"A little boy," Eve said, talking fast now, words tumbling over each other on their way out. "This high," she said, gesturing with her hand a little above her waist. "Said he was lost, couldn't find his mother."

That was the setup. He could feel it. "What did he look like?"

"Uh ... uh ..." Eve's hands were flapping in front of her as if she were flicking water off them.

"What color was his hair? What was he wearing?"

"Light blond hair. Saggy black T-shirt. It was dusty, with a couple of little rips on the back of the shoulder— left, right? I don't know. Pants—dark color, not clean. Maybe five or six years old."

"Thanks, Eve. Very good. Now, which direction did they go?"

She pointed, and he was off, vaulting over the top of their table.

When he landed, he realized his mistake. "Idiot," he muttered. He'd forgotten about his injury, and now his leg was convulsing in agonizing spasms. "Text Gunner and Colt," he spat out through clenched teeth. "Inform them of the situation and what we're looking for."

"Right," Eve said. "Want me to come?"

"No. Stay here and let me know if Maggie shows up." And then he ran, his fist grinding into his old wound to try to ease the spasm. He ran in the direction Maggie had disappeared as hard and fast as possible. He would deal with the pain later.

Thirty-Eight

*M*aggie had hoped that by appearing to acquiesce and go quietly, she would be able to get them far enough away from the little boy so he wouldn't be in danger. Then she would kick up a noisy ruckus. If he was a shooter, then she would be dead, but at least it would be fast, and there would be witnesses to testify and get him thrown in prison. And if he wasn't planning to kill her, was just bluffing, then she might manage to get away.

It was a good plan.

Unfortunately, the boy followed them. He was limping slightly, poor thing. Trailing them at a distance. The man hadn't noticed. But as long as Maggie could see the boy, her assailant might, too, and she had to behave.

The woman had disappeared before Maggie could see her face, but Maggie was holding on to what details she could remember. *Red manicured nails, the forefinger and middle finger on the right hand either broken or bitten down. Five-foot-four or -five. Seemed a little dumpy from behind, but wasn't wearing form-fitting clothes, so difficult to tell.* The descriptions would be important if—no, *when*—she got to safety. *That woman is going to pay for hitting that defenseless boy.* Maggie took a calming breath and exhaled.

It helped, to make plans.

Her other plan, she was discovering in hindsight, perhaps hadn't been the smartest.

When dickhead started escorting her away, she'd slipped off one of her brown leather sandals and flipped it with her foot through the gap between the stalls and into the crowd. Her hope was that Luke would notice she was missing and, while searching, would see the sandal, realize she was in danger and come racing to her rescue.

Well, she was regretting that move now. Traversing a large gravel parking lot with one sandal was no fun. Even if she managed a getaway, it would be incredibly difficult to outrun her buffed-up buddy, but to attempt it when she was missing a shoe? Not good odds.

She scanned the parking lot for anyone who could possibly help.

The only human she could see was the little boy, hovering at the perimeter of the parking lot, his head peeking out from behind a bush. He was crying.

"Run!" she mouthed urgently. "Get help!"

The donkey's ass jerked his head around to face her. She quickly looked forward, hoping the boy had ducked out of sight.

"What were you looking at?" he demanded, ice-cube gaze drilling into her.

"I was hoping to see a restroom," she said, keeping her voice nonchalant, as she gazed up at him. "I have to go."

"Nice try," he said.

A gray Dodge Caravan with tinted windows squealed to a stop in front of them, scattering gravel and dirt. *Dammit. A different vehicle. Colt and Gunner are chasing after an Escalade.*

The jerk wrapped his thick forearm around her neck in a choke hold and reached for the door with his gun hand.

It's now or never. She heard her mom's voice in her head: *You must fight!* Maggie knew from her mom's keep-my-girls-safe lectures and hands-on demonstrations that things were likely to get a million times worse if he managed to get her into that vehicle.

She tucked her chin down against her neck to protect her windpipe from being crushed, then dropped her weight down toward the ground, at the same time slamming her elbow upward with all her might.

"What the—" he started to say, but then her elbow drove into his solar plexus. An *oof* escaped as the air slammed out of his lungs. His body caved forward, his arm around her neck flew outward—only a few inches but enough for her to drop from his grasp and onto the ground. She felt the gravel tear into her knees.

"Run!" she screamed as loud as she could, scrambling to her feet, hoping the boy could hear her. "Get help!"

Maggie started to run, too, but managed only a couple of steps before she was yanked backward by her hair. Her feet almost went out from under her, but she regained her balance and pivoted around. She was aware of three other men jumping out of the vehicle, the black grip of her captor's gun swinging toward her. She lunged forward, thrusting her fingers up toward his eyes, her guttural cry fracturing the air around them.

Something crashed down onto her head. Crushing pain blurred her vision. Men converged on her. *Did I get him?* Maggie wondered, swaying, her vision shrinking to barely a pinprick. *Hope I blinded the bastard,* she thought, as her knees gave away and darkness swallowed her up.

Thirty-Nine

*L*uke bent over to pick up Maggie's sandal. He straightened abruptly and scanned the area but couldn't see anything out of place. Just vendors with crowds of market-goers milling around the various stalls.

Still the feeling was strong. He shut his eyes for a second and focused inward. *There … to your right,* his inner voice whispered. He turned slightly and opened his eyes, looking hard in the new direction.

Her energy was flowing through the sandal gripped in his hand, and with it, a sense of knowing. *She's alive, but time's running out.* A surge of fear rose from his gut, threatening to boil over.

He needed to be calm and balanced if he was to help Maggie at all.

And then he saw what he was waiting for. A blur. He almost missed it. A little blond-haired boy in a faded black T-shirt darting through the crowd, approaching fast.

Luke grabbed him by the scruff of his neck.

He was a feisty little bugger, squirming and kicking. "Lemme go! Lemme go!" he cried fiercely, scratching and biting.

"Stop it," Luke ordered, wrapping his arms tightly around the boy to contain his flailing limbs.

"I gotta help the lady," the boy sobbed.

"The one with hair like a new penny, who smells like fresh grass and honeysuckle, and makes kick-ass apple tarts?"

The boy stilled in his arms.

Forty

*M*aggie shook her head, feeling groggy. She could hear dripping water, the sound of the suck and pull of the ocean. She could smell the salt on the air, and something else.

What is it?

She didn't know. Her brain felt scrambled.

There was the copper taste of blood and bile in her mouth. She spat. It didn't help. Why were the left side of her face and her temple throbbing so badly?

She tried to lift her hand, but it wouldn't move.

Panic rose, threatening to engulf her as the events of the afternoon came flooding back.

The most important thing now is to keep calm and suss out the situation.

On the ground near her feet sat a wooden crate with a kerosene lantern on top, casting a pool of light around her. She appeared to be in a dark cave; the air around her was dank. The rough rope securing her wrists behind her was chafing her skin. Her ankles were bound as well. She seemed to be alone, too, but listened hard. She heard the low sound of men's voices discussing something, but they weren't close; she couldn't make out words. *They must be guarding the entrance of the cave.*

She was on her feet, tied upright to something. *Is it breakable?* She rounded her shoulders and pressed her back into the object. *A wooden stake. Too sturdy to break. But can I dislodge it?* She pulled forward as far as the binding would let her and slammed her body backward.

It didn't budge.

I'm screwed, Maggie thought, panic rising and choking off her air.

Nonsense! she told herself sharply. She took a long, healing breath and released it, then reopened her eyes. Still, her vision was blurry.

Damn. Now her stupid nose was running, and she had no way to wipe it. *No more crying,* she told herself sternly. She wiggled the rope constricting her wrists down the stake until she was in a crouching position. She strained forward and, with shoulder sockets protesting, was able to wipe the moisture off her face onto her knee.

Maggie's head snapped up. *What was that noise?* She stared into the shadows in front of her where the noise had come from. *Is someone there, in the shadows, watching me? Or is it my mind playing tricks?*

"Hello …?" Maggie said, a little hesitant, because if no one was there, she didn't want to bring the guards running.

She held her breath, listening hard.

No answer.

Maybe she was looking in the wrong place. The sound could have ricocheted off the rock surfaces. She scanned the cave slowly, noticing a dim lightening of the darkness to the right of her. *The way out must be in that direction.* The tiny hairs on the back of her neck shot up. She froze. Her heart slammed up into her throat.

Something's there.

Forty-One

*T*here was no sign of Maggie in the parking lot; no people who might have witnessed the abduction.

Luke glanced down at the little boy. "I need you to let go of my hand," he told him.

The boy looked at him, his large, fearful eyes filling.

"What's your name?" Luke asked.

"Adam," the boy whispered.

"Well, Adam, I'm not going to leave you. But I need to call for help for the lady who gave you the treats, and I need my hand in order to do that. Can you help me out, let go?"

And the kid finally relented, released Luke's hand, but the poor kid was shaking. Blood seeped from the wound on his head.

"Thank you," Luke told him and dialed his brother's phone. "Jake, I'm texting you a mobile number. I need you to bypass the opt-in, then triangulate her location ASAP. Thanks." He disconnected, then texted Maggie's cell number.

Gunner's SUV pulled up with Colt, Gunner, and Eve; Samson was in the back.

"Ethelwyn and Lavina are watching the stall," Eve said. "They said they'd handle the sales and breakdown, and would call if Maggie shows up."

"Maggie's not going to show up," Luke said, picking up the poor, frightened kid. The boy threw his arms around Luke's neck.

"You don't know that," Eve said, her face going pale.

"Eve, she's been abducted." He opened the back door of the vehicle and placed the boy inside.

"You can't just pluck a kid off the streets, Luke," Gunner said.

"Adam's a witness," Luke said, strapping the boy in and sliding onto the seat next to him. "We don't have the time or a safe house to drop him at, so he's coming with us."

His cell rang. His brother.

Luke slid his finger across the screen to answer. "What did you get?"

"I was able to track her movements until the point where Armand intersects Finlayson Creek Road, and then the trail went cold."

Luke squeezed his eyes shut. *Dammit.*

"Sorry," he heard Jake say. "Wish I could have been more help."

"Not your fault. The satellite transmission on this island sucks. It's either that or they found her phone and confiscated it." Luke wanted to curse, break something. "Thanks for trying," he said instead.

Forty-Two

*M*aggie peered into the dark, trying to glean details, anything.

A woman was bound to a stake about ten feet away from Maggie. Her head was slumped forward, her unkempt, strawberry-blond hair obscuring her face. *How long has she been there? Is she unconscious ... or dead?*

There was something familiar about her body, her hair. If only Maggie could see her face.

"Hey," Maggie whispered, but even that seemed loud, bouncing off the rock walls of the cave.

The woman didn't move or respond.

Maggie shimmied herself back to a standing position, urgency rising. "Hello?" she said a little bit louder.

"Well," a voice drawled, cutting through the darkness from in front of her, sending shivers skittering over her skin. "Will you look at that? The two little sluts are relegated to pole dancing."

Maggie knew that voice.

She knew it, but it didn't make sense.

"Carol ...?" Maggie ventured, having a difficult time wrapping her mind around what her ears were telling her. "Carol Endercott? From the office?"

"In the flesh," Carol chortled, stepping into the pool of light, throwing up her outstretched arms. "Ta-dah!"

"I don't understand. What are you doing here?"

Carol dropped her arms and sneered at Maggie. "Oh, poor baby. Let me explain."

Carol disappeared into the shadows briefly, then returned with a bottle tucked under her left arm and two crystal champagne glasses in her hand, and a folding metal chair in the other. She opened it and sat, tucked the champagne glasses into the crook of her arm, and peeled the foil off the top of the bottle. "You see, Brett and I—"

"What do you mean—Brett and you?" Maggie broke in.

Carol shrieked with laughter. "You didn't know, did you?" she asked, leaning in, eyes glittering, malice on her face. "Brett and I were close. We were more than close. We were a family."

"But you're married, you have a kid ..."

"Brett and I would have been married years ago if he hadn't been assigned to do temp work at the esteemed law office of Greenblatt and Mayer. Another typical example of my fucking luck. But one day, you waltz in with your stupid 'Great-Aunt Clare,' who needed to sign her will. An additional witness was needed. And there he was: my ever-enterprising Brett saved a copy of the document on his handy-dandy flash drive."

She popped the cork from the champagne bottle, sending it shooting past Maggie's head.

Carol glanced at her with a smirk. "Back to our story." She poured champagne into the crystal flutes. "Your aunt, as you know, was planning to leave all her substantial worldly goods to you—her ass-kissing, plain-as-hell niece."

She placed the partially emptied champagne bottle on the ground beside her chair. "A godsend, really—we were living on ramen noodles. Although the timing left a bit to be desired." Carol chuckled and shook her head. "Me pregnant and all."

"Pregnant?" Maggie felt ill. "Your child was ... Brett's? My Brett's?"

Carol nodded, her eyes vague, lost in memories. "He never loved you. He loved me. He promised that once we had access to your money and Comfort Homes was up and running ..." Her voice trailed off. "You have no idea how much I hate you, do you?"

"I thought we were—"

"What? Colleagues? Oh, friends, perhaps?" Carol snorted. "That's priceless. We should drink to that." She rose to her feet and walked over to Maggie, extending a champagne flute toward her. "Oh!" Carol said in fake surprise. "Your hands are tied. *Quel dommage.*"

"You're welcome to untie them," Maggie retorted.

Carol let out a brittle laugh. "I tell you what—I'll hold your glass for you." A tormented, bitter expression flicked across her face. "After all," she said, her voice dropping to a growl, "you held my nearest and dearest for all those endless, heart-crushing years."

Fear flared in Maggie's throat. "I didn't know, Carol. I never would have—"

"Cheers!" Carol said brightly as she clinked the champagne flutes together. "To friends." Carol downed her glass, then spat into the other flute and pressed it hard against Maggie's lips. "Open wide."

"Carol," Maggie started to say, but Carol tipped the flute up, spilling the contents into Maggie's mouth, over her face, and down her throat.

"Yummy, huh?" Carol said in a singsong voice. Her gaze traveled downward to Maggie's soaked blouse. "Oh ... you have such tiny little titties. No wonder he couldn't stand fucking you. What next? Oh! We can't forget about our other little friend, can we? That would be ruuuude." She danced back over to the champagne bottle, droplets of water kicking off her heels.

Water? Why is there water? Maggie thought, simultaneously clocking that water was gently lapping over her toes, against her arches.

Carol topped up both flutes.

"Carol," Maggie said, trying to keep the desperation out of her voice. "I'm so sorry for any pain I inadvertently caused you. I didn't know you were with Brett. I never would have—"

Carol whirled around. "Of course you didn't know, you dumb shit! That was my whole master plan. Duh! He marries you. I knock off your feeble old aunt. Tee-hee! He didn't know about that part of the plan until after I implemented it. Boy, was he surprised." Carol giggled. "Then he was supposed to marry you, and then— whoopsie! But he got cold feet, the dipshit."

"Wait a minute," Maggie said, rage and sorrow roaring through her body. "Are you telling me," tears flooded her eyes, "that you killed my Great-Aunt Clare?!"

"Yep," Carol said, nonchalantly, turning her back on Maggie. "Cyanide sprinkled in her bed sheets. Easy-peasy."

Grief ripped through Maggie. Poor, sweet, kind Great-Aunt Clare, who had taught her to cook, bandaged up her knees, and never hurt anyone in her life. "I'm going to kill you!" Maggie cried out, bucking against her restraints.

"No, sweetie," Carol tossed over her shoulder. "That's what I'm going to do to you." She sashayed over to where the other woman was staked. "Hello, Kristal," she cooed. "Not so glamorous now, are you?"

Kristal? Kristal Barrington? The one Brett took the honeymoon trip with? Oh, God. The girl is thoughtless and spoiled, but she doesn't deserve this.

"It's been a whole day and a half," Carol said in a singsong voice, "since you've had some champagne. I'll bet you're thirsty. Say *pretty please*, and I'll give you some."

Kristal didn't respond, didn't move.

"Stuck-up bitch!" Carol howled, all traces of baby talk gone. "Stealing my man with your fucking trust fund!" She drew back her arm and slapped Kristal with incredible force. Kristal's head whipped to the side.

"Not so pretty anymore, are you?" Carol was screaming, laughing maniacally, the sound magnified as it bounced off the walls of the cave. "Bet he wouldn't want to get within a mile of your skanky crotch now." She laughed, slapped her thigh, then grabbed Kristal's hair and yanked it so her face was angled toward Maggie. Kristal was clearly dead: her mouth was agape, her eyes half rolled back and vacant, blisters on her face. "See this?" Carol said, gleefully. "This is going to be you in a couple hours."

Oh my God, that smell is Kristal. Maggie shut her eyes, but she couldn't shut her ears.

"The tide goes in," Carol was singing, "and the tide goes out."

You will not get sick, she told herself determinedly. *You will not. You will be strong. You will have courage.*

"It's amazing," Carol mused, "what a combination of salt water and air will do to a body."

Maggie pushed her nausea down and forced herself to open her eyes.

"But it wasn't just looks, was it, Bretty-baby," Carol said mournfully, her shoulders slumping. "I couldn't compete with her kind of wealth. Her millions and millions. I couldn't ..." Heartbroken sobs filled the cave. "I took out loans, I mortgaged my life, I hired staff I couldn't afford, but that wasn't good enough, was it?" Buckling over with grief, Carol sank down to her knees. "After all those years," she wailed, "of waiting and waiting ..."

"So you killed him," Maggie said coolly, cutting into Carol's pity party. The crazy bitch had murdered her beloved aunt. Yes, Maggie was tied to a pole. And yes, she was probably going to die. But until that time came, Carol would pay.

"It wasn't my fault." Carol looked up, as if she had almost forgotten she wasn't alone.

"Oh, really? It wasn't your fault? He. Dumped. You," Maggie said, succinctly, staring into Carol's tear-streaked face, ice running through her veins. *No panic,* she told herself. *No fear.* "And so, you shot him. *In* the face." Maggie glanced quickly at the lantern. The water in the cave was rising. Another six inches of water and the flame would be doused.

"I didn't mean to. But he was going to leave—"

"So you killed him, because he was playing you like he played me. He didn't love you—"

"Yes, he—"

"He was *never* going to marry you," she screamed.

"Shut up!" Carol screeched, surging to her feet.

"Why the hell would he?" Maggie laughed derisively. "Look at you. You're a mess. Not to mention a fucked-up, sick, murdering bitch—"

"Shut up!" Carol roared, flinging the champagne flutes at her, but Maggie jerked her head out of the way, and the glasses shattered on the stone wall behind her.

"And now," she said, in a superior, know-it-all voice, "you are buried up to your frizzy blond bangs in monstrous debt, which you will never, *ever* be able to pay off, because you were trying to *buy* the love—" *Bingo!* Maggie thought, with a surge of triumph, as the champagne bottle flew past her head and smashed into the wall, splintering around her, "—of a man who was just using you."

"He *loved* me!" Carol howled in anguish.

"No, I don't think so," Maggie said. "I would venture a guess that the word *hate* would describe what he felt for you."

Carol grabbed the back of the metal chair. "Shut the fuck up, you dumb bitch!"

"*Fear*," Maggie said brightly, "perhaps is another good word. *Trapped*—"

An inhuman noise erupted from Carol as she hoisted the metal chair over her head and hurled it. It slammed into Maggie, striking her hard on the head.

She slumped down, knees banging against the wet cave floor, her body limp.

Forty-Three

*G*unner slowed the SUV. "This is it," he said. "Armand and Finlayson Creek."

Jesus. Luke rubbed his face. They were in the middle of a gravel and dirt road, no structures visible from the road. No driveways leading off it. Daylight was fading, which was going to make their search even tougher. "All right," he said, "let's get out and take a look around. We should keep quiet, in case her assailants are nearby."

"Got it," Eve said, her eyes worried.

Gunner pulled to the side of the road.

When Luke tried to exit, the boy clung to his shirt. He suppressed a sigh, unstrapped the kid, and lifted him out.

"You want a piggyback?" he asked the kid, his voice barely audible. Adam nodded, his face too serious for someone so young. "Up you go," he whispered, as he swung the boy onto his back. Then he strode over to join Gunner and Colt, walking the road, looking for trails, disturbed foliage, broken branches.

"Mister?" The boy tapped Luke's shoulder.

"Shhh," Luke said.

"Mister?" The boy tapped him again.

Luke felt the flicker of irritation, but suppressed it. Adam was just a scared little kid. "What," he asked him quietly.

"See way down there, where the road ends?" the boy said, his forefinger pointing over Luke's shoulder.

"Yeah," Luke replied, half-listening while looking to see if there were fresh footprints in the muddy ditches.

"That's the gray van my mom and the bad men stole her in."

"Your ... mom?" Luke said slowly.

"Yeah."

"Okay," Luke said. He swung the boy down to the ground and knelt so they were face to face. "I need you to tell me whatever you can remember about the men and your mom. What they looked like, what the plan was. This way we'll know what we're looking for, where to look."

"Which would really help us, Adam." Eve's soft voice came from behind him. "The nice lady who gave you those yummy apple tarts? She's my sister, and I love her very much and I'm worried about her. We need your help. And if we're able to find her, I bet she'd be so pleased with you that she'd make a whole batch of apple tarts and give you every single one of them."

"I'd do it even without the tarts," the boy said, his head tipped down, eyes on his feet, "'cause she was nice to me and ..."

"There now," Luke said, his voice gruff. He took the boy's hands in his. "Don't cry. We men cry later, when the danger's over. Right now, we gotta get down to business."

"That's right," Colt said gently. Gunner stepped up beside him. "That's what we men do."

"Okay," the boy said, scrubbing the tears from his eyes with a grubby fist that left dirt streaks in its wake. He squared his thin shoulders and looked Luke in the face, teardrops shimmering on his long, dark lashes. "There's four men," he said, holding up four fingers. "I don't like 'em. They're scary. They wear guns. One has a knife in his boot. I saw it. I don't know about the others. They're taking her to that cave where they took the other lady." His lower lip started to tremble again, eyes flooding and spilling over. "Sorry," he said, trying to dash the tears away, but more just took their place. "Sorry …"

"It's okay," Luke said. "You're doing great." He tried to keep his voice calm and measured. "Have you been to this cave? Do you know where it is?"

Forty-Four

*T*he clatter of the metal chair smashing against the wall had brought men swarming into the cave. Maggie could see their shadowy shapes through the lowered fringe of her eyelashes. She stayed slumped over, didn't move, the coppery taste of blood in her mouth.

Carol waded angrily toward her. "Get up!" she yelled, jerking Maggie's head back and slapping her hard across the face.

Maggie kept herself limp, unresponsive, letting her head flop from side to side with each blow.

"It's not fair," Carol screamed, almost in tears. "There's more I have to tell you!"

A man stepped into the light. "Ms. Endercott?"

Maggie recognized the voice. It was the dickhead who had accosted her at the market.

Carol released her hair. Maggie could feel the shift in the air as Carol whirled around, could hear the slosh of the water.

"Get out! Get the fuck out!" she screamed.

"The men want to be paid."

"Fuck off," Carol said, turning her back on him. "I'm busy."

"Both packages have been delivered." There was a dangerous edge of steel in his voice.

Maggie lifted her lashes just a fraction. Yes, it was him. The other men were in the shadows. She wished she could make out distinguishing features to describe them to Luke. Because he was coming. She knew it. She could feel him searching for her.

"She might not be dead yet," Carol snapped.

"Fine." A gun suddenly appeared in his hand. "I can remedy that."

Carol stepped in front of Maggie. "No! She's mine. And if she isn't dead, I want her death to be slow and long. I want her to be alone and in the dark with time to think about what she did to me. That was the deal. Just like Kristal."

"Then our contract is complete," he stated. "You need to pay us."

"Later."

"Now," he said. "The boat's standing by. If my men and I don't leave in the next fifteen minutes, we'd have to use docking lights, which might attract attention to your little adventure." As he spoke, the other men silently moved to form a tight, threatening circle around Carol.

The seawater was lapping higher and higher. Maggie used everything she had to keep tremors from the cold racking through her.

"Jesus Christ, you money-grubbing, fucking little shits." Carol shoved her way through them and plunged into the darkness. Maggie could hear her churning and splashing around in the water. She returned a few seconds later, dragging a soaking-wet backpack behind her. "Here," she snarled, hurling the backpack at him. "Here's your blood money. Now get the hell out of here!"

Tssss

The lantern hissed out, and the cave plunged into darkness.

Maggie used the opportunity to sink even further, the water reaching to her collarbone as she fumbled around behind her, trying to find a broken glass shard. *Ahh.* Her fingers closed around one. *Thank God!* Quietly, she sawed at the rope binding her wrists.

A light suddenly flared on. A flashlight, shining into the backpack. In its peripheral light, she could see Carol edging toward the entrance.

"What the fuck?" one of the men roared. "A few bills on top, and the rest is fucking paper!" He flung fistfuls of paper into the air.

Carol made it a few steps before the cave reverberated with the sounds of a gunshot. Carol staggered. The gun roared again, and Carol fell facedown in the water.

"Stupid bitch!" someone muttered, and the men headed out of the cave.

Maggie was shaking violently. Ice-cold water swirled around her ribs. *Need to work fast,* she told herself, sawing frantically at her bindings. The glass slipped, sliced the base of her thumb. "Great," she muttered, continuing to saw. "That's all I need. More blood in the water to attract predators of the sea." The seawater was filling the cave, now up over the curve of her breasts. Claustrophobia and fear rose, but she pushed it down.

Later, she told herself firmly. *You can fall apart later. No time for that now.*

Forty-Five

Stealth be damned, time was running out. Luke could feel it in his bones. He tore down the winding forest path, his flashlight lighting the way. The boy clung to him like a monkey, his little arms wrapped tightly around Luke's neck, head pressed against Luke's shoulder to avoid the branches slashing against their bodies as he ran. Gunner, Colt and Eve ran too, not far behind him.

Hold on, Maggie. Hold on. He'd heard two gunshots a few minutes ago. *She has to be safe.*

He'd tried to convince Eve and the boy to stay behind, to hide in the bushes away from the vehicles. But Eve got ferocious at the suggestion. Her sister had been abducted, and she bloody well wasn't going to stay behind, quaking behind some bush. And the boy picked up his cuss from Eve: "Hell, no! I'm comin' with you too!"

He heard the sound of a boat engine firing up.

"Hear that?" Gunner growled.

"Yeah," Luke answered. The deep-throated thrum of the outboard motor built in intensity, revved into high speed.

Please ... God ... Please keep her safe ...

Luke took the last ten yards at a balls-to-the-wall sprint, his leg screaming in protest. They burst out of the undergrowth and onto the rocky bluff just in time to see the shadowy shape of a speedboat disappear around the curve of the cove. It was too dark and too far away to see how many people were onboard.

He lifted the boy off his back. "Okay, we're here. Which direction is the cave?"

"It was right over there," Adam said, gesturing to his right. "But ..." The boy trailed off, looking confused.

"But what?"

"But there was beach before and rocks to climb ..."

"Where?" Luke said, the agony in his leg not coming even close to the torment in his heart. "Where exactly was the cave? Can you remember?"

"Yes." The boy nodded. "You see that big tree sticking out over the water? It was right below that."

"You're sure?" Luke asked, kicking off his shoes and stripping down to his boxer briefs.

"Uh-huh. But it's all water now. I can't see the cave—"

"You stay here," Luke said. "I'm going to get Maggie." And he dived off the bluff into the icy black water below.

Forty-Six

*M*aggie swam toward the entrance of the cave. She prayed she was going in the right direction. The men had left that way, and then there had been the noise of the boat to confirm it. But now, all was silent.

A swell of water splashed over her face, causing her to choke and sputter. The wounds on her head and face stung like hell. Fear and panic rose in her throat, engulfing her. She felt light-headed, her limbs heavy, movements awkward. She didn't have much time.

Another swell splashed over her face.

She tried to calm the wild staccato of her heart, taking several deep breaths and blowing them out. She took one last breath, filled her lungs as deeply as she could, and dived under the water, praying she would find the cave entrance.

Forty-Seven

*L*uke was powering swiftly through the water, arms slicing forward, cupped hands pulling back, his legs helping to add momentum and speed.

He paused for a second, treading water while he shook his head to clear the water streaming over his face and check his progress. Thank God, the moon had come out from behind the clouds. He could see the arc of the tree stretching out over the water about twelve feet away, and the dark figures of Colt, Gunner, Eve, and the boy racing along the bluff, mirroring his journey through the water.

He scanned the shoreline. *Where's the damn cave?* And then he saw it: the inward curve of the shoreline. He shifted, heading in that direction, his bum leg screaming in pain.

Suddenly, something surged to the surface of the water, splintering the quiet. Luke's heart slammed into his throat, and adrenaline pumped through his body. And then ... he saw her. Maggie. Coughing and spluttering, gasping for air, arms flailing, her long hair streaming around her pale, up-tilted face.

Forty-Eight

*M*aggie snuggled deeper into the blanket and took another sip of the hot toddy Gunner had made, enjoying the soothing comfort of the steaming hot water, lemon, honey, whiskey, and cloves. Samson had managed to wedge himself between the coffee table and the sofa and was sprawled out on the floor, a luxuriously furry, warm footrest for her defrosting toes.

Eve had been quite the tyrant when they got back to Luke's house. She insisted on cleansing Maggie's wounds, and dressing them with antibiotic cream and bandages. "Don't you ever, ever scare me like that again," she told Maggie, giving her sister a fierce shake that morphed into a long hug.

Afterward, the sisters went into the living room to join the men, who had built a roaring fire in the stone fireplace. Eve put some cheeses, cold cuts, hand-churned butter, and fresh bread on a wooden cutting board. Maggie was ravenous, and had sunk down on the sofa beside Luke and made the two of them a plate of food.

The boy was curled up on the other side of sofa, using Luke's thigh for a pillow. Someone had covered Adam with a chenille throw blanket. Asleep, he looked even smaller. He was a beautiful child under all that grit, with his golden hair and flushed cheeks. So young. So vulnerable.

An orphan now. *Poor kid,* Maggie thought sadly, *to lose both his mother and father in the last three days.*

She shook her head. It was not a conversation she was looking forward to having with Adam. No matter how terrible or negligent his parents had been, they were all he'd had, and it would be a profound sorrow and a loss for the small boy.

Maggie took another sip of her hot toddy, relishing the warmth and comfort of Luke's body next to hers.

She should have been exhausted and ready for bed, but she wasn't. She felt exhilarated.

It was over.

She was *alive.* She was *safe.*

She nestled into the crook of Luke's arm and he pulled her even closer still, making her feel protected and cherished. She glanced up and smiled at him. "I love you," she said for the hundredth time that evening.

"I love you, too." He dropped a tender kiss on her forehead. "I love you with everything I have, and everything I will be."

She turned her head sideways, pressing her ear and her cheek against him, so she could hear and feel the rumble of his voice through his chest.

"You are …," he continued, his hand rising tenderly to cradle her head, "my heart, my breath, my reason for living."

Epilogue

*H*ave a lovely afternoon, and thanks for coming," Maggie said, unlocking the door and letting the last two straggling customers out.

"This is going to be our daily hotspot," one of them said. "I'm already having withdrawal symptoms."

"Lois," the other woman laughed, shaking her head, "how is that possible? You devoured a slice of that delectable chocolate cake, a wedge of the rhubarb-strawberry pie, *and* a toasted ham and cheese sandwich with a bowl of fresh tomato soup."

"I'm coming back tomorrow. Don't try to stop me," the woman laughed as they stepped off the porch and onto the sidewalk.

"Well, I am so glad you liked it," Maggie said. "See you tomorrow." She closed the door, flipped the sign in the window to *Closed* and flung her arms over her head. "The first day of the Intrepid Café is over!"

"Woo-hoo!" Eve cheered, grabbing Maggie by the hands and pulling her into a jig. Apron strings flew as they whirled past wooden tables and white slat-back chairs, pale cream hydrangeas in square silver vases, and Eve's spectacular art adorning the walls.

"We did it!" Maggie sang out. "We really did it!"

"And what a success!" Eve crowed. "We're going to be rich!"

There was a knock on the door.

"Go away," Eve called loudly. "Business hours are eight to three ... Come back tooomorrrrow!"

"Eve," Maggie laughed, slowing to a halt. "That's no way to treat potential customers." She turned toward the door, and her heart leaped.

There was Luke, bending over and looking in through the window, with Adam at his side.

"Hello," Luke said, shading his eyes to cut the glare from the sun on the glass.

Maggie ran over, opened the door, and threw herself into Luke's arms. "It went really, really, really well!"

"So I heard," Luke said, smiling down at her.

"No, but *really* well!" Maggie said. "I know you were here earlier, but right after you left, we were flooded with customers and lots of advance orders, too. It was wonderful! Just wonderful and my feet are tired!"

Luke laughed. "What's so wonderful about sore feet?"

"It's proof of how busy we were," Maggie explained. "There wasn't a spare second to sit down. We're going to have to hire additional staff, because there is no way ..." Her voice faded. She looked from Luke to Adam and back to Luke, suddenly realizing they were both in full black-tie regalia. "Why ... why are you guys so dressed up?" she asked. Her eyes widened. "Did we have something fancy on the calendar and I forgot?"

The strains of Albinoni's *Adagio* came to her, filling the café, the street, with glorious sound. Maggie peeked around Luke and saw a string quartet and an accordion player, all in black tie.

Her gaze flew back to Luke. "Oh my," she whispered, as Adam pulled a fragrant bouquet of cream and pale-purple lilacs from behind his back and put them into her trembling hands.

Luke dropped to bended knee, and held out an opened black velvet ring box with the most gorgeous engagement ring she had ever seen in her life.

"Maggie, my love," Luke said, "from the moment you leaped into my arms, red long johns wrapped around your head, I was lost. You've filled my life with love and laughter, made my house and home—oh, sweetheart, don't cry—"

"—It's a happy thing," Adam said, tugging on her arm, looking concerned. "He's asking you to marry him. Please say you will. He's been practicing all day."

"Say you'll marry me," Luke said, laughing, reaching down and giving Adam's hair an affectionate ruffle, his warm, twinkling gaze locked on hers, "and put us both out of our misery."

"Yes!" Maggie cried, bending down and flinging her arms around the two of them. "Yes! A hundred million times, yes!"

Laughter and tears intermingled. Applause broke out from the crowd that had gathered outside the café. The musicians broke into a joyous rendition of the *Ruslan and Ludmilla Overture*.

Luke slid the stunning oval diamond ring onto Maggie's trembling finger.

"I love you so, so much," Maggie said, looking into his beloved face.

Eve was dancing around them, waving her apron over her head like a flag, an enormous smile on her face.

"Hey, Adam," Eve said, stopping to catch her breath, gazing at Maggie with joy-filled eyes. "Why don't we go into the kitchen, see if we can find a spare sugar cookie or two. Give these two lovebirds some alone time."

"Or maybe an apple tart?" Adam said hopefully, slipping his hand into Eve's as the two of them disappeared through the swinging doors.

The music from outside was swirling around them as Maggie lifted her face. Her lips met his. Her heart, so full. Full, and overflowing.

"I love you, Luke Benson," she murmured, her arms entwined around his neck, hands fisted in his hair, "so very, *very* much."

He leaned back slightly, slid his hands forward to frame her face. The warmth and love in his gaze made her knees feel wobbly.

"And I love you," he said, as if he were making a sacred vow, "and *will* love you, to forever and beyond."

Acknowledgments

Three years ago, my friend Ken Freeman decided to publish his novel, on Amazon. He has been after me ever since, to join in on the fun.

"Sure, Ken," I'd say. "Hmm… Yeah, sounds like it really makes sense, but …"

"You have all these manuscripts you've written that you've never sent out," he'd say, his face and entire body animated. "Novels where the rights have reverted back to you. Throw them online! I'm telling you, it's amazing!"

"Maybe someday," I'd say soothingly. I had *no* intention of doing it. Had been traditionally published for years; had other streams of income so didn't require the small advance I would receive in order to pay my bills. I was happy puttering along, writing my little books, and sending them out there into the world.

But last April, Ken came for a visit, and he seemed older, more frail. Of course, my husband and I have known Ken for eighteen years; during that time, I've put on some weight, my hair has gone gray, and my husband's hair … well, a good portion of that is gone for good. But you notice it more when a friend ages. It's like when your friends' children are suddenly grown. You aren't there for the day-to-day, and the realization that time is passing hits you harder.

I got scared that night, lying in bed with my husband. Realized that Ken is twenty years older than me, and that someday he won't be there when we want to reach out by phone, email or Skype. That we won't always be able to sit around the living room on big comfy sofas, drinking red wine, reading our new pieces, critiquing, sometimes laughing so hard that we have to clutch our bellies and wipe away the tears running down our faces.

"I want Ken to live forever," I said.

"Me, too," Don said.

"I'm glad he's so healthy, exercises and eats good food," I said, snuggled into my husband's furry chest, hoping that he would live forever, too.

"Mm…" Don said. He was falling asleep.

And as I lay there in our darkened bedroom, listening to my husband gently snore, I made a decision. I was going to write a book under a different name and put it up on Amazon. No literary tome: a *romance* novel. My guilty pleasure. My sister introduced me to my first one when I was sixteen, and I've been devouring them ever since.

The next morning at breakfast, I told Ken and Don my plan. Ken was super excited, his face aglow, and I knew that this was something I would never regret.

Well, little did I know how much fun I would have. This last year has been an ABSOLUTE BLAST! I love writing romance! And my husband, my family and friends have been super supportive, and I'd like to thank them all:

*Ken Freeman, for being our dear friend and for all the reasons above, and for sharing his experience on what worked, and what didn't, and helping me get set up.

*Don, as always, was my first reader and, even more impressive, it was *his* first foray into the … ahem… pleasures of the romance novel, and he even *enjoyed* it!

*Dawna, for brainstorming with me on our walks.

*My three grown children, who were bemusedly cheering me on from the sidelines.

*kcDyer, of *Finding Fraser* fame, for the multitude of Skype calls, advice, helping me navigate my way.

*My more recent friend, Mary, who gave me courage to stand proudly in my love for a well-written romance.

*Nancy Berland, for taking me and my book on and then going through my manuscript like a top-notch sushi chef on speed, chopping and dicing and giving me the most beautiful, thoughtful and thorough notes.

*Eleanor Gasparik and Victoria Bell, who helped me smooth out the bumps and gave wonderful suggestions, as well as copious notes on the copy-edits and proofs.

*Denaye Baker, for the gorgeous cover design.

*I'd also like to thank Cissy Harley for designing the SaraFlynn.com website; the team at Writerspace and the Writerspace community; and the team at Nancy Berland Public Relations for their help getting the word out.

*And lastly, my thanks to my agent for not freaking out about this whole crazy venture.

Thank you, thank you, thank you!

SARA FLYNN

Sara Flynn is the pen name for author/actress Meg Tilly. Tilly has written five standout adult and YA novels and starred in such films as *The Big Chill*, *Valmont* and *Agnes of God*—for which she won a Golden Globe Award and an Oscar nomination. Tilly has three grown children and resides with her husband in the Pacific Northwest. She is currently at work writing the second novel in the Solace Island series.

CPSIA information can be obtained
at www.ICGtesting.com
Printed in the USA
LVOW12s0310290617
539750LV00001B/28/P

9 780995 811805